WEEKEND

IN

TROY

HELLE RINK

CONTENTS

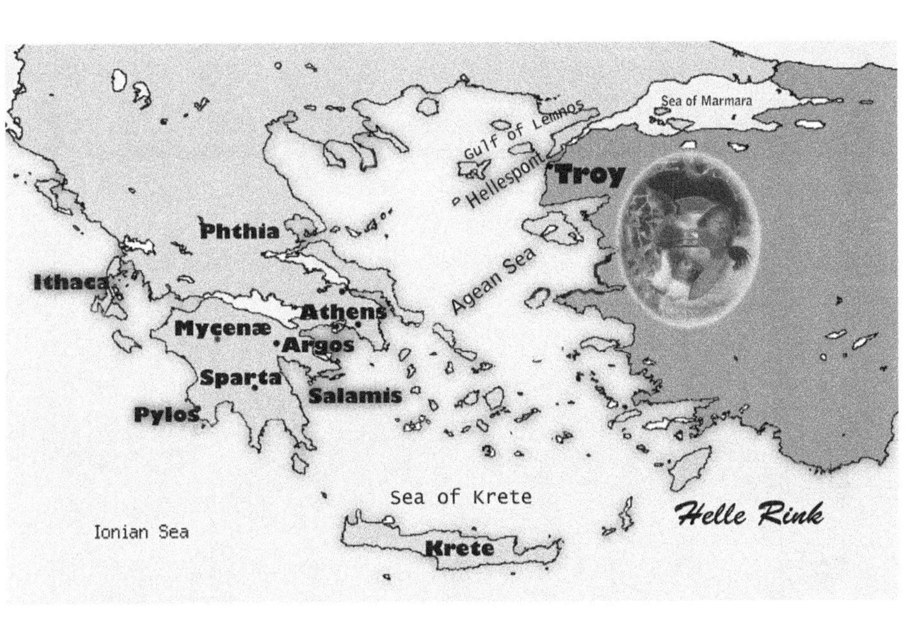

Sea of Marmara
Gulf of Lemnos
Hellespont
Troy
Phthia
Agean Sea
Ithaca
Athens
Mycenæ
Argos
Sparta
Salamis
Pylos
Sea of Krete
Ionian Sea
Krete
Helle Rink

INTRODUCTION
LONG AGO AND FAR AWAY

Once upon a time, there lived a queen in a marble palace by the sea. This queen, Helen, was the most beautiful woman in the world. She was a daughter of the king of Sparta and her husband was now the king of Sparta. Helen didn't like this because, as the true daughter of a king, she should have been his heir and a queen in her own right. But such was not the law in those days. Her husband was Menelaus, a brother to the powerful king of Mycenae, Agamemnon.

Then, one day, an embassy from a faraway land arrived, and with it a young man with all the masculine beauty a man can have: a chiselled face, aquiline nose, huge soulful brown eyes, long eyelashes and well traced eyebrows, silky brown hair, a sculpted physique and whatever else makes a man stand out among other men. His name was Paris and his father was Priam, king of Troy. When Paris looked upon Queen Helen, he instantly fell deeply in love as she did with him. It was a meeting of souls.

So, one day Paris returned to Sparta and took Helen away in his bireme and they sailed blissfully to his father's land, the fabled Troy, across the sea.

Now, Menelaus, Helen's husband was not happy about this. He called together the other kings of Greece and reminded them of a vow they had taken that all would protect Helen, the most beautiful woman in the world. They decide they must take Helen back for their joint honours and so set sail from Greece.

Now, on Dardan plain [before Troy]
the fresh and yet unbruised
Greeks do pitch their brave pavilions
Now, expectation, tickling skittish spirits,
On one and other side, Trojan and Greek,
Set all at hazard.
Now, good or bad, 'tis but the chance of war

Wm Shakespeare, *Troilus and Cressida*

1

FRIDAY

1.1 IN TROY, THERE LIES THE SCENE

Imagine. Imagine a pure blue sky with a few fluffy white clouds lazing about, going nowhere in particular. Imagine a sea as blue as the sky, although of a somewhat darker shade. There is almost no wind and the waters are calm, shimmering and glimmering under the rays of the sun. Far, but not too far, a fleet of vessels is anchored close to an island, oars stowed, sails furled, bobbing gently following the drift of the waves.

Now imagine a beach, a beach of unblemished white sands stretching as far as the eye can see, waves lapping gently on the shore, leaving a white froth behind as they retreat. The sandy beach reaches about five meters inland; then a slight rise leads onto a gravely plain, sparsely covered with dry grass. A hill rises about 1 km from the sea, topped by a flat plateau. To the right of the hill, a headland curves around, facing another headland across the water; the strait of water between these two points is known as the Hellespont, connecting the Ægean Sea to the inland Sea of Marmara.

The geography has remained much the same over the ages, except that the sea is today much farther away. The sea is still - the Ægean. Sail due west across it, and you will reach the Greek mainland. On a clear day, from the hilltop you can see the Acropolis. Well, perhaps not. Once, on the plateau, there rose a city, a city of high, strong walls, many gated, known as Troy, Troy the beautiful, Troy the rich, Troy the glamorous, the envy of the world. It is not there today. But stood in all its glory thousands and thousands of years ago.

But let me introduce myself. My name is Gaius Marius – through no fault of my own – and I am cat – a Siamese cross. That means that I have blue eyes and the markings on my face, ears and tail are typical Siamese. However, no judge of cats in his right mind would give me a second glance – purebred I am not. I am a cat of the 21ˢᵗ century. So what am I doing in Troy? Well, many tourists ask themselves: why did we come to Costa del Sol or the Algarve or whatever. The moral is: when on holiday, one must go somewhere.

It was a peaceful late morning in late summer. Now, close to zenith, the sun was going strong and I decided I needed a bit of shade. I had found a cheap and cheerful establishment whose main feature and attraction was being right by the beach – and the only one around. It went under the quaint name of *At the sign of the Greek Olive Tree*, announced proudly on a signboard painted by a willing but inartistic hand and nailed over the entrance. The fare at *The sign of the Greek Olive Tree* was plain. On good days, there was moussaka. At all other times, olives, cheese and bread. They also served snacks since most of its patrons drank rather than ate. The tuna ones were my favourites. From an architectural point of view, *The Greek Olive Tree* wouldn't have won any prizes. It was a ramshackle place, made up, it seemed, of bits of wood from cashiered vessels, which would explain the strange holes in odd places on its walls, through which oars might once have dipped into the water, moving a proud vessel forward.

The Greek Olive Tree was of a good length, with a bar running from end to end. It was a three-sided building with a roof of sorts but no front or door. Instead, there was a low picket – of sticks – fence separating the bar itself from a terrace that extended well beyond the roof. The décor reflected the owner's penchant for local materials and, as this was a war zone, it was rich in cloven helmets, bits of armour and notched swords adorning walls, hanging from ceiling and fixed on and along the bar. These relics were both Trojan, and Greek and what have you. Broken weapons, as dead men, have no nation. One day, if I have nothing better to do, I might amuse myself trying to figure out how the late owners met their untimely ends. It shouldn't be too hard; a bit of forensic science, picked up from TV shows, is all one really needs.

I was sitting on the bar, at the end nearest the beach, with a splendid view of sea and harbour. At the other end, the owner leaned against the wall, eyes half closed, apparently without a care in the world. A snotty seven-year old, obviously his son, for what other kid would be inside on such a glorious day, pretended to wipe tables with the help of a filthy wet rag. The wife, I suppose, was in the kitchen, where all good Greek wives are kept. In a dark corner, a big strapping fellow I took to be a bouncer of sorts was sound asleep and who could blame him since it was a slow time of day and, besides myself, there was only one other patron in the place. He'd been there some time, lapping up watered raki and mumbling to himself. I sipped at my designer water and watched my fellow barfly. One didn't need Freud to see that this fellow was not a happy camper. He was reaching the stage where drunks want an audience, someone with a sympathetic ear. And, as if on cue, he wailed:

"Almost ten years! Almost ten years we've been in this Gods forsaken hole." He started sobbing into his raki, watering it even further. "I've never had any home leave. My wife has a six year old boy." He turned to the bartender: "What do you think of that?" That clever fellow didn't answer but waggled his eyebrows. What can one say? The drunk continued: "She says he's a gift from the gods." Good thinking. Smart lady. The drunk had another swig but the booze just seemed to make him sadder. He turned to me as being, perhaps, a more sympathetic listener. "Do you realize that when the Greeks sailed, the fleet had a thousand ships? Why, 69 kings joined the expedition, with troops, weapons, siege engines and all. You should have seen the scene at Aulis. Would have taken your breath away, it would. Bands playing, girls strewing flowers before the kings' feet, banners flying, drums and trumpets going full blast. Everyone was there to watch. Women cried, kids ran about all over the place.

"Before we embarked, the commander-in-chief, Agamemnon, may he rot in Hades, told us the whole thing would be a piece of cake. Sail out, clobber the yokels, pick up lady and booty and sail home. But here we still are. And what do we have to show for it? I ask you, what has been the point?" I swished my tail. Don't look at me, pal. I just came out for the weekend. But drunks at this stage are happy to ask the questions and supply the answers themselves. "It's all because of that dumb blonde Helen and her fancy toy boy Paris. I ask you, why would anyone bother? I mean, she wasn't a spring chicken 10 years ago when she left Sparta so what's she like now?" Truth to tell, I'd always been rather dubious about the 'ravished lady' story. But this wasn't the fellow I wanted to discuss conspiracy theories with.

Anyway, he was still going strong without any help from me:

"Is any broad worth it? And do we hear about a scheduled troop withdrawal or an exit strategy? That's what comes from having a king as a commander-in-chief. Responsibility without accountability. And we still use our original tents and equipment, I mean, after ten years, you can imagine the wear and tear." I looked to my left as if by instinct. There, on the Dardan plain, the Greek camp was clearly visible, pennants flying for each of the Greek City States. "Given the time we've been here," sobbed my new pal, "we could have built a load of beach cottages with all the home comforts and mod coms. Why, it could have been a holiday resort, bring the wife and kiddies. Garrison duty, you know. Six months on, six months off. After all, the war isn't going anywhere. But, no.

"The powers that be are forever telling us: 'Boys, we just need another season to wrap this thing up. We'll all be home by Christmas'." He flung his arms out as if calling for divine judgement. "Look at it," he pointed towards the city on the hill. "Does that look like it'll be 'taken care of' by next Christmas? We'll be here when the next millennium dawns!" O.K., pal, not to worry. That's just 200 years away, time will fly, you'll see. Just then, however, my drunk passed out and slowly slid to the floor; a nod from the owner and the bouncer dragged him out to sleep it off on the beach.

I considered the city on the hill. Troy of song and legend. Its standard, a white horse rampant on a green background, fluttered gently in the breeze from city's highest point, a massive tower. The walls looked solid enough from where I was. In fact, for a city that had been under siege for nine years, it looked pretty sturdy. Between the Greek camp and the hill, where the battles take place, nothing much seemed to be going on. I could see clouds of dust here and there that I took to be from single riders, maybe scouts or messengers.

I asked the owner if he was a local lad. He grinned, showing about six gaps where teeth should have been, dentistry in the time of the Trojan War being somewhat primitive.

"Not on your life, I came from Ithaca with Odysseus. But after a year or so, Odysseus saw the whole expedition was a shambles. So he says to me: 'Eurybates, we might as well make a bit of money since it looks as if we'll be stuck here for some time.' So we set up this partnership. And we're doing well, you know. This war can't go on forever; at one point, the Greeks will either win or leave. In either case, me and Odysseus will have a nice nest egg and it'll be off back to Ithaca." Well, I wasn't about to rain on his parade[1]. I asked discreetly:

"You wouldn't fancy staying on? After all, bars are good money machines, why, business might even pick up once the city has fallen, there'll be so many depressed people about, to say nothing of celebrating troops. You'd be raking it in." Eurybates shook his head.

"Naah," he said, "you'll see, the bottom will fall out of the property market. It'll take years to pick up. No, I'm off home."

We were interrupted by the arrival of a tall old man, white hair, thin on top, white beard, both streaked with grey. He was wearing a long robe which may once – many moons ago – have been white, and leaned on a staff. On his feet, the ubiquitous sandals worn by all at the time. He must have been blind since a small boy was leading him by the hand, making sure he didn't fall over stools or upset tables. Eurybates sighed.

"Bloody sponger," he whispered. "Guy's always hanging about and asking for handouts. Says he's a poet. Who's to know? It's all the same with these academics. Why don't they work for a living like the rest of us?" But Eurybates was really a softy, or maybe a closet intellectual snob, for he called out: "Well, Homerys, how's the boy?" Homerys waved a shaky paw, took a dramatic stance and declaimed:

---

[1]   It took Odysseus 10 years to get back to Ithaca from Troy. None of his crew made it. See Homerys's *The Odyssey*

"Sing, O goddess, the anger of Akhilleus son of Peleus,
that brought countless ills upon the Achaeans [Greeks].
Many a brave soul did it send hurrying down to Hades,
and many a hero did it yield a prey to dogs and vultures,
for so were the counsels of Zeus fulfilled from the day on
which the son of Atreus [Agamemnon], king of men, and
great Akhilleus, first fell out with one another.

Homerys turned to me: I can only guess how he knew I was there. "How did you like the opening?"

"Great. Grabs you right away," I answered. "I especially like the bit about the vultures." I whispered urgently to Eurybates.

"Give him some wine or he'll go on and on. His epic poem has about 2 000 lines." As Eurybates didn't move as quickly as I wanted, I added: "I'll go halves with you!" Eurybates got busy with the wine – well watered. Homerys sat down gratefully, his poem forgotten for the nonce.

"You are a lord of hosts," he declared, holding up his beaker in salutation. Eurybates frowned:

"Well, I confess it sounded good," he said to me, "but I'm not too sure I understood what it's about." It was my turn to waggle my eyebrows.

"Believe me, my friend, you're not supposed to! That is the beauty of epic poetry." The point of epic poetry being to bore unborn generations of schoolchildren to death and keep academics out of the public houses.

I wandered down to my favourite tree by the beach, and, after a long stretch and wide yawn, curled up within its roots for a late morning snooze. The sighing of the wind and the soft warm breeze soon sent me off. I awoke refreshed and had a nice slow waking up stretch. It was about lunchtime so I ambled back to *The Greek Olive Tree*.

1.2 THE PRINCES ORGULOUS

I had hardly settled down, on the bar as usual, to my tuna snacks and designer water when the peace of *the Greek Olive Tree* was rudely shattered by what seemed to be an invasion of the Goths and Vandals.

A hoard of great strapping fellows appeared covered in bronze and gold – armour, helmet, greaves – with ornately designed bronze weapons in their hands. I gapped. But it soon dawned to me that this was the flower of Greek chivalry, the Greek High Command. Akhilleus I recognized by his physique – hours at the gym, I'll warrant – and golden hair. An older man, black haired with a wreath on his helmet, a beard and an attitude you could throw darts at, started laying down the law in no uncertain fashion.

"You!" he cried, pointing to a younger man in bronze armour – no gold. "Out!" Akhilleus bounded forward, enraged:

"That is my special friend, Patroklos! I demand he stay!"

"Your special friend, indeed!" sneered the guy with the wreath maliciously. "Of course he is. But he has no place in the Greek High Council! Out, I say! I am Agamemnon of Mycenæ, and I am in command!" Well, Akhilleus had to knuckle under and Patroklos went. But Agamemnon wasn't done yet.

"Out!" he shouted, pointing at an ill kept, squint-eyed dirty fellow in rags sitting alone in a corner. "Out!" This time no one complained so off the fellow went. Agamemnon looked around, I suppose to see if there was anyone else to bully. He sneered at Eurybates, pointing again:

"There's a cat on your bar!" Eurybates was a confirmed eyebrow raiser.

"And?" But now someone else got up; not as old as Agamemnon although his brown hair was already touched with grey.

"Agamemnon, it's a cat. It's got a bowl of water and some snacks. Can we please get on with it? Or do you want to start looking for lizards and cockroaches, too?"

I was distracted by a sour smell next to me that certainly hadn't been there before. I looked around, wrinkling my nose and saw that the chap Agamemnon had last chucked out was next to me, trying to make himself look small and inconspicuous. I asked:

"Haven't you ever heard of a bath? Or deodorants and shampoo? What about a trip to the mall for some new togs?" He sneered, showing nasty broken yellow teeth. Lord of Cats, what a mess he was!

"Keep your voice down, you stupid cat, or Agamemnon will kick us both out. I'm Thersites and a slave, so who do you think is going to give me a day at the spa and a whirl in the city shops?"

"You've got a master, don't you, if you're a slave! He's responsible for you. You're an eyesore and a public health hazard!" I got a leer:

"After 10 years, do you think anyone remembers who my master is? I don't remember myself. I serve all which means I serve none." I'm an intelligent cat as cats go but this was getting beyond me so I dropped the subject. Thersites didn't look as he was about to go anywhere and was too big for me to wrestle out. Then Eurybates joined us and leaned against the bar next to me. He didn't seem to mind Thersites. Being a cat, my besetting sin is information gathering so I asked:

"What can you tell me this lot? I recognize Akhilleus of Phtia, right? Guy with golden curls and muscles, posh togs. What about the others?"

"Well," said Thersites, "the guy doing the chucking-out is Agamemnon of Mycenæ..." Eurybates interrupted:

"Extremely conscious of his self-importance as leader of the Greek Expeditionary Forces. He's brave enough in the field but as a leader I think his pride and arrogance do the Greeks more harm than good. Also, he ain't so hot at people management." I nodded:

"I know the kind," was my comment. There are plenty of those where I come from. Not to be left out, Thersites added:

"He's married to Helen's sister, Clytemnestra."

"Yes," interjected Eurybates, "and the chap next to him, the burly one with whiskers, is his brother, Menelaus of Sparta, the world's most famous cuckold." Thersites snickered:

"His main claim to fame." I look at Menelaus and felt quite sorry for him. Everyone wants 10 minutes of fame; poor Menelaus had got 10 years of it with no end in sight. He was much like his brother but blond, more muscular and without the haughtiness and arrogance. A family can only have one alpha male. At this point, Eurybates was called back to his duties as bartender and hurried off. Pleased to have the floor to himself, Thersites continued

"Then you have that huge fellow, all muscles, thick neck and no brains, that's Ajax of Salamis, the glory of Greece although he's really half Trojan." He tittered, getting spittle all over me. Ugh! "Formidable fighter, of course; myself, I think just the sight of him, with that weird shield of his, is enough to send anyone running away, Greek or Trojan." I never did get a look at this wonder-shield but it seems to have been something along the line of a barrel, wholly encompassing the body. Eurybates, having quenched the thirst of the valiant warriors, came back.

"The younger guy, good looking, good height, brown hair and so on, is Diomedes leader of the men of Argos and Tiryns." I frowned:

"Tyrins? Never heard of it." Eurybates answered vaguely:

"Probably a smallish island somewhere. Then there's Idomeneus, leader of the Cretans. Guy with moustache and mousy brown hair. And then you have Odysseus of Ithaca and the old fellow is Nestor of Pylos."

"Why do you mention them together?" I asked. "Are they joined at the hip?" Thersites tittered.

"They might as well be. Where one goes, the other is not far behind. They are the two most dangerous men in the Greek army." I looked. Odysseus with his brown hair turning silver, a long nose, needing a shave, not particularly tall or muscular but with a penetrating eye that made me shiver. I didn't think I would want to tangle with that one. Eurybates continued. He was obviously very proud of his boss.

"Odysseus, the master manipulator. No one can outwit him and if anyone is going to win this war, he will." And so there it was, the Greek High Command at the time of the Trojan War. They had now settled down at various tables and Eurybates' bouncer was busy getting everyone plates of moussaka. But Thersites wasn't done yet.

"And that fellow standing at the other end of the bar, that's Calchas, the Trojan seer, who defected to the Greek side." I looked at Calchas, a sort of non-descript middle-aged fellow, brown hair, brown eyes, wearing a long belted gown embroidered with strange symbols and a skullcap with more symbols. Now, had I been Commander-in-Chief of any army and my chief seer absconded to the other side in the middle of a war, I would have packed up there and then and gone to look for another job. However, things were starting to happen and we turned our attention back to the lunchers.

Agamemnon took a swig at his beaker and said in a lordly fashion:

"So, here we are, and, besides it being lunch time, I would like to know why. I did not call any meeting." Talk about arrogance. Akhilleus jumped up, almost in a frenzy.

"But I did, I did, Agamemnon, and could we please have less of your airs and graces. You are the Commander in Chief because we, your peers, have so decided. You are the first among equals. Don't run away with the idea that you own us." He looked around for someone to disagree with this but no one did. "Nine years we've been at Troy and we're getting nowhere. There must be a reason. There has to be a reason. Is it that the Trojans have superior technology, more manpower, top-of-the-line military strategy or better supply lines? I don't think so. Every man lost on the Greek side can be replaced from our homelands but every dead Trojan is one Trojan less. If nothing else, that should give us an edge."

"Pride, pride, the hubris of the Greeks," quavered Homerys, who was still around and whom Agamemnon hadn't seen or had decided to ignore. "Until the Greeks acknowledge the might of the Gods and make the proper hecatombs, all their efforts in war will be in vain." Eurybates hastily refilled Homerys's beaker to keep him quiet. But Akhilleus was right on it.

"Yes, old man. That is what I think, too. Our gods have turned against us. Our men are sick and dispirited. Our best efforts get us nowhere. If all else is for us, what can be against us? Only the Gods. Calchas, what say you? Speak freely, no man here shall touch you whatever you may prophesy." Calchas did not look pleased in getting involved in this brawl. He cleared his throat a few times and then intoned sorrowfully:

"I am afraid, my friends, I must agree with Akhilleus. The Greeks have lost the Gods' favour, to be specific, the favour of Apollo." He looked increasingly embarrassed. But seeing no way out, he continued: "And not because of broken or unfulfilled vows or lack of hecatombs." Calchas looked around and, seeing they were hanging on his words, went on: "You will remember how, on your way to Troy, the sacred city of Thebes was sacked and the spoils shared among you, the Greek High Command." He turned and faced Agamemnon directly. "Your share, Great King," Calchas bowed, "included the maiden Crisies. Her father, Chryses, a priest of Apollo, came to you as a supplicant, offering you a great ransom to redeem his daughter. You well know, my King, that you refused the ransom; you spurned the old man, scorned him and had him thrown out of the camp." Before he could go on, Homerys sprang to his feet and declaimed:

"Dotard [Chryses]! Avoid our fleet;
where lingering be not found by me, nor thy returning feet
Let ever visit us again, lest nor thy godhead's crown nor
sceptre save thee!
Her [Crisies] whom thy seekest I [Agamemnon] will hold
mine own
"till age deflower her."

Homerys nodded several times.

"That is what you said, great king, to the priest Chryses." He brought out a dirty little notebook and waved it about. "I have it all here, in my notes." Everyone ignored Homerys's outburst since they all knew Agamemnon did not use such elegant language. Eurybates gave Homerys some cheese and olives to take his mind off poetry. In the meantime, Calchas took a step back and continued: "That, in my view, is the cause of Apollo's quarrel with the Greeks and the reason for your recent setbacks. The priest Chryses prayed to Apollo, who stands in high regard on Olympus and has a long reach. He will not be appeased before daughter and father are reunited without fee or ransom." All eyes went to Agamemnon, who stared back defiantly. He rose and walked threateningly towards Calchas who, to do him justice, didn't move a muscle. Agamemnon was so enraged he could hardly speak:

"You, you, evil prophet! When have you ever prophesized victories for me? Instead, all I hear from you are maledictions. And now, you dare cast upon me the full responsibility for our failures at Troy! So I am to pay the price to appease the Gods by giving up what is my own, my share of the Thebes loot, given to me in agreement with other members of the High command. That is very convenient, isn't it, Calchas? But hear you me, all of you, she is my property, mine, to do with as I see fit." Murmurs of disapproval all around. Thersites sniggered:

"And who can blame him? She's a real looker, all blonde hair and blue eyes and very, oh, so very young." Calchas said, bowing:

"Worthy and great king, I speak as the Gods command me. As for myself, I am neither for nor against you. Take my words as Theirs – not my own." Useful, if you want to be unpleasant: the Gods made me say it. Agamemnon continued his tirade:

"What proof do we have that Calchas' interpretation is correct? After all, it could be mere speculation on his part. Or else he just made it up. All this 'seer' stuff may be just so much snake oil."

"Because," said Akhilleus through clenched teeth, "if all other possibilities have been ruled out, what is left, no matter how improbable, must be the truth." Odysseus stood up.

"I agree with Akhilleus," he said. "The girl must be returned. True or not, we cannot risk our fortunes and the lives of our soldiers for so paltry a reason." Old Nestor nodded his head, as did Ajax, Diomedes and Idomeneus.

"Brother," said Menelaus, "you must agree." Agamemnon got to his feet and swept his cloak back.

"I must!" he roared. "I must! I, Agamemnon, king of Mycenæ! Commander of the Greek Expeditionary Forces! I must! Am I to be ordered about like a slave or a dog? I must! I will not! And, you, my brother. What are we doing here but trying to get back that no good slut of a wife of yours!" Menelaus murmured something about an oath. Agamemnon continued standing in the centre of the group, glaring at each one in turn. Ajax held up a finger as if he wanted to say something but was slapped down by his neighbour, Diomedes. Akhilleus said:

"Do you want to be remembered down the ages as the idiot who lost a war for the sake of a woman? Not a queen, or a goddess or a matchless beauty but the daughter of a mere priest. Because that, my dear Agamemnon, will be your fate." Nestor then rose:

"My friends, I hope you may listen to me with kindness; I am old and have seen and experienced many things and known great men, yes, men greater than any here today. Do you not see how decisions made in the present determine the future? Bad judgements lead to more bad judgements; injustices committed today bring new miseries tomorrow. You, my friend Agamemnon, are not looking beyond your immediate lust. If you channelled your tremendous gifts and powers to further our war efforts instead of trying to hang on to the body of one young girl, what might we not accomplish?"

Sounded good from where I sat. Everyone stood waiting for Agamemnon' answer. He strolled around the room, looking each man in the eye. Ajax fidgeted. Diomedes rubbed his chin. Idomeneus inspected the ceiling. Nestor and Odysseus moved not a muscle. Agamemnon said through his teeth, bringing out an ornate dagger and smiting the nearest table with it:

"So that is it. You are all in league against me! If so, I suppose I must bow to the will of the majority." He stopped and drew his dagger out of the table top, pointing it at Calchas who, once again, did not bat an eyelid while everyone else held their breath. Agamemnon went on: "Calchas, go to my tent and see that Crisies is reunited with her father, Chryses." Calchas bowed, turned and left. Agamemnon continued, turning and looking straight at Akhilleus: "However, to make up for her loss, I will take another Theban in her place so that I, alone among the Greeks commanders, may not be without a prize. That would never do; I, king of Mycenæ and commander-in-chief, to be left empty handed." Agamemnon almost beat his breast. Akhilleus eyes narrowed and his breathing quickened:

"Most noble king," he said barely holding his temper in check, "indeed, you are the most covetous and greedy of mankind. Tell me, how should we find you such a replacement? It's not as if we have a chest of girls we can just dip into. I say, then, give the girl back as the God Apollo demands and when we sack Troy we will repay you three- and fourfold." Well, this sounded fair to me but not to Agamemnon who sneered:

"So, Akhilleus, you would outwit me and outsmart me, take what is mine and keep what is yours. If I am to give up Crisies, I shall take Brisies, the Theban captive allotted to you. I have spoken." There was a common gasp and Akhilleus jumped to his feet, pointed his finger at Agamemnon, trembling with fury.

"You are steeped in insolence and lust of gain. How can any Greek follow the orders of one such as you whether on foray or in open battle? And why am I here, laying down treasure and men's lives for a quarrel that is not mine. Troy has not raided my cattle, stolen my horses, or cut down my harvests. I and my men have followed you for your pleasure, not ours: to gain satisfaction from the Trojans for your shameless self and Menelaus in what I thought was a just cause. And now you threaten to rob me of the prize I toiled for and that was freely given to me. Though my hands do most of the fighting, when it comes to sharing, your share is always far the largest, while I must take what I can get. But this is the end: I shall return home with my ships, for I will not stay here as a slave to gather gold and booty for you." Agamemnon turned his back on Akhilleus as if he had not spoken at all and shouted to a couple of footsloggers outside:

"Guards, go immediately to Akhilleus' ship, take the girl Brisies and bring her to my tent! I, Agamemnon, leader of the Greek Expeditionary Forces, command it!" The guards left smartly and a horrible silence settled over the party.

"Oh, my," whispered Thersites. "Watch for the fireworks!" Agamemnon turned to Akhilleus with a haughty look, haughtier manner, waved an insolent hand and said dismissively:

"Go if you want to; I shall not stop you. There is no king here whom I despise more than you, always quarrelsome and ill tempered. Go home, with your ships and your Myrmidons. I care neither for you nor for your anger." Akhilleus drew his sword and lunged at Agamemnon but Nestor intervened, placing himself between them. Nestor cried out:

"If only the Trojans could see us now! How Priam and all his sons would mock us and what delight they would take in our quarrels. We, who excel in numbers, in counsel and skill in fighting, conquered by our own disunity! You are like quarrelsome children, fighting over a toy you will cast away as soon as you see a newer one! For shame!" Agamemnon twirled his cape:

"That is all well and good, Nestor, and do not think I despise your wise counsels. But this man is beyond all bounds; he thinks himself better than any of us; he deserves more than we do. He feels his strength and prowess in battle makes him the premier warrior in the field, giving him the right to command and demand. He is an arrogant scoundrel."

"Who are you to revile me like this," Akhilleus snarled back. "If there is greed and arrogance within our command it is you, Agamemnon, who have brought them. You are uncouth, selfish, an incompetent nincompoop and a swine. I should cut your throat right now and do us all a favour!" Akhilleus looked around but saw that none of the others would back him up. He then declared, sheathing his sword: "I will not kill over any woman!"

And, turning on his heel, headed for the open terrace where he stopped and shouted. "If this be a coalition of the willing, I and my Myrmidons are no longer willing. Have a good war." He was gone. We heard him shout: "Patroklos!" and Patroklos' sandaled feet running after him. Thersites whispered:

"Truth to tell, Akhilleus needs a war, any war, after all he's good for nothing else, he was designed for war. Don't run away with all his talk of 'just causes'. Any fight is a 'just cause' for Akhilleus."

There was a slight interval after all this commotion. Then, Odysseus got to his feet and walked about, head bowed. He stopped in front of Agamemnon and said:

"You must be the wisest fool in the Greek world." Agamemnon started to protest but Odysseus stopped him with an upraised hand. "No, say no more. It seems our lot to pick quarrels over women. Why are we here? Helen. At least that's what we claim. And now: we've lost our best warrior over yet another woman and, worse, a lesser woman, a woman who might have been any woman but turned out, by chance, to be the daughter of a priest of Apollo. Nestor," turning to that ancient worthy, "I've had enough. Let's go." And they went. Then the others went too, until only Agamemnon and Menelaus remained. Agamemnon was seething, trembling with rage. Then he, too, got up and left, followed by his brother. Agamemnon ambitions to become a tyrant was clearly uphill work. I could have told him it was hopeless. He still had a lot to learn. I would advise he take Stalin's correspondence course.

Homerys was still around and, of course, there was no stopping him. He got to his feet and opened his arms wide:

"The Greeks have forgotten the Gods. They dream of mighty deeds and honour and glory. But the Gods will not be mocked; the fate of men is in the hands of the Gods. I've written it all down, you know." Waving his notebook some more "My epic," he continued grandly, "will remain a monument for countless ages after this war is over and the men who fought and died here are forgotten." Right. Never mind the women and children. Homerys stared dreamily at nothing. In the meantime, Thersites had cadged a free drink from Eurybates and was quaffing noisily.

"I just love a good quarrel," he said gleefully, "it's all great fun. And by the way," pointing at Homerys, "who is the old gaffer?" I looked at him sagaciously.

"Today, a little old blind man. Tomorrow, a colossus bestriding the millennia." Thersites stared.

"You are one weird cat." Homerys got up again before anyone could stop him and declaimed:

> *And Thetis' son [Akhilleus] said: "Fearful and vile I might be thought, if the exactions you [Agamemnon] laid upon me be true. Others you may command who will obey, thou shalt not me; or, if thou dost, far my free spirit is from serving thy command. Impress this upon thy soul – I will not use my sword on thee or any for a wench. But if whatever else you should take from my ship, then comes my part; then be sure thy blood upon my lance shall flow in vengeance."*

Thersites, Eurybates and I looked at each other.

"Well," I said, "it sounds a lot better than what Akhilleus did say." Seeing no more freebies were to be had from Eurybates, Thersites took himself off and I made my way to my tree on the beach.

As I approached, I became aware of a young man sitting quite close to my personal root, so to speak, hands around his knees, staring at the sea. I sat down and examined him. Medium height. Slim. Blond hair that I swore had been blow dried. Chiselled features and a long thin nose. Good physique without exaggeration. Blue eyes. He wore a silver helmet, white tunic with gold trimmings, a golden belt and lace up sandals with gold laces. He had wings on his feet. Wings?

"You have wings on your feet," was my first remark. "If you were a bird, I really feel it to be my duty to try and catch you."

"Indeed," came the answer, "and I would expect no less, if I were a bird but I am not. I am Hermes, messenger of the Gods." I rolled my eyes.

"I don't believe in the Gods, no offence meant," I answered. Hermes shrugged.

"That's OK, they don't mind that you don't." I felt nonplussed. The conversation seemed to have come to a grinding halt. I tried another tack:

"So, if you are the messenger of the Gods, what message do you bring?" Hermes replied:

"None. It's not like I'm a carrier pigeon and only let out when there's a message to be carried." Well, that begged the question:

"Then what are you doing here? And where's your caduceus?" Hermes rolled his neck as if trying to get rid of a crick.

"I got bored up in Olympus," he answered glumly, "there's nothing to do and no one to talk to if you don't want to join endless debates about the Trojan War. As far as I'm concerned, the Trojan War has been done to death. So, I took a personal day. And I don't carry that stupid rod when I'm off duty." I considered this.

"Tell me, just as a matter of interest," I asked at last, "if you're bored with the Trojan War, what are you doing in Troy?" Hermes sighed:

"I said," as if addressing none too bright a pupil, "I was bored with the debates. Not the war. I've come to have a look at the action from the human point of view." This was a boring subject to me so I asked him:

"Hermes, what's a hecatomb?" Hermes was drawing symbols in the sand with a stick and started on what seemed to be a line of bulls:

"It's an offering of one hundred of a species to the gods." I panicked. For a minute, I thought the Greeks might consider a cat hecatomb appropriate (although finding one hundred cats outside Troy would take some doing). Hermes continued reflectively: "You have no idea how Zeus abominates this sort of thing. He cannot stand the smell of roasting meat and he feels slighted that he, a God, should be thought to have any interest in dead animals, whether cooked or uncooked." I thought about that for a bit. How had humanity gotten it all so wrong? As if Hermes had read my thoughts, he continued: "Humans feel that whatever is essential to them will please the Gods. Plain stupidity and short-sightedness." I mulled over this:

"You might consider," I remarked, "that if a man owns two sheep and gives one to the Gods, he is making a great sacrifice as that one sheep represented half his property. But I suppose the priests just eat the meat and no sacrifices, no matter how great, ever get anywhere near Olympus." Hermes shuddered:

"The Gods forbid. Zeus would come out in spots." We now seemed to have exhausted this subject, so I took the conversation another way:

"There was a frightful row at lunch and Agamemnon and Akhilleus almost came to blows. Calchas says the Greeks have had a message from the Gods," I said, "If you say you didn't bring it, being on a personal day, who did?" Hermes sighed in irritation.

"It could have been any of the minor gods or goddesses. Iris or ..." I interrupted him before he could rain a long list of minor Olympians down on me and instead gave him a brief outline of what had taken place, concluding:

"So we only have Calchas' word that there was a message at all."

"True," said Hermes, "besides, I'd take anything Calchas' says with a grain of salt." I pondered.

"So he's not trustworthy, that's what you are saying?" Hermes rubbed his hands together and looked at the horizon:

"As a seer, Calchas is better than most. Seeing, as I am sure you know, is just using your common sense or, failing that, your imagination to interpret facts: the future is a consequence of the past and the present. Easy. Anyone can do it, but most humans are too stupid and lazy. They'd rather have it done for them. However, I can tell you the message doesn't sound very likely. It's not the way Zeus does things." After a pause, he continued: "Why do you ask so many questions? You're a cat, what do you care?" I bristled.

"I think you're being offensive. If there was no message from the Gods, what was all that to-do about then? Are you telling me that the Gods have nothing to do with the Greeks' reverses?" Hermes gave me a pitying look.

"Since when did humans need outside help to mess things up? But, of course, when the going gets rough, they must have someone to blame; humans are not good at MEA CULPEA." Just then, Homerys came along the sand, his hands reaching out blindly for his boy who was hiding behind a bush. Not finding him, Homerys took the opportunity to unload more poetry:

And Akhilleus cried to his mother, Thetis:
... of all this tell Zeus; kneel to him,
embrace his knee, and pray,
If Troy's aid he will ever deign,
that now their forces may
Beat home the Greeks to fleet and sea, embruing
[drenching] their retreat in slaughter, their pains paying
the wreak of their proud sovereign's heart...

"Jeez," I said in disgust. "That Akhilleus! What a sore loser! As an ally, I'd choose a rattlesnake any day." Homerys was getting ready to declaim some more when Hermes shooed his boy towards him and they went off along the beach.

"A little bit of Homerys," said Hermes, turning back to me, "goes a long way." I could but agree.

"Do you really want to know why the Greeks are losing the war?" asked Hermes suddenly. Well, I did but in three words of one syllable; unfortunately, that was probably not what Hermes had in mind. To divert him, I said hurriedly:

"I was about to go into Troy for a cup of tea. Wanna come along?" and Hermes answered:

"Don't mind if I do," so off we went.

1.3 PRIAM'S MANY-GATED CITY

Hermes and I walked across the plain and up the hill towards the city. The plain was desolate. Nothing but scrub grass or a few stunted bushes seemed to grow there. I said:

"Whoever decided to build a city here? I mean, except for the sea, the view is appalling." Hermes shook his head and answered:

"Anatolia, especially in the late Bronze Age, had an abundance of flora: maquis (dwarf forests), red pines and cypresses, and lots and lots of olive trees. Flowers, too, in season; variations on tulips, snowdrops and crocuses." He sighed. "But nine years of war has taken a toll on the environment. The countryside had been devastated, the villages destroyed. Not much grows now where, in better times, peasants harvested chickpeas, figs, barley and lentils and kept the odd goat and chicken." Hermes looked sad. I could understand him. Gone, baby, gone. Hermes looked at me:

"A pity, really, isn't it?" I nodded. "Although nothing to what the place looks like in your time."

"True," I nodded, "it's much worse now. The whole coast, all the way down to Smyrna, is chock-a-block with holiday homes. Something between Costa de Sol and Palma de Majorca."

"Wouldn't go anywhere near them," was Hermes' answer. I said:

"The perfect world only existed before man moved from homus erectus to homus sapiens. Somebody sure screwed up!"

Troy, the many-gated city, actually had six: Dardan, Tymbria, Helias, Chetas, Troien and Antenorides, all well-guarded; you couldn't just knock and get admitted. But I'm a cat and if a cat wants to get in anywhere, he will. I'd found a convenient bolthole near Antenorides. I said to Hermes:

"I'm slipping through here but it looks too small for you."

"Don't worry," came the answer, "see you on the other side." And he just walked straight into the wall and vanished. I slipped through my hole feeling silly and there, on the other side, waiting for me, was Hermes.

"Want me to brush you down? You've collected a bit of dust." I shook myself.

From Antenorides, it was just a short hop to Priam Square, the heart of Troy. Here, the city's main avenues converged at a roundabout in the centre of which was a square, a bronze lion at each corner, their backs to one another, looking outward in different directions. In the centre of the square was a fountain, from the centre of which rose a very very tall marble column with a Trojan worthy, also in bronze, looking down, with disdain, no doubt, at the petty doings of scurrying humanity below. I called Hermes' attention to the chap on the column and asked if he knew who this had been. Hermes said:

"That's Tithonius, uncle of the present king. Won a great sea battle, I seem to recall." Thanks.

"They tell me that the bronze for the lions was smelted down from enemy weapons."

"I wouldn't put it past them," came the somewhat enigmatic answer.

Priam Square was where the government buildings, museum and temples and, of course, the best bars, were to be found. This being middle of the afternoon, there was a lot going on. Ramshackle booths sold all kinds of goods from fruit and vegetables to shoes and cheap clothing. No signs of rationing or shortages. The Greeks had never managed to encircle the whole city, so the Trojans still had links inland and allied kingdoms supplied them with goods, produce and, on occasion, soldiers. That made sense because, once Troy fell, who'd be next on the Greeks' hit list? The temple to Pallas Athena, a wonderful building all in white marble, stood on the city's highest point, a magnet for tourists but, given the need to climb 200 steps to reach it, I had decided to leave this treat for later, although I had promised myself to get around to it before I left. The royal palace, neighbouring the temple, was less grand and had fewer steps. Made sense. Kings come and go but a goddess is forever.

As I had been in Troy before, I had already sussed out the best bars and eateries. The one I led Hermes to was more like a café than a bar. It was called, ominously, *The Trojan Horse*. Despite its name, the café was really cozy, pleasantly darkish inside: dim light came in through small windows to which was added the light from a scattering of lamps in sconces set at varying distances along the walls. It had a welcoming shabby-gentile look, with tables and chairs arranged in cosy groups. The décor ran on familiar lines: cute bits of pottery such as china dogs and cow creamers and a wall painting of what must have been Priam Square a hundred years ago. Another wall painting depicted King Priam and his sons – what with 50 of them, wall space was at a premium.

A board listed 'today's specials', another, the Trojan heroes' latest battle scores, with Hector as top scorer; no surprises there. A bar ran along one side of the establishment, with a wall-to-wall mirror behind it and glass shelves holding the mandatory array of bottles. Hermes and I chose a corner table near a window. A petite, comfortably plump blonde whom I had met previously and was called Marianne presided over the place. She wore flowing draperies in gay colours with gold fringe here and there. She'd seen better days but then, who hadn't. There was a waiter of sorts, little old guy in a what had once been a white apron, reading the local sports page. Marianne flicked at him with her teacloth, nodding at me. The guy took one look, and with all the ill grace he could muster, brought me a high chair. I showed my incisors in gratitude. He shuffled back to his newspaper. Marianne then came over.

"Hi, and what can I get you?" .

"I'm having a tea and scones, jam and fresh cream." I said and looked at Hermes. He shrugged.

"Sounds good."

"Two teas and scones," I said to Marianne. She frowned.

"Are you expecting a friend to join you?" she asked. I stared at her.

"She can't see me," drawled Hermes. "or hear me for that matter." Now this was embarrassing. How was I going to justify two teas? I decided to brazen it out.

"No, I am not." I said with a nonchalant air. "Two cream teas, please." Marianne wrung her hands; waitresses don't like anything out of the ordinary:

"You want one now and another later?" I shook my head.

"No. Both now, please." Marianne shrugged.

"OK, you're the customer." I gave her my best purr and she went off. I turned to Hermes.

"Man, that was embarrassing. She's going to think I'm some kind of a fruitcake." Hermes replied with a complete lack of interest:

"Does it matter?"

"Yes, it jolly well does. You think it's easy being a feline tourist. I have trouble enough as it is without an imaginary companion and going in fear of people calling the animal control cops." Hermes held up his hands.

"OK, OK, I get the point. But just take it easy; after all, I do have certain powers. Anything goes wrong, I'm on it. The fact is, humanity believes in the Gods therefore they cannot see us or hear us if we choose they should not."

"And?" I asked as there must be more.

"You, being a feline, on the other hand, don't believe in the Gods, ergo, I am visible to you." Well, I didn't feel any easier but there was not much I could do about it since Hermes appeared to be a fixture.

I must say I enjoyed my tea; the jam was just perfect and the cream a dream. I only hoped Marianne wasn't looking our way since Hermes was enjoying his too, and wolfing it down. A bark next to him announced the arrival of the café dog, one Antonia, begging for a share. Hermes gave her some scone. "She can obviously see you," I said and Hermes nodded.

"I already explained that." Then Marianne collected our tea things and I asked for a raki and tonic and one Perrier water. We sat enjoying our drinks in companionable silence, looking at the other patrons. I said to Hermes:

"Since you are here, there is something I want to discuss with you." Hermes looked at me sideways as if he wasn't in the mood. But I was adamant.

"The Trojan War," I said, "is said to have lasted ten years. But how do you count time? From the time the Greeks left Athens ..." Hermes interrupted me:

"Actually, they gathered and left from Aulis." I ignored him:

"Whatever. We know all about it. The winds that weren't there and the fleet that couldn't sail. What I am asking is: How long did it take the Greeks to reach Troy? Not forgetting they stopped along the way to pillage cities – such as Thebes." Hermes shrugged.

"Truth to tell, Gaius, I haven't a clue." I went on:

"And there's something else. Until quite recently, wars were fought in what was called 'campaigning seasons', which meant that you tilled your land, seeded your fields, brought in the harvest and then went to war. How did the Greeks manage this? How could they be away from home for ten years? Why, even WWII started in September, post harvest. Did they go backwards and forwards? Sail home at the end of the campaigning season and come back the following year?" Hermes looked at me intently:

"I hate to say this, Gaius, but I just don't know. No one has ever bothered about these details. Ask Homerys." I felt frustrated and disappointed:

"You kidding? Homerys wouldn't care as long as it didn't mess up his metric flow."

Feeling miffed, I turned my back on Hermes and looked around. It was still earliesh so there weren't too many people. A couple of soldiers with shop girls, lost in each other's eyes and blind to anything else. Only one other table was occupied. An elderly gentleman, running slightly to fat and thinning hair, fairly well dressed, and a young fellow very well dressed, all gold fringes and bronze buckles. Good looking, too; dark hair and brown eyes and a manly figure, square chin with a dimple in it, although he would never threaten Akhilleus. While I put down the older guy as, so to speak, 'county', the younger one was definitely aristocracy or even royalty. Both were having raki and water. The two had been talking in whispers but now the younger man's voice rose.

"I don't care," he cried petulantly, like a spoiled kid who wasn't getting his way. "I'm not going onto the field today; they'll have to manage without me. With my heart breaking for unrequited love, how can I possibly concentrate on killing people?" he clutched at his heart. "I'm in torment, in torment, Pandarus! It's making me weak; I can't sleep at night, I can't get up in the morning – I can't focus." Oh dear, there's nothing as boring as people who go on and on about their unsuccessful love affairs. Why they imagine anyone cares has always been beyond me. The older chap appeared to be playing some game of his own. He said:

"I've tried to help you as best I could but, honestly, you're quite hopeless. You'll have to sort yourself out without me." He stopped for a second and then waggled his finger in the other's face. "My dear Troilus, remember: faint heart never won fair lady; you need to work at it." He then declaimed in a high nasal voice: "None but the brave deserve the fair!"

"Troilus," I asked Hermes. "Who's he?"

"One of the younger of Priam's brood," was the answer. Oh, well. I tuned in again to the conversation.

"But I have, I have," moaned the victim. "You can't say I haven't tried."

"It's obvious," came the reply, "that you haven't tried hard enough. You've got to put your back into it, your shoulder to the wheel, you know. Give it your all! Nothing ventured, nothing gained! She's not going to drop into your lap just for the asking. Where there is a will there is a way."

"No one has suffered as much for love or tried as hard to please a lady as I have," wailed Troilus, now totally oblivious to anyone around him. Hermes looked at me:

"Eros seems to have been up to his old tricks around here." I raised my eyebrows. Eros? "The god of love," explained Hermes impatiently. "You might know him as Cupid!"

"Oh, that Eros," I exclaimed. It would explain a lot; no one could make such a fool of himself as Troilus without a bit of help.

"It seems," I said, "that Eros has made a sloppy job of it since the lady is not playing along!"

"Eros," came the answer, "is fond of his little joke." We turned our attention back to the lovelorn youth.

"I've sent her flowers, I've sent her bonbons, I've sent her verses wrested from my very soul and written down in my blood. Shall I read you some?" His hand went into his tunic. Hermes and I stiffened. The prospect was awful. But Pandarus held up a hand and averted the disaster.

"Not now, my friend, later, later, when we are a bit more private." Troilus, however, had already moved on.

"I can't get her out of my mind," he was now weeping, "I haven't got a minute to myself. And how am I to hide my pain? Each night I must face my family since mother insists we all dine together!" Not a bad idea, thinks I, seeing no one knew how many chairs will be empty the next evening. But Troilus continued: "I sit at the king's table, I can't eat or concentrate on what is being said around me because Cressida fills my mind." Now, at least we had a name. But why the secrecy? What's new about a lovesick young man? Was there something wrong about this Cressida? I looked at the uncle. He did look a bit shifty and furtive. Now here was a mystery. Troilus, however, wasn't done: "My evenings are a torment, and how long do you think it will be before someone notices I'm not myself? Already Hector accuses me of not pulling my weight. He wants to talk about strategy – what do I care about strategy if it's not how to win Cressida? It's getting to the point where Hector ignores me!" Quite right, too. In the middle of a major war, you don't really need staff officers mooning about and not paying attention. On the other hand, younger sons often don't count for much anyway. But how Troilus could keep a secret, any secret, without the whole world knowing, was another question, seeing how he was carrying on. And he wasn't done yet. "Where, oh, where is she, Pandarus?" Pandarus said musingly:

"I saw her yesterday – she sure is a fine gal. I don't want to disparage your sister Cassandra but, really, Cressida is so witty ..." It was like a conversation between the deaf.

"I'm telling you," moaned Troilus. "I'm drowning, drowning. And if someone's drowning, what difference does it make whether it's in a puddle or the Ægean? And all you can say is, 'oh, she's so wonderful'. What's the good of that? You're just rubbing salt into my wounds. Have you no mercy?" Poor Troilus wrung his hands. His Pa and Hector might not know all about Cressida but, by this time, everyone in *The Trojan Horse* did. I could see Marianne's ears flapping. Really, this lad was beyond a joke. Pandarus said solemnly:

"I'm just telling you the truth. You need to commit yourself totally. In for a penny, in for a pound!" Troilus retorted:

"You talk too much." Which was really unfair since, with Troilus, it was difficult to get a word in edgewise. Pandarus looked offended, got up and started to leave.

"Well, I'm done with this business," he said firmly. "Do it your own way." Of course this brought the reaction he'd probably been aiming for:

"You can't do this to me," cried Troilus hanging on to Pandarus' sleeve. "You can't leave me like this! Pandarus, you have to help me."

"She's my niece," answered Pandarus haughtily, "and I'm not going to put up with you abusing her, that she isn't as clever as Cassandra or as beautiful as Helen. But I no longer care. I'm off. Good day to you." Being off was difficult since Troilus still clung to him:

"I didn't say that," he moaned, "I didn't say that at all! There's no one more beautiful than Cressida, there's no one wittier than Cressida!" But Pandarus shook himself lose and was out the door. Troilus put his arms on the table and his head on his arms.

"This is so unfair," he wailed, still completely oblivious to anyone else around. "I can't get to Cressida except through her uncle and now he's as mad as a bear with a sore head. What am I to do? What am I to do?" Really, I felt quite sorry for him. It would have been sad if it hadn't been so comical.

"So, messenger of the Gods," I asked Hermes, "what's your take on this?"

"He loves," came the answer, "while she does not."

"Probably wise of her," I added, "since he talked of himself the whole time and never mentioned her – as a person, that is, rather than as an object of his passion – at all."

At that precise moment, there was a diversion. One of the shop girls got up in a fury and gave her companion a good stinging slap.

"How dare you!" she screeched. "What kind of girl do you think I am?" And to her girlfriend: "Come on, Aurelia, these two losers will never be good for anything!" The ladies stormed out. Hermes and I looked at each other.

"What did you make of that?" I asked. Hermes answered:

"Wrong words at the wrong time in the wrong place to the wrong person." He sighed. "The more I see, the more I sympathise with Eros. Making two humans love each other is a labour for Hercules." We were then distracted by marching boots on the pavement outside. The army was on the move. One warrior looked through the window and bounded in. He went up to Troilus and barked:

"Troilus, why aren't you on the field? The Greeks are launching a major offensive and we need every man. This is no time to sit around in cafés! Get booted and suited, and be quick about it." I looked at Hermes.

"Priam's son." Everyone is Troy seemed to be Priam's son. Deiphobus then espied the two abandoned swains and turned on them. "You, two. Get with it! Join your units – now!" The two scuttled off but Troilus still hung his head:

"Deiphobus, I don't feel well."

"You can be sick – or dead – tomorrow for as long as you like. Today, it's every man's shoulder to the wheel. Do you think the rest of us do it for our health?" Deiphobus stalked out. And so, after saying he wouldn't, Troilus did.

1.4 PARIS IS GORED WITH MENELAUS' HORN

I called for another couple of drinks and Hermes and I sat there quietly for a bit, both, no doubt, mulling all we had just witnessed. At last I asked Hermes:

"What do you think this Pandarus is up to? Is he trying to get an aristocratic husband for the niece? Is he trying to get Troilus into an embarrassing position and then blackmail him? Or he's just an old busybody with nothing to do? Too old for the army and a city under siege is not a fun place. All the theatres closed, all the best restaurants, too, as the waiters have probably all been drafted."

"Well, Gaius, you have come up with so many solutions I'm spoilt for choice. Any of the above, I would say." I could see Hermes was completely uninterested. Then he went on: "I suggest we go up to the battlements of the Tower and see what's going on in the field." Well, war isn't really my thing even as a spectator sport but I suppose one must be tolerant of others' interests, so I followed Hermes out of the café, along to the wall near Antenorides and up I don't know how many steps to the battlements. There was quite a crowd there already. For my life, it looked like a British upper class tea party. Ascot or maybe Wimbledon or Lords, all that was missing were the hats and strawberries. Chairs and parasols had been set up, small tables scattered around holding refreshments and various items of sustenance. Menials moved around, bringing in supplies and making sure everyone was served. I suppose in Troy war was the only game in town. Most of the party was made up of old ladies and gentlemen, the ladies conspicuous for their veils and the gentlemen for sporting medals from bygone wars. I jumped up on one of the lower crenulations and looked down. Down was very far indeed.

"Hermes," I said, "I'm not happy here. A gust of wind would blow me over."

"Stop snivelling," was the unsympathetic answer, "there aren't going to be any gusts of wind this afternoon." I sniffed but was distracted when some stupid old lady cried out:

"Oh, look what a sweet Pussy! Puss, puss, puss," twiddling her fingers the way humans think attracts cats. I arched my back and hissed, showing claws and incisors and she backed off with a hurt look. "Not a very friendly pussy," she said to her companions. Well, too bad, lady, that's the draw of the cards. Some pussies are, some aren't. I was more interested in knowing who all these people were so I asked Hermes. He pointed to two elderly gentlemen who had bagged the best seats.

"Ucalegon and Antenor, elders of Troy. Priam is sitting in that throne like chair and behind him are Panthous, Thymoetes, Lampus, Clytius, and Hiketaon. Too old to fight, you know, but not too old to lavish their opinions on everyone and drown them in useless advise." Go figure. PLUS ÇA CHANGE, PLUS C'EST LA MEME CHOSE. Old soldiers never die, they just become more boring with each passing year.

From where we were, Hermes and I had a superb view of the whole field. I sat sedately as far back as I could and still have a view. Hermes was a nice guy but I had never known that the messenger of the Gods was also into weather forecasting. However, I took his word about the wind – with reservations. Hermes sat on the high crenulation next to mine, his legs swinging over the void. Seeing he had wings on his feet, he was perfectly safe. You may say I should have been too, since cats have nine lives but I had never seen this scientifically proven and wasn't about to become the subject in a clinical test.

Down on the field, the Greeks and Trojans, in serried ranks, faced each other. The Trojans suddenly burst forward, each soldier seemingly bent on doing his own thing, while the Greeks held their line and stayed shoulder to shoulder. Then Paris stood out from the general Trojan melée, all dressed up, leopard skin – I pursed my lips in disapproval – two swords, bow and arrows and spears. How did I know it was Paris? Well, he had that pretty boy look and by the richness of his armour and other accruements it couldn't be anyone. Don't ask me how he managed to hold all his arms with only two hands. As for the finer points of the rules of engagement at the time of the Trojan War, I didn't have a clue. Not, mind you, that I understand them today either. Paris lifted his weapons and seemed to be ranting on.

"What's Paris on about?" I asked Hermes. "Can't hear a thing!"

"He's challenging one of the Greeks to single combat," came the short answer, his whole attention on the goings-on in the field. Then he turned to me and seemed to waggle his ears and suddenly I could hear perfectly. Hector had now come up to Paris.

"Paris, what game is this?" Paris flushed:

"Game? This is no game. I will fight Menelaus in single battle for Helen and all her wealth." I was astounded.

"Wealth?" I said, "and here am I thinking it's all about love." Hermes looked at me significantly.

"More fool you," was his comment. Then Menelaus came forward, broad and muscular, raised his sword and shield to the sky and cried out:

"Let him who shall die, die, and let the others fight no more."

We were diverted from these goings-on by a breathless herald falling through the archway onto the terrace and kneeling before Priam.

"August lord," he said, "there is to be a single combat between Paris and Menelaus to determine the outcome of the war." A gasp of wonder from the tea partiers. "The Trojans are bringing two lambs to the field, a white ram and a black ewe, representing Earth and Sun, and the Greeks a goat as a sacrifice to Zeus. And, lord, you are bid come also, so you yourself may witness and swear to this covenant." Priam became quite agitated.

"Go get Helen," he quavered. "I think Helen should be here." A servant girl rushed off. The question was, why hadn't she been here to begin with? And then a vision of perfection sauntered on to the battlements.

Helen. Was she beautiful? Of course, I'm a cat so cannot judge but I could see she was ... perfect. Tall, a lovely head balanced on a swan-like neck onto ever so slightly sloping shoulders; long arms, slim wrists with long thin hands, tapering fingers and perfect pearl-like nails: her form was elegant: small bosom, narrow waist and hips, and the legs that shimmered through the gauze dress were long and shapely. Perfect heart-shaped face, Grecian nose; high forehead, high cheek bones; full rose coloured lips, creamy unblemished skin; blond hair streaked with silver and golden strands, held up with golden pins and falling down her neck and shoulder in broad coils; and her eyes ... deep blue fringed with unbelievably dark lashes. Eyebrows a dark blonde. I won't go into details of her dress because Helen would be perfect in the beggar maid's rags. Yep, that Helen, she was something all right. But there was a look about her I couldn't quite place. On instinct, not a lady I would guess.

"Does my Lord Priam call me?" she said in a low musical voice devoid of emotion.

"Yes, my dear," answered the good old man, even at his age not insensible to her charms. He gave her a breakdown of what was going on. "Sweet Helen," he concluded kindly, "take your seat beside me and if the Gods are good to us we will see the matter settled this day." But Helen ignored him. She walked up to the ramparts, placing herself between me and Hermes, and looked over the field.

"Indeed, there are all my kinsmen: my husband Menelaus and Agamemnon, his brother, Odysseus, that crafty villain, and so many others. And your Trojans, Priam, your many sons and your kinsmen." Silent for a moment, she murmured in a low voice only Hermes and I could hear. "But there are two I would see but not here. Castor and Pollux, my dear brothers: you have not come nor should you. Stay away, this is not an honourable war." I looked at Hermes and whispered:

"What's she on about? I've heard of these guys but where escapes me." Hermes murmured sotto voce:

"They are – or where – her brothers, Gaius. Both lie under the earth in their land of Lacedœmon."

"Oh, then she doesn't know," was my comment. Hermes countered:

"Ignorance is bliss." How true. Helen turned back to Priam, her face haughty, eyes cold and said:

"War is a man's business. It would be a sorry day were women reduced to settling their differences in such a wasteful and messy manner. I have no interest in battles, this or any other. When it is all over, you will find me on my balcony with my embroidery." She turned but just before she left she caught sight of me. We exchanged a long glance. Her look was pure steel and I purred, as cats do when they know they don't have the upper hand. I didn't think she'd say 'oh, what a sweet pussy', and she didn't. Then she was gone. Priam, nonplussed, said nothing, but the aunts were all over it.

"Why," said one, "can you imagine! Not caring whether your husbands live or die!" The second aunt cackled:

"Husbands is right. Perhaps she'd be glad to see the last of one of them."

"Ahh," said the third, "but which one!" The three cackled together and sipped their tea. Priam rose and left with his principal councillor, Antenor. We saw them come out of the tower, mount a waiting chariot and leave through the Antenorides gate towards the battlefield. Hermes gritted his teeth.

"Here we go again," he said as the sacrifices began, blood and guts all over the place. "Disgusting! Zeus will be as mad as a wet hen. Don't be surprised if there is thunder when the barbecue starts."

"I take it," was my comment, "he is a strict vegan."

"His favourite food is grape – specially in liquid form," was Hermes' answer. I combed my whiskers with my claws:

"My, I would never have guessed."

In the field, Agamemnon appeared to be leading a prayer meeting:

"Great Zeus," he cried, "most glorious, and Sun, that sees and gives ear to all things, Earth and Rivers, and the Gods who in the realm of Hades chastise the soul of the oath breaker, witness these rites and guard them, so they not be vain. Should Paris kills Menelaus, let him keep Helen and all her wealth, and we shall sail home for Greece; if Menelaus kills Paris, Helen and all that she has will return with us to Sparta."

There was a rumbling in the sky that was otherwise blue and clear.

"Oh, oh," said Hermes, "here we go." Below, Priam in his turn invoked the power of the Gods and swore that Troy would back the agreement to the hilt. Having done his bit, so to speak, he said:

"I will now go back to Troy as I have not the strength to witness my son and Menelaus fighting to the death. The Gods' will be done." He got in the chariot with Antenor, and off they went; they did not return to the battlements.

"Yeah," sneered Hermes, "the Gods will indeed. Just blame it on the Gods. Your son is a no good skirt chaser who gets well deservedly clobbered by an irate husband and it's the will of the Gods, not your kid's bad behaviour and lack of guts."

On the field, Trojans and Greeks formed a circle around the combatants. Hermes and I were so intent on what was going on that we were almost scared out of our wits by a woosh and the arrival of a lady from what seemed nowhere who settled down to the right of Hermes. He looked at her and raised his eyebrows.

"Aphrodite[2]. Why am I not surprised?" Aphrodite, all charm and blond hair but still no match to Helen, crossed long slim legs and inspected her nails.

"Others, besides yourself, are interested in the Trojan War. And don't tell me you're here just to keep the cat company." Cat, I mean! Hermes bristled.

"I know why you are here, Aphrodite, so don't give me any gumph. You've got the hots for that pretty boy, don't you? But let me make it clear: if you interfere in any way, if you as much as lift a finger or blink an eye to help Paris I will shop you to Zeus in a twinkling. Be warned!" Aphrodite put her head to one side, pouting her lips and trying to look cute and coy at the same time.

"Hermes, my sweet friend, I know you wouldn't do that." Hermes looked away.

"Aphrodite, my dear love, I advise you not to test what I would or would not do. I know all your tricks." Aphrodite fell silent and looked glum.

Down on the field, the combatants faced each other. If I were a betting cat, I would have put my money on Menelaus. Right makes might. O.k., so Paris had age on his side but Menelaus was a big strong man, bred for war, and a lot heavier than the slim elegant Paris. Menelaus raised his spear and hurled it at Paris; although it passed though shield and cuirass and tore his shirt, Paris managed to side step and get away with a flesh wound. Then Menelaus drew his sword, driving it at Paris' helmet, but the sword broke into three or four pieces as it hit and Paris – and helmet - were unhurt. Hermes looked sharply at Aphrodite who had fluttered just a bit.

"You have been warned," he said menacingly. Aphrodite protested:

---

[2]   Greek Goddess of Love

"I haven't done anything!" Hermes drummed his fingers on the stone. Then Menelaus rushed at Paris, caught him by the horsehair plume of his helmet, and began dragging him towards the Greek lines. The oxhide strap was choking Paris, and Menelaus would have strangled him to death, to his own greater glory, had the strap not broken and the empty helmet come away in his hand. He flung it at his comrades, grabbed his spear and sprang at Paris. I closed my eyes. Menelaus was sure to run him through and blood makes me sick. Then, to everyone's surprise, Paris turned and ran, the Trojans parting to give him passage and then closing their circle again. Menelaus gave a shout of rage and threw his spear, hitting some unfortunate Trojan in the shoulder. By that time, Paris was already at the Antenorides gate. Aphrodite, Hermes and I looked at each other.

"I swear, Hermes, I swear I had nothing to do with this," Aphrodite pleaded.

"I believe her," I said, "Paris is a coward and cowards can run really fast." There seemed to be nothing left to see. The warriors on the field were just standing around or sitting down, pulling up their socks and taking swigs of water from their canteens. I said to Hermes:

"The Greek Olive Tree will have a full house tonight." Hermes raised his eyebrows. Aphrodite had disappeared. So we left it at that. The entertainment seeming to be over, we started down the myriad steps to Priam Square. On one of the landings, we saw Helen sitting at a balcony, intent on her embroidery. A maid came running up to her.

"Lady," she cried, "the Lord Paris is in his chamber. He is sore hurt and is asking for you." Helen compared silks in deep concentration.

"Tell my lord Paris," she said icily, "that I am otherwise engaged. Send one of the manservants to him. Or go yourself." The maidservant looked embarrassed:

"Madam…" she tried again. Helen's ice-cold blue eyes looked right through her.

"Was there anything else?" she asked in a voice of steel. The girl, frightened out of her wits, shook her head and scuttled away. Helen turned her full attention back to her embroidery. Wow. Sir Walter Scott got it all wrong when he said:

O woman!- In our hours of ease,
uncertain, coy, and hard to please,
[...]
when pain and anguish wring the brow,
a ministering angel thou[3]

Was it Helen of Troy Sir Walter was thinking of? I think not. On the next landing, Hector was standing at the door of a chamber, talking to someone inside. And Hector was really pissed:

"Paris," he exclaimed hotly, "I wish you had never been born. How the Greeks will mock us for coming up with a champion fair of face but lacking both wit and courage! You who had the audacity to carry off a married woman from a far country, bringing sorrow upon your father, your friends and your whole country. That you should run from Menelaus, her lawful husband, like a whipped cur. Is this how you prove what mettle Trojans are made of! What price now your lyre, love-tricks, comely locks and fair face when you have allowed yourself to be branded as a coward!" Paris came to the door, his head hanging like a naughty schoolboy.

"Hector, you are absolutely right. However, do not taunt my gifts for I assure you they are worth having." Hector snorted:

"I can't see that your 'gifts', as you call them, have done anyone any good – except yourself, of course, and even then it's debatable." Hector stamped his foot, turned his back on Paris and stomped off. Hermes and I continued down the stairs. As we reached the street, I asked Hermes:

"What do you think Homerys will make of all this?" Hermes shrugged.

"You'll soon find out," as indeed I did. Arriving at Priam square, there was Homerys in full throttle:

Again he [Menelaus] intends to force the lifeblood of his
foe [Paris] and ran on him [Paris] aiming, with shaken
javelin when the Queen that lovers love [Aphrodite],
ravished him from that encounter quite. She hid him in

---

[3]   *Marmion*, Canto VI, st. 30. Sir Walter Scott (1771-1832)

> *a cloud of gold and never made him known till in his*
> *chamber, fresh and sweet, she gently set him.*

"For Aprodite's sake," was Hermes' comment, "let's hope Zeus never reads Homerys." I added sanctimoniously:

"Truth is in the ear of the hearer."

1.5 THEY ARE COMING FROM THE FIELD

Hermes and I walked back to *The Trojan Horse.* It was time for something strengthening.

"Well," I said taking a sip of my water, "that was a washout."

"Yep," answered Hermes staring into his raki, "but no war ever ends with single combat. Too easy by far." Then a servant of sorts came in and holding up a finger, declaimed:

"A table for my lord and lady!" He got a look from Marianne.

"The Lady Helen and Lord Paris, I suppose?" The servant looked slightly embarrassed.

"Well, no, not really, my lady Cressida and Lord Pandarus!" Marianne rolled her eyes.

"Well, my good lad, there are plenty of free tables. Take your pick," and smartly turned her back on him. But servants are never nonplussed for long. He chose a table near the window – in fact, the one next to me and Hermes – and made a great show of wiping it down and dusting the chairs. As Pandarus came in, he indicated the table and bowed as low as he could. Marianne said:

"Ah, Pandarus, back again, are you? A lady this time, is it? Tea, I suppose?" Pandarus smiled most graciously and sat down, taking care to arrange his clothes just so.

"Please, my dear Marianne, tea for my lady Cressida and watered wine for me." Marianne flicked her dishcloth to show what she thought of them. Hermes and I looked at each other. A rather tall, willowy young lady entered the ETABLISSEMENT . Long dark brown hair, soft brown eyes flecked with green. Her dress was in the usual Greek style with a touch of the oriental: a coloured shawl with a golden fringe. This appeared to be The Cressida.

"Nice," was Hermes' remark. "One can see why Troilus is smitten." However, there was a sadness about her, a listlessness in the way she stirred her tea. She said in a low voice:

"Uncle Pandarus, you know I don't like coming out in public like this. People stare so. You saw how Marianne looked at us." Pandarus pooh-poohed all this.

"My dear," he said, "if you feel guilty you will look guilty. Hold your head up high. You haven't done anything. And think of your prospects!" Marianne arrived with their order and the conversation stopped until she was gone.

"Yes," said Pandarus into his watered wine. "There was a great battle today. You should have seen the Greeks and Trojans lined up, their shields gleaming in the sun. There's a rumour going round," he added SOTTO VOCE, "that this may be the end of the war."

"What a blessing that would be," sighed Cressida, "why, I was a little girl when it all started out. I can hardly remember what it was like then."

"Deiphobus had to come and get Troilus, you know; Troilus had sworn he wasn't taking the field today. But of course the Trojan side couldn't do without him." This remark was received by Cressida with a stony face. Pandarus tried again:

"Yes, Troilus is vital to the Trojans' war effort."

"Are you telling me that Troilus is more important than Hector? Why, there's no comparison. Troilus is a mere boy. You must be delirious, uncle, I've told you often enough not to go out in the sun without your hat. You know how easily you get heatstroke." Pandarus waved his arms about impatiently.

"You just don't understand, do you? Troilus is Troilus!"

"But you seem to compare him to Hector!"

"Alas, alas, poor Troilus, he is not himself these days!"

"Not if he's like Hector, he isn't," was the amused answered. Well, I had an inkling where Pandarus was going but he wasn't about to get there anytime soon. He took another stab at it.

"Do you know that Helen considers Troilus the most handsome of Priam's sons? She says there is no complexion to compare with his, his nose is the most aristocratic and none of his siblings has his thick curly hair. And, as for his dimpled chin, why, she finds it irresistible."

Cressida drank her tea and poor old Pandarus saw that he would have to go straight to the point.

"Niece, I told you something yesterday."

"So you did."

"Niece, think of it."

"I have. I do. I will." Suddenly, Pandarus leaned forward. His eyes narrowed, his brow creased and the good-natured foolish old uncle seemed to have been replaced by something a lot more dangerous. His fingers tapped Cressida's hand.

"Niece, you had better think and quickly. You know what our situation is. Just tell me, when was the last time you were asked out to dinner?" Cressida looked flustered.

"Well, I ..." Pandarus interrupted her rudely.

"Exactly. And your friend, Lydia, when was the last time she came visiting?"

"What with the war and her husband and the new baby ..."

"Don't fool yourself. You no longer have any friends. You no longer have any standing in the community. You are a pariah[4]! Your continued existence – and mine – depends entirely on the forbearance of those who ostracized us but let us live. If you were to become the intimate friend of Troilus it would take us a long way, dear niece, to regaining some of the standing we lost when your father Calchas dumped the both of us and went over to the Greeks." Cressida drew herself back.

"Why don't you, dearest uncle, say it right out?"

"If your dear Papa, Cressida, comes up trumps for the Greeks, a thunderbolt from heaven or some such thing was to strike Troy, how long do you think you and I would last?"

"Are you trying to say, uncle dearest, that our lives depends on my father's continued failure to hand victory to the Greeks?"

"That's my clever girl; I knew you would get it. Exactly. However, there is an option. Can you guess, dearest relative?"

"Troilus." Pandarus became the kind uncle once again.

---

4   An Indian word meaning 'outcast'.

"Yes, my dear, if Troilus were to become your good friend ... your protector ..."

"My lover!" Pandarus shrugged.

"Wife, who knows? It all depends on how you play your cards, sweetheart! Be it all as it may, the day may well come when only Troilus will stand between you and I both and a one way ticket to Hades." Cressida got up.

"I'm not listening to this anymore," she said and flounced out. Pandarus drummed his fingers on the table.

"The Gods damn all virtuous maidens! They'll be the death of us yet," and left himself. Hermes and I were again alone in our corner. I looked at Hermes and he looked at me.

"I never knew," I said, "that being a girl could be so complicated." Hermes sighed.

"Ask anyone. Ask Europa. Ask Leda[5]. In fact, ask Helen." I mussed on this for a bit.

"I take it," I said at length, "that if Paris had run off with Menelaus there wouldn't have been such a fuss." Hermes raised his eyebrows but didn't deign to answer me.

After a while, Hermes and I left *The Trojan Horse* and took a wander around the square. Besides the usual booths selling brick-a-brac, some wily entrepreneurs had set up shop selling war memorabilia – bronze gloves, arrowheads, the odd helmet, medals and so on. They were doing a brisk business. We looked at this lot for a while. Hermes said:

"Well, Gaius, taking any souvenirs home?" I shook my head.

"Don't think so. There's always the problem, you know, of overweight baggage and, anyhow, if I wanted something I could just go out to the battlefield and pick it up for nothing." Hermes nodded.

"Too true, my friend." I had another thought:

"I could, of course, sell it to a museum as a real artefact from the Trojan War. But I'm afraid no curator would believe me." So that was a washout and we went on.

---

[5]　Europa and Leda were both victims of Zeus' lust, to seduce them, he took, respectively, the form of a Bull and a Swan

Then we heard the blaring of trumpets, drums beating and the sound of tramping feet, the jingling of chains and weapons and harnesses, the sound of chariot wheels on stone paving. The fearless warriors were back, passing through Antenorides on their way to Priam square and a Te Deum at the Temple of Diana. The crowd grew frenzied and came rushing up, waving Trojan flags and cheering madly. Troops were rushed in to push them back, and Hermes and I were pressed into the throng. For a moment it looked as if I was about to be trod under foot when Hermes picked me up and set me on a window ledge. In the middle of the melee, Pandarus arrived, dragging Cressida with him, and they took up positions close to my window. Pandarus was in high spirits and eulogized each warrior as he passed. Æneas and Hector were first. Pandarus rhapsodised loudly:

"Oh, brave, brave warriors!" and, in aside to Cressida, "these guys are good enough, I suppose, but wait until you see Troilus." Cressida asked:

"Where's Paris? Didn't he go to the field today?" Pandarus seemed not to know of Paris' exploits which was curious since he seemed to know everything that went on in Troy. He waved the question away as if irrelevant, and he wasn't far wrong. Then came Helenus and Deiphobus, and Pandarus repeated his little act. Cressida looked bored. At last Troilus appeared, covered in dust and mud, a glum expression on his face. Pandarus went into ecstasies. "Here's a hero!" he exclaimed. "A parfait knight. What a warrior! What a commander! An arm of chilled steel; no one can compare with him and here I include the Greeks, too." Laying it on a bit thick but at least the wicked uncle seemed to have taken a few hours off. Cressida wasn't buying it:

"I hear Akhilleus is quite good and so is Agamemnon," she said.

"Akhilleus? Agamemnon? Why, they're just a rag and a tag and a hank of hair compared to Troilus." Pandarus waved his arms about. "Any girl would give her eyeteeth for such a lover as Troilus. Why, he's got it all. Birth, beauty, good looks, youth, excellent public speaker – you mark my words, Troilus is going places. But for his sadness, I do pity him." But Cressida had had enough. She turned to Pandarus and rapped out, quite forgetting she was on a public street with a mass of people around her. This habit of babbling about your most intimate matters just anywhere seemed to be a Trojan peculiarity.

"Let's see if we understand each other, uncle, shall we? Are you trying to sell me to Troilus or perhaps sell Troilus to me?" Pandarus looked embarrassed.

"My dear girl, what a thing to say! I'm trying to tell you that Troilus likes you. Likes you a lot, in fact."

"And so what, uncle? Even if Troilus loved me more than anyone ever loved Helen, what good could it do me? Am I to be a wife? Me, the daughter of a traitor? Am I to be a mistress, kept in the shadows, casting away my good name and my future? What happens when Troilus tires of me? Am I to become a whore? Turning tricks in allies with any scum possessing a coin just to keep alive?" Pandarus looked both shocked and frightened and tried to shush her up. But now Cressida was really angry. "So spare me all this Troilus chatter. Forget Troilus. He's not for the likes of us." She looked at him with a gimlet eye. "Sorry, uncle, you'll have to take your chances just as I will. There are more important things than merely being alive." Pandarus looked as if he didn't think so. But Cressida wasn't done. "And one thing I will never accept is someone 'protecting' me – 'If you will be nice to me, why, baby, I'll take care of you'. I'll tell you who knows what's good for me. I do. So let's hear no more of this Troilus nonsense." She stalked off, leaving Pandarus gobsmacked.

"What a virago!" he shuddered and then he too left. Right, Cressida, with relatives like that you don't need any enemies. I turned to Hermes:

"What do you know, Cressida is Calchas' daughter." I'd had my suspicions back at the *Trojan Horse*. "Not really fair, going off and leaving her behind!" Hermes sighed:

"The world," he said, "is a shithole." How original. I gave him a sideways squint.

"You knew all along, didn't you?" Hermes didn't bother to deny it, merely saying:

"A God is a God is a God." Muy amigo. "I'm off, Gaius. Think I've had enough excitement for one day." And so had I. Life in Troy was all go go go.

Hermes just disappeared, one minute he was there, the next he wasn't. I walked around Priam Square for a bit. Dinner was over and people were strolling about; the shops were still open and pretty busy; kids were everywhere, in the fountain (to the horror of mothers) and climbing all over the lions. Seeing Homerys on a bench with his fidgety boy next to him and not being in the mood for more epic poetry, I decided to go back to the *The Trojan Horse*. However, I wasn't quick enough and Homerys's voice floated behind me:

> *"O Zeus! Vouchsafe [grant] me [Menelaus] now revenge, and that my enemy [Paris] for doing wrong so undeserved, may pay deservedly the pains he forfeited [escaped]; and let these hands [Menelaus'] inflict those pains, by conquering, ay, by conquering dead, him [Paris] on whom life complains. That any now, or any one of all the brood of men to live hereafter may with fear from all offence abstain. Much more from all such foul offence to his host [Menelaus], and entertained him [Paris], as the man whom he [Paris] affected most.*

Well, Homerys, your heart is in the right place but I hate to tell you that wife stealing and husband cheating will go on merrily, I imagine, until humanity is no more.

1.6 SHE'S A VERY MERRY GREEK INDEED

The Trojan Horse was pretty empty since the action was all out of doors, on the sidewalk cafés, where a balmy evening and a starlit sky came for free. Marianne and the waiter were busy at their outside tables. I decided this was a good time for an evening snooze before my nightcap and I jumped up on the seat of a wooden armchair filled with cushions. I pummelled them to my satisfaction, stretched and curled up. I had the place for myself for about half an hour before a large party came in, with Marianne bustling after them. It was Priam and what looked like the Trojan High Command. By this time, I knew most of them. Hector, Helenus, Deiphobus, the counsellor Antenor, Paris and Troilus plus a few others such as two sons of Priam's I hadn't seen before, Echemmon and Chromius. They were all pretty banged up, bandages and slings and plasters being in obvious evidence. The action, following the Paris debacle, must have turned savage. Hector, his head swathed in bandages, turned to Marianne:

"Please close the café, Marianne. We wish to be private." Marianne bobbed a curtsy and hurried off. Helenus (arm in a sling, one foot bandaged) said:

"Don't sit in that chair, father, there's a cat lying in it." Priam looked down at me. I looked back through slits in my gimlet blue eyes. Priam seemed uncertain.

"Perhaps we can move him," he suggested without conviction. Deiphobus came over and I flexed my claws, my eyes boring into his, my ears laid back. Deiphobus thought better of it.

"Never mind, father," he said, "you have my chair and I'll take that one over there." Indeed. If you want the best seat in the house, you need to move the cat, which is not always wise, cats having uncertain tempers.

Marianne closed the doors and the old waiter brought beakers of wine and water and mugs for everyone. Once everyone had been served, silence reigned. I wondered if they had come to discuss the matter of the one-to-one between Paris and Menelaus but it seemed the general attitude was least said soonest mended. An eerie embarrassed silence followed until at last Priam sighed deeply. He looked around at his sons – out of the fifty sons, I wondered how many were still alive? – and his councillors. He turned to Hector:

"My son, you and I have discussed Troy's situation. Would you be so good as to sum it up for our friends?" Vintage Priam. Let someone else do the heavy lifting. Hector looked around, took a swig and then said:

"I hardly have to tell any of you how many years, lives and resources have been lost in this war – oh, I can't remember all the friends and kindred who have died over these nine years, the list is too long!" For a moment, Hector covered his eyes with his hand, a futile gesture, you can't shut out what has been. He got himself together: "In spite of the price we have paid, we are exactly where we were nine years ago except that the Greeks demand, besides Helen's return with her treasure, heavy war reparations." I cocked an ear.

This could be interesting. I bet every Trojan wished Helen at the antipodes. Too bad. Hector continued: "I very much fear that, after today, another battle may finish us off. Our soldiers are exhausted as are our people and our allies. The question therefore is: do we make a treaty with the Greeks, returning Helen and her treasure and acknowledge as lost all we have invested so far in this affair – honour, dead, wounded, cash, to say nothing of hardship and sorrow." Priam buried his head in his hands as he well might. Then he seemed to collect the pieces and said:

"Hector has laid out our situation exactly. This council has been called to discuss what our next move should be. Hector, please." Hector moved about uneasily in his chair.

"No one fears the Greeks less than I do; however, there is the future to consider, not only mine: if we lose on the battlefield, if the city is taken, what will become of our people? A humiliating peace means safety and from safety comes security. Or, are we willing to take our chances on the battlefield and hope to prevail at last? Stake all and win all – or lose all." Hector looked around and then addressed Antenor: "As the wisest of our councillors, Antenor, let us have your opinion." Antenor shook his grey head slowly:

"Trojans and allies, I will speak as my experience and wisdom commands. Let us give up Helen and her wealth. Every soul lost since the first sword was drawn over Helen was as dear to us as she has become." Doubtful looks all around. To my mind, Helen wouldn't be winning popularity contests anytime soon. Antenor went on: "We can all agree, I take it, on the importance of ownership, the very pillar on which our civilization rests. And is there any relationship closer than husband and wife? You steal another man's wife and what price then our legal system, the very fabric of our society?" He stopped and looked around. "Why should we continue fighting to keep what doesn't belong to us and is of no use to us? Let's cut our losses while we can. Send her back." Well, old Antenor had my vote and Hector's, who nodded in agreement. To my surprise, Troilus jumped up all in a rage, his broken heart seemingly forgotten. He was all a-fire to solve problems as long as they weren't his own.

"With all respect, Antenor – and Hector – how can you even suggest such an outcome? What price our father's honour and that of Troy? Isn't our father's greatness a treasure beyond measure to be protected and not discarded? Are we afraid of a future we know nothing of? Are we going to allow ourselves to be bullied in our own country? We did not seek the Greeks, they sought us. I say, Helen stays and may the chips fall where they may!"

Indeed. What war was not started in the name of self-interest wrapped decorously in the national flag? Helenus, a non-descript blonde whom I later learned was also a priest, smiled at Troilus in a superior and condescending way.

"Well, little brother," he said, "you're very ready to sneer at Antenor and Hector but I don't see you coming up with any alternate solution other than returning to the battlefield. The wise predict the future by looking at the past which has shown us that we may win a battle here and there, but in the long run we cannot prevail over the assembled might of the Greek city states. We have lasted this long because our walls are strong and cannot be breeched. But they may not shield us forever. Abstract values like honour and glory are all very well but you're not being reasonable, just emotional."

"And I suppose, Helenus," Troilus snapped back, "you will rely on dreams and portents? Examine a calf's liver or read the stars?" He was all fired up; perhaps not as much of a wimp as I had thought. "You say we cannot win this war in the long term – that the Greek city states are stronger than we are. But hear me: I say the future is wide open and anything is possible." He was so red in the face I was afraid he'd burst a blood vessel. But he continued: "And what price courage, what price honour, what price valour? And what price glory?" Hector held up his hand for silence.

"Brother," he said gently, "Helen is not worth the price we're paying for her." That made Troilus wilder still.

"That's it, is it? Everything has a price?" shouted the warmonger. But Hector was all patience.

"Any object needs to be measured by its intrinsic value so we, the buyers, may judge the price we're willing to pay for it." Indeed. CAVEAT EMPTOR[6]. Hector continued: "The will must be subject to

---

[6]   Buyer beware

what the mind considers reasonable." Troilus took a deep breath. The Gods keep us from the young. They'll blow up the planet yet as sure as eggs is eggs.

"When all this started, everyone applauded Paris for abducting Helen, in fact, he was given ship and crew to go and do it and the whole of Troy watched from the ramparts as he sailed off. So I ask again: What is Helen's worth? A woman for whom a coalition of the Greek city states launched a thousand ships." Troilus stopped for a sip of wine; not big drinkers this lot, unlike the Greeks. I was impressed although I wasn't sure I could get around his logic. Yet I would never have guessed Troilus had so much reasoning in him

A commotion came from outside. A girl, all filmy draperies, flying hair and wild eyes, burst through the café door and flung herself upon Priam.

"Weep, Trojans, weep!" she cried. "Listen, oh listen before it's too late. We are all doomed."

Hector got a chair for her.

"Calm down, Cassandra," he said gently. "Let me get you a drink." So this was Cassandra. Good looking girl but definitely unbalanced. Cassandra started sobbing wildly, hiccupped and then managed to go on:

"Cry, Trojans, cry! The sea has not as many drops of water as we must shed in blood and tears before this is over. Troy will be destroyed and cease to exist. Our irresponsible brother Paris has condemned us all. Helen will bring us nothing but sorrow. Let her go or Troy will burn." I checked my return ticket; I still had it in my back pocket. I could also hitch a ride with Odysseus. Scratch that.

"Well, Troilus, my young brother," says Hector, stroking Cassandra's hair, his arm around her shoulder. "Doesn't our sister's anguish touch you? Or the peril to our citizens, young and old alike? Have you so hardened yourself by your ideas of honour and glory that no reason, no fears of a disastrous defeat from a worthless cause can stop you in your mad dash to immortality?" But Troilus was unimpressed.

"My brother, are you really suggesting that we should be guided by our sister's mad ravings?" he said. For my part, I'd believe

Cassandra any day of the week before this young firebrand. Priam then turned to Paris:

"Paris, you are the most directly involved. What do you say?" Paris said:

"I give notice to both Trojans and Greeks that I will not give up this woman; but the wealth I brought with her I will restore, and will add to that more of my own. I am committed to this course and be assured I will see it through to the bitter end." Deiphobus interrupted him:

"Paris, Helen's fate is now way above you pay grade." Too true. In fact, Helen's fate should really be put to the vote by the entire population of Troy. Then Antenor spoke again:

"Deiphobus is right. The fate of Helen is not just beyond Paris but beyond all of us. Paris' solution is a non-starter, anyway. The Greeks will not take the gold and leave the lady. They want both or none." A silence ensued.

Priam at last spoke again, addressing Paris:

"You say you will see it to the bitter end, my son, but so must your family, friends and the people of Troy, to be paid for with our lives and the future of our state." The Trojan leadership was fatally flawed. Priam, a weak old man; Hector, brave and decent who loved his home and family but totally without guile or cunning, both essential in war or diplomacy. I bet he had scruples, too, another setback. So neither Priam nor Hector, although nominally in charge, could not or would take the tough decisions called for. Oh, for an Odysseus or even an Agamemnon. Paris continued, intent on dragging everyone with him on the merry road to ruin:

"Well, father, shall we get rid of Helen, wipe the slate clean, as if she had never been? But I give you notice: if I must, I'll stand alone to defend her." Sure, *and through it all, I stood tall and did it my way.* Paris, you're a hypocrite. Anyway, you gave us a sample of your steadfastness this afternoon. Priam sighed. Hector said:

"My brothers and friends, you have all put your cases well." All this brotherly love seemed a sure road to nowhere. "Now, Helen is without doubt Menelaus' wife. Both law and nature command that she belong to him. To persist in an error is foolish; the wise man is he who changes his mind once he has seen he is in error." He stopped, hoping, I presume, this would sink in. But no one reacted. Hector looked at each one in turn. "It seems, however, I am outvoted. You are resolved to keep Helen, cost what it may. I suppose I must agree, since it does indeed touch on our individual dignities and that of Troy. So be it."

So they were all agreed to let the whole thing go south as they, in their hearts of hearts, knew it would. As Cassandra was only a woman, her word counted for nothing. Paris and Troilus were jubilant and Troilus said in exultation:

"Brother, that is the exact point I was trying to make. If I was just a hot head, as you and father think, why, not one drop of Trojan blood should be spilt in Helen's defence. But she is worth keeping, by her very renown; she is a catalyst of valiant and great deeds. Not even you, Hector, would give up such an advantage of promised glory." Hector continued looking glum. But then he bestirred himself.

"Very well. We will discuss this no further." The doomed party went off, taking Cassandra with them. I watched them leave thinking that Hector at least would be spared the terrible bitter end. As for Paris - *He that troubleth his own house shall inherit the wind*[7]. I never quite understood this but now it seemed to mean: once you have destroyed your home, there is nowhere to live.

I was so lost in thought that I never noticed Homerys coming in and sitting down at the table the Trojans had just vacated. I couldn't see his boy so I supposed he was fooling around outside with the other kids. Marianne, like Eurybates, seemed to know all about Homerys and brought him a beaker of watered wine and some bread and cheese. Homerys addressed me; don't ask me how he knew I was there.

"That Troilus," he said. "I don't like him. Who is he, anyway? There's only one Troilus in my book:" if you're not in Homerys's book, you've no right to exist. Homerys declaimed with an exaggerated arm movement: *"Troilus, the dauntless charioteer."* Then he fell on his bread and cheese: "He's dead before the action starts. This Troilus, I

---

[7]   Proverbs. Old Testament

disown him." That didn't sound good for Troilus. Homerys continued glumly: "And I'm still waiting for one single word about the Gods from the Trojans. Oh, are they asking for it! No one is going to look good when the Gods get through with them! They forget! They forget!" I slipped out but Homerys's sonorous voice followed me:

> *... our [Troy's] most fatal war*
> *let us importune [pursue] still,*
> *till Zeus the conquest has disposed*
> *to his unconquered will.*

1.7 TROY IN OUR WEAKNESS STANDS

Feeling depressed after hearing all of Troy's woes, I decided to go back to the *Greek Olive Tree* and took up my usual position on the bar. Happy Hour was in full swing, Eurybates and the bouncer being all a-bustle. Everyone was there: Agamemnon, Odysseus, Diomedes, Nestor, Ajax, Menelaus and Idomeneus, as well as the enlisted men still standing. Naturally, the groups kept themselves separate, the nobs inside and the rest on the terrace. Snobbery has a very long history indeed. As in the case of the Trojans, nobody was looking his best: Menelaus had a large dressing on his thigh, Diomedes one around his head while Idomeneus had his arm in a sling. They were all bruised and scratched; as for the enlisted men, I was surprised there were any left.

They were discussing what happened on the battlefield after the Menelaus and Paris imbroglio, when, it seemed, both sides had gone at it with a will. So the talk was about who had killed whom. Who was maimed or mortally wounded or taken prisoner. It all sounded gory, exaggerated and uninteresting. Menelaus was busy getting pissed but managed to say, between gulps:

"If there was any justice in the world, the Trojans would have had to return Helen and her goods and chattels. I won that bout fair and square."

"Be that as it may," answered Odysseus, "you did not kill Paris and that was part of the deal." Menelaus got to his feet and threatened Odysseus with his beaker.

"I would have if I could have caught him!" He sat down again. "Bastard must have set a new record for the Olympic 100 m dash." Yep, thinks I. Nothing like being scared out of your wits to give you that extra rush of adrenalin. Nestor patted Menelaus kindly on the shoulder.

"You did great, Menelaus. No one could have done better," he said soothingly and signed to Eurybates for a top up for Menelaus. I sniffed the air and to my misfortune confirmed that Thersites was there. Really, I needed a pocket full of poses to stand the smell. He whispered:

"This battle – if you could call it that – I was not impressed." I looked at him askance.

"What do you mean? There was a challenge, single combat – the single meaning Menelaus – a foot race, followed by lots of mayhem, blood and gore. Look around you. Each and every Greek should be in the sickbay. So, yes, I was impressed, although I missed the second act." Thersites squinted at me. I continued: "And, talking of blood and gore, what did you do for the side? Can't see any bruises or scratches or missing limbs." Thersites grinned wickedly.

"Have you forgotten, pal, I am a slave? Slaves don't fight."

"Now, isn't that just hunker-dory!"

"You got it."

Agamemnon looked round at his fellow commanders. The alcohol was giving a shine to past events and they were all looking a tad more hopeful, except for Odysseus who knew that, no matter how bad things were, there was no reason they couldn't get worse. Agamemnon started walking forwards and backwards in front of them, one hand behind his back, beaker in the other. I surmised a peptalk was the order of the moment.

"My friends, comrades and invaluable allies. First of all, I want to congratulate my brother Menelaus. Menelaus, you were magnificent and by rights Paris should be dead and the war over. Brother, you did us proud." Approving murmurs all around. Menelaus said nothing but called for another drink. Agamemnon went on: "I don't think we could have done better even if Akhilleus had been there, which makes me wonder how much we really need him." He turned to the plebs on the terrace and spread his arms: "But our lads were in fine fettle and I cannot think of one who did not do his duty." He waggled a finger. "And more! Eurybates! Drinks all around for our brave lads! I'm buying!" This sent up a cheer that could be heard in Priam Square as nothing touched a Greek's heart more than a free drink. Agamemnon slurped some wine down and turned back to the nobs. "I think this is a good moment to take stock of our situation." No one disagreed; while Agamemnon talked himself hoarse, they could enjoy their drinks and let their minds wander. He went on:

"Be proud, friends, of our accomplishments and think not of our failures." Think positive, that's the motto. Everybody applauded loudly and Agamemnon ordered another rounds of drinks. Thersites whispered:

"You ever saw Agamemnon more popular? Hey, Eurybates, where's my drink?" Eurybates frowned at him and was about to say something but decided against it. Instead, he slid a brimming mug to Thersites who grabbed it and drank deeply before Eurybates could change his mind and take it back. Agamemnon went on:

"You, Nestor, you could have been a man in his prime the way you lay about with your sword. As for telling the boys they should kill as many Trojans as possible and loot the dead later, why, that was a stroke of genius!" I was aghast and Odysseus frowned. Nestor! That old fellow who should be thinking of the hereafter, laying about him like a ten-year old! On the other hand, everyone took Nestor to be an old man and so he was by the standards of the time. Personally, I thought him about the age as Hitler or Stalin at their demise. Nestor looked embarrassed:

"I sort of got carried away," he said in an apologetic voice, an eye on Odysseus. Agamemnon then turned his attention to Odysseus. He massaged his chin and then said in a low voice: "I fear I was disappointed in you, Odysseus. It seemed you were hanging back when the Greeks were forming their lines of attack. You are deep in cunning with a heart of guile. Did you not see the Greeks were engaging the enemy and that we needed every hand? If we do not pull together, where will we be?" Odysseus frowned:

"Agamemnon, my guile and my cunning, as you put it, advise me not to put myself or my men in harm's way just because harm is there. You," and he looked around at the other members of the High Command, "fight because you wish to. Me and my men, we fight to win. And when that happens, you shall see us all in the front line. We will not throw our lives away for glory or medals." Well, that shut Agamemnon up. He glared at Odysseus then broke into the falsest smile I've yet encountered.

"My dear Odysseus, you quite misunderstand me. Excellent in counsel, I have neither fault to find with you or orders to give you, for I know your heart is right and that you and I are of the same mind. If any ill has been spoken, I will make you amends." They embraced but I could see Odysseus putting away this little episode for future use.

Thersites giggled.

"Ain't it always the same thing," he said. "One guy says something then explains it means quite the opposite." I ignored Thersites to ponder on deeper matters such as what good teamwork meant on the battlefield. But when the going gets rough, you can't beat paraphrasing Adam Smith:

> *In battle, every soldier generally neither directly intends*
> *to promote victory for his own side, nor by his actions*
> *knows how much he is promoting it. By fighting he*
> *intends only his own survival; and by directing his*
> *efforts in such a manner as to produce what will have*
> *the greatest impact, he intends only his own gain, and*
> *he is in this, as in many other cases, led by an invisible*
> *hand to promote an end which was no part of his*
> *intention.*

And who was it that said: '*The best laid strategy only survives five minutes into the battle.* Sorry, I got carried away. Nestor was handed a fresh beaker and sat down. Odysseus having been given the word, so to speak, got to his feet.

"The problem as I see it," he said: "is that teamwork only takes one so far. We Greeks have teamed up, as Agamemnon says, all

69 city states of us, but there Troy still stands; Hector, their best warrior, dominates the field and we do not, at the moment, have his match. Our best chance came today and we all know what the upshot was." He held up his hand as Menelaus opened his mouth. "Peace, friend Menelaus. You did all you could and no one can fault you. So, my friends, the long and the short of it is that we're still where we were yesterday afternoon: the war's a bloody stalemate. Either we break it or we'll be here until kingdom come." Murmurs of assent. Agamemnon and Nestor nodded their heads wisely. Odysseus took a swig of wine and went on: "This is the greatest coalition in Greek history and there's no reason we shouldn't be able to destroy this two-bit town." He looked around. Every face looked back at him expectantly. "It is my opinion that Troy will not fall by force of arms. And we have other problems, too." Doubtful looks. I murmured:

"A house divided cannot stand." Odysseus spun around:

"Who said that?" As no one took responsibility, he gave me the eye but continued: "Whoever it was, it is perfectly correct. A house divided. Everyone loses!" Odysseus had a sip and continued: "Our best fighter, Akhilleus, the only Greek to match Hector, is sulking in his tent. His absence, and in such a manner, is bad for discipline and morale. In fact, we would be better off if Akhilleus just went home." Nestor said, with Agamemnon nodding vigorously:

"So, what would you recommend?" Odysseus scratched his chin.

"I know this war cannot be won by battle; we need the Trojans to come to the same conclusion." But Agamemnon would have none of it:

"Nonsense, my dear fellow, we shall prevail. All things comes to he who waits." Weird. Didn't sound like much of a strategy to me.

1.8 ZEUS FORBID!

When I got back to the beach and my special tree, I had bit of a wash, a good stretch and was just dropping off when I was, literarily, swept off my feet. Someone had grabbed me around the middle – not how one holds a cat to make sure he stays with you. But as I found myself being carried at great speed through space, clawing myself away was not an option, so I dug my claws into the arms holding me, closed my eyes and hung on for dear life. As suddenly as the trip had begun, it was over and I found myself – literarily – thrown on the ground. An irate female voice said:

"Bloody cat scratched me!" As I came out of shock and had a chance to look around me, I saw that my lady abductor and I were standing on a marble plaza at the foot of marble steps leading to a grand marble temple, all white, Doric columns, tryphanium, liberally populated by gods and goddesses topped by a dome that seemed to be encrusted with twinkling diamonds. Then I realised that the dome reflected the heavens above as if it were a mirror image. My jaw hanging open, I followed my abductress up the steps to heavy gold encrusted oak doors, beautifully carved with flowers and animals, where a huge fellow in a worn tunic of lion skin stood leaning on a heavy club. He looked askance at me.

"No animals admitted," his voice was totally devoid of interest. The lady said fiercely:

"Now, Herakles, don't give me any of your lip. Where does it say no animals are allowed on Olympus?" Herakles scratched his chin.

"No precedent," he said in the same voice. My abductress' eyes flashed dangerously.

"If you don't open the doors this minute," she screamed, "I shall have a temper tantrum like you've never imagined!" She tensed herself up, gathered in her breath but Herakles caved in and the doors swung open before the storm could break.

"Bloody woman," he snarled as we went past. "What on earth did she bring a cat for? Now, a shark or a dolphin I might understand ..." What this was all about stymied me. Personally, I would take a cat before a shark any day.

Anyhow, we entered and found ourselves in an immense circular marble chamber. An amazing sight: the walls and ceiling were white marble veined in all colours of the rainbow in every shape imaginable. The floor was fantastic mosaics, with more designs that I could take in even if I returned once a year until I died. My companion and I were on a sort of mezzanine surrounded by a gold railing that turned into banisters where three steps lead down to the main hall. Marble couches were scattered with cushions embroidered with gold and silver thread and hung with gold and silver tassels. Especially large cushions lay on the floor. At the far end, on a raised dais, two great ivory armchairs adorned with even larger cushions, with more on the floor for, I supposed, footrests. An imposing looking man, not young, not old, with shoulder length black hair and beard to match, strong features, piercing eyes, wearing a crown of gold leaves twinkling with diamonds, sat on the right, his chair slightly larger and higher than the one next to him. This in turn contained a lady, also neither young not old young, hair still golden with the faintest traces of silver, her figure good, sharp blue eyes with just the beginning of crows' feet; otherwise she had wonderful clear skin. She wore a golden coronet. There were plenty of other people around and the din of raised voices and laughter was deafening. It must be Happy Hour. Everyone was dressed in the Greek style, the men in white tunics with gold geometric embroidery, green laurel wreaths on their heads, the ladies in long diaphanous sleeveless gowns, all shades of blue, with high waists, their hair bound with golden ribbons, curls falling around their faces. The glitterati and the literati. Nymphs in short dresses were serving, under the direction of a smiling major domo, a bit on the chubby side, his face gleaming with sweat and his laurel wreath slightly askew.

As the gathering caught sight of us, the noise died away and everyone stared. I was completely gobsmacked, never having seen anything remotely like this. I looked up at the lady who had brought me. She was much like everyone else but with sharper features, mouth set as if she meant business and her gown was pale green, her black hair dressed in what appeared to be gold encrusted seaweed. A deep male voice greeted her.

"Thetis, you are a rare visitor to our festivities. And to what may we thank this honour, that you should leave your home in the sea to visit us in Olympus? Come closer, my dear. Don't be such a stranger." She walked down the steps into the main hall and I followed her. The little fat major domo installed her on an empty coach; I chose a damask pillow with golden thread, gave it a good pummelling and curled up comfortably. Thetis said:

"Great Zeus, always the gentleman." Zeus gave me the eye:

"Thetis, my sweet, welcome as always. Might I ask why you have brought a cat with you?" She answered stiffly:

"He's my witness!" I gasped and looked up at her.

"Witness?" I yowled. "I'm a cat, lady, and cats can't be witnesses. No court of law would allow it. There is," to clinch it, "no precedent." She turned as if to slap me then remembered the claws so she snapped instead:

"Shut up!" I whined:

"I thought you wanted a witness. I can't be one if I'm not allowed to open my mouth." There was a discreet cough and to my relief my old pal Hermes strode forward, holding what looked like a whiskey and soda. He'd changed his winged cap for a winged laurel wreath. He bowed slightly and addressed the man with the black hair and beard:

"Mighty Zeus," he said, "this is the cat I have been telling you about. He is far away from his home in both time and space. He is named Gaius Marius."

"Oh," said Zeus, "isn't that the fellow who's going to turn the Roman Republic upside down one of these days? Perhaps the old fella came back as a cat – or was a cat in a previous life." He laughed mightily at own his joke and every one followed suit except Thetis who glared at him. I was not amused and shook my vigorously.

"A cat is a cat is a cat. Once a cat, always a cat. You can't start out as a human and become a cat or start out as a cat and become a human. It's a scientific impossibility."

Hermes gave me a sharp look – mind your manners. I wanted to stick out my tongue at him but thought better of it as Ares said thoughtfully:

"Re-incarnation is a scientific impossibility!"

There was a pause and I was wondering how long this subject would continue as I, for one, was already tired of it. Hermes then came forward: "Gaius, I think you need to be officially introduced to the Olympians." He held his hand out towards Zeus: "This is mighty Zeus, king of the Gods, ruler of sky and weather, master of law, order and fate. Next to him is his wife, Hera, Queen of Gods and goddess of women and marriage, sky and starry heavens. The lady who brought you here is Thetis, daughter of the Old Man of the Sea – otherwise known as Poseidon – and mother of Akhilleus." I sniffed. No wonder Akhilleus was so rude and bad tempered. Hermes went on:

"The man with the lyre to your left is Apollo, master of prophecy and oracles, healing, disease, music and poetry. And a master of archery." I wondered how many master's degrees he'd taken to cover that lot. I looked at him. Good looking fellow, all blond curls and muscles. Next to him lay a golden lyre as well as a bow and arrows. Hermes droned on:

"On the couch next to him is Artemis, Apollo's twin, Goddess of the Hunt, wilderness and wild animals." I looked at Artemis through slit eyes. A huntress. I put her on my shit list right there and then. She gave me a long look as if evaluating what kind of sport I could give her. Right good looking but what are good looks if you are a bitch. I was going to ask whether she protected or devastated the wilderness and protected or culled wild animals but decided it might not be safe. Hermes called me back to the here and now:

"There is Hephaistus, God of fire, metalworking, stonemasonry and sculpture." Hephaistus was nothing to write home about in the looks department. As far as I could see, one leg was shorter than the other and his face was asymmetrical. I thought being perfect was one of the requirements to become an Olympian God. Perhaps not.

"Ares," Hermes was saying, "is God of war..." I would never have guessed; huge fellow wearing armour as if the next battle was just around the corner. His helmet lay on the couch beside him. "... battlelust, civil order and manly courage," finished Hermes. Well, seemed odd to me; surely he couldn't have it both ways – order and disorder. Hephaistus and Ares looked a lot older than the others, no doubt because of their lifestyles. Metallurgy is demanding work and so is war if you want to do either properly. Hermes went on:

"Then we have Athena, goddess of war, wise counsel, defence of towns, heroic endeavour, weaving and pottery." My head swam. The idea of such multitasking made me dizzy. Athena had blond curls, blue eyes and all the trimmings, looked cool and collected. I bet she lorded it over Hephaistus and Ares, sitting behind a desk and laying down the law. Hermes went on pitilessly:

"Demeter is the goddess of agriculture." Demeter was a mature woman; all that hoeing and planting does that to you. "Next to her is Dionysus, god of wine, pleasure and festivity." Dionysus had a happy go lucky look to him and would probably be a laugh in a pub over a few beers.

Hermes then clapped the chubby fellow on the shoulder and straightened his laurel wreath. "And this is Ganymede, cupbearer to Zeus, and in charge of all festivities on Olympus." Hermes added, pointing to a very beautiful lady on a splendid couch: "Last but not least, Aphrodite, the Goddess of Love." Yeah, right. Paris' divine groupie. We'd met. Aphrodite gave me a look which I read as: discretion is the better part of valor. I must confess that at that moment the cat had got my tongue. I hoped the introductions were over. What was I supposed to say to this lot?

"Hi, everyone," was all I managed. "Nice to meet you." Artemis said:

"Considering he's a cat, I must say he is quite handsome. Beautiful coat with wonderful markings. Pity he is not purebred." I swished my tail and laid back my ears. Yeah, and I love you, too. I hate being patronized. This was not going well. I looked at Zeus. I suppose a cat may look at a god. He waved his glass, whisky on the rocks as far as I could tell; Ganymede clapped his hands and a nymph appeared with a fresh drink. Zeus combed his beard with his fingers and looked at Hera, who was holding a highball glass – gin and tonic, no doubt. .

"Well," he said, "hadn't we better offer our guest something?" Hera looked at Ganymede who came forward and addressed me with a smirk:

"Saucer of milk?"

"Very kind, I'm sure," I drawled, "but I'm lactose intolerant." Raised eyebrows all around. "That means," I explained, "that I can't digest milk. But some nice sparkling water would be appreciated." At once, a very pretty girl came out with the bottle and a saucer and served it. I lapped it up. Vintage Perrier, without a doubt. Hera looked at me curiously.

"How very strange," she said, "The word 'intolerant' used in connection with any state of health will only become current about 3 000 years in the future. Usually, mammals can – and do – eat anything. They are, of course, intolerant in the other meaning of the word." I shook my head.

"Dear lady, as you say, in the old days, humans – or animals – if they were intolerant to anything edible, would die after ingesting a fatal amount. In my time, everyone is carefully diagnosed, put on special diets, and survive to ensure they pass on the bad genes to the next generation." Hera shook her head, swallowed some gin and tonic, and said:

"Well, that's survival of the fittest turned on its head. But do have a tuna sandwich." So I tucked into the tuna but left the bread alone. I do not do carbohydrates.

When I resurfaced, Zeus was saying platitudes to Thetis who was holding a glass that looked very much as if contained lemonade. I wouldn't put it beyond her, either. A born party pooper if I ever saw one. After all this, I thought they might have forgotten about Akhilleus and the witness stuff but Ares, who had been stroking his chin for some time with a frown on his brow, suddenly brought us all back to the business at hand:

"This is quite unorthodox, Thetis, having an animal for a witness," he said shaking his head. Artemis nodded:

"I am an expert of animals," she said, "and let me tell you that a cat does not see the same things a human does. And, of course, their interpretation is vastly different. She touched the tip of her nose: "However, I doubt animals have the capacity of lying; so as a witness, he might be as good, or even better, than humans." What a poseur, I thought to myself. Much she knows about anything. Why, lying and cheating is second nature to cats. But then, again, I do not think cats were the subject of her goddess thesis. "But surely," Artemis cut in "there were humans present who could serve as witnesses." I thought: *right! Get me off the hook.* No such luck, though, as Thetis said sourly:

"I don't know. The cat must know." I sighed and stroked my whiskers and said:

"Well, yes, there was the whole of the Greek High Command." Hephaistion shook his head.

"Not a one among them to be trusted." Rats!

"And there was Thersites." Apollo laughed so loudly the walls almost shook.

"Oh, no, Thersites! A swindler, a coward, a rogue and a cheat. You must be joking." Well, I wasn't but I could see Apollo's point.

"Also," I added, "he should bathe more often. It was hard for a fastidious cat to stand next to him." Silence. Hera prompted me:

"Well? Is that it?" I just my eyes and thought back.

"There was Eurybates..." Dionysius shook his head.

"Odysseus' man. And Odysseus is a man you can't trust." He laughed wildly at his own joke and had some more wine that choked him and a nymph had to pat him on the back. I was pissed by being so rudely interrupted and continued as if no one had said anything.

"There was Homerys!" Dead silence as the Olympians looked at each other. At length Zeus coughed.

"An admirable poet and a great one. But hardly someone you would trust to know the truth, let alone tell it, even in a court of law. That vivid imagination, you know..." There seemed to be a general consensus to this. Zeus then turned to Thetis and continued: "Very well, my dear, if you have come here, which you seldom do, bringing a witness, I can only imagine you have some complaint to lodge. And I suppose we must accept your witness such as he is." Keep it up, thinks I, and I'll scratch your eyes out.

"Certainly I do," answered Thetis, curling and uncurling her fingers as she had been doing all through Hermes' introduction and the discussion on having a cat for a witness. "It is with regard to my son, Akhilleus." Zeus looked none too pleased. He said with a frown:

"Now, Thetis, Akhilleus has all the gifts the Gods can give a mortal – beauty, strength and skill in arms. He has had the best education available, and if he has an ungovernable temper he inherited it from you, and I can't see there is much I can do about that." Zeus took a final swallow of his drink, immediately replaced. I gave the nymph the eye and got some fresh Perrier. Thetis stamped her foot in rage and cried:

"But he has been unfairly treated by that, that tyrant, Agamemnon." Zeus was unimpressed.

"So? Don't tell me Akhilleus can't handle a knucklehead like Agamemnon." Thet is started to snap, gritting her teeth, leaning over backwards and clinching her hands. But then she thought better of it and said, in an almost normal tone.

"Great Zeus, I don't want to discuss this in open assembly. I beseech you to hear me in private!" Hera raised her eyebrows and looked fixedly at Thetis.

"Indeed?" she queried, lifting her chin and giving Thetis the eye. "And what can Thetis have to say in private to Great Zeus that I, his wife, confident and counsellor, must be excluded from?" Zeus looked annoyed and turned to Hera:

"Dammit, woman, do you have to stick your nose into everything? Do you not know there are matters that go beyond a woman's understanding and should be dealt with by Zeus and Zeus alone?" Hera looked at her almost empty highball glass, a nymph ran up with a refill; she stirred her drink with its little stick, then murmured:

"Most certainly there are such matters, my lord, but I hardly think a quarrel between Akhilleus and Agamemnon can be classed as one." Zeus cleared his throat several times as men do when their wives have them cornered. He said in a lofty manner:

"My dear, now that I think of it, you are quite right. In fact, I want all the Olympians to hear the case and give me their advice." Thetis ground her teeth in frustration. I could see she was about to call Zeus a henpecked husband but then decided it wouldn't help her cause. So she took a deep breath and started off:

"Immortal Zeus, Agamemnon has ..." but Zeus held up a hand:

"Thetis, I presume you were not yourself a witness to what took place between Akhilleus and Agamemnon, am I correct?" Thetis stopped short. Then she said sullenly:

"I was not. My son told me all about it later."

"Therefore," continued Zeus, "I take it that is the reason you have brought a witness – albeit a rather unconventional one – who actually saw – and heard – what went on – Gaius Marius, the cat, no offence meant."

"And none taken," I said. Zeus ignored the interruption.

"So, it is his first hand testimony I would like to hear, not yours which is second hand and must be classed as hearsay." After this, there was a lull while everyone got their drinks topped up and settled down comfortably for the show. I got some more Perrier. And found all eyes fixed on me.

"This is very irregular," I said. "I know Zeus is the judge of all things and Thetis is the prosecutor in this case but where is the defence? You can't have a trial without a defence."

"My dear Gaius Marius the cat," interrupted Zeus in a weary voice. "Be aware that on Olympus I am prosecutor, defence, jury and judge." I shut up at once. Zeus waved at me to start so I did.

"Well, there were these two girls."

"What two girls?" Ares asked. So, from the word go, it was becoming difficult. I answered:

"I didn't actually see them but since they were the cause of the quarrel, I can only infer that they actually existed." The Gods looked at each other doubtfully.

"This is not satisfactory," said Demeter, "part of the testimony cannot rely on inferences without direct observation." I was getting hot under the collar, but Zeus intervened:

"Let us accept, for the time being, the existence of the girls," he said and, nodding his head at me: "go on." I did.

"As far as I could understand, these were girls captured on a raid the Greeks made on Thebes before they arrived in Troy. The girls' names were – supposedly – Chrissies and Brisies." I paused as Dionysius interrupted:

"This raid on Thebes," he said, looking straight at me, "I take it you were not there."

"I was not."

"So," he continued, losing all interest in me and looking around at his fellow Olympians, "can anyone confirm that the raid on Thebes actually took place?" Athena raised her hand.

"I can," she said, "and I can certainly testify to the fact that the place was a right mess when the Greeks left. But I know nothing of the women." I decided that being a witness was no fun.

"I must say," I said, "that I disapprove of women being taken as war loot as if they were a good cloak or a new sword or a sack of potatoes..." Zeus held up his hand.

"As a witness, you are not allowed to have an opinion, Gaius Marius. Just stick to the facts." Demeter bristled:

"I know what it is to have a daughter abducted," she said in a teary voice, wiping her eyes. The rest of the party sighed. This was obviously an oft told story. Hera got up to pat Demeter on the shoulder:

"Yes, dear," she said soothingly, "and we feel your pain, we do indeed." Demeter went on doggedly:

"And Hades was never brought to justice at all!" Zeus bristled.

"Indeed he was, Demeter, as you well remember!" Hera added soothingly: "And you do have Persephone six months of the year as a result." I considered whether to take a nap while this matter was thrashed out and was just curling up on my damask pillow when Zeus boomed out:

"We mustn't get sidetracked like this. That all happened long ago. So, witness, let's get on with it." I uncurled myself shook the cobwebs out of my brain and drawled:

"Well, the facts are: by common agreement, Agamemnon got Chrissies and Akhilleus, Brisies."

"So," was Hephaestus' comment, "each guy got a girl. What's the problem?"

"But is so happened," I continued, my eyes closed to show what I thought of these interruptions, "that Chrissies' father wanted his daughter back, I cannot imagine why. No one seems to have cared about Brisies. She probably didn't have a family." Zeus was going to say something so I held up a paw. "Sorry. That was just an assumption. Anyway, Chrissies' father, who's name was Chryses, which I found very confusing, went to Agamemnon and offered him fabulous wealth if he, Agamemnon, would return his, Chryses', daughter, Chrissies. But Agamemnon refused, was very rude and had Chryses, the father, thrown out of the Greek camp." Apollo asked in an aloof tone:

"And what proof do we have of this matter of Chryses and his daughter?" I ground my teeth.

"None from me," I snarled. "I never had the pleasure of being introduced to either." Hephaestus took of swig of whatever he was drinking.

"This is some witness you brought, Thetis. He can't confirm anything."

"It was the best I could do," snapped Thetis.

"However," continued Hephaestus, "the behaviour he describes is characteristic of Agamemnon, so I think we can accept it on principle, based on past evidence." A murmur of approval. I had some more water in the hope they'd forget about the whole thing. But no. Zeus waved at me. I continued:

"Now, the foregoing is background. Akhilleus called a meeting of the Greek High Command and this I did witness. The upshot of their discussions was that the war had been going very badly for them. The reason for this, Akhilleus said, was that they had lost the favour of the Gods." Murmurs all around.

"And this conjecture – for that is what it is –was based on?" This was Hera. I coughed:

"There seems to have been a plague in the Greek camp and lots of men were sick; further, some archer or other has been shooting Greeks indiscriminately. I cannot confirm either." Zeus sat up straight and glared at Apollo.

"What have I told you a thousand times? I don't want you going about with bow and arrows until you've learned to use them properly!" Apollo whined:

"I just had a couple of accidental slips during practise, you know. I didn't hit those guys on purpose. Anyway, no one died, they just got a bit wounded!"

"Shut up!" shouted Zeus and, to me, "go on." I sighed. This was very tiresome.

"So, the Greek command invited Calchas, the Trojan seer, you know, to give his opinion." Murmurs all around. Everyone seemed to know Calchas. Dionysus murmured:

"Calchas, that turncoat! I'm not sure how far he can be trusted." Ares waved this away:

"As far as any seer can be trusted." He glanced at Apollo who just looked at the ceiling. I rushed on before anyone else could interrupt. "Calchas said that the Gods were angry with the Greeks, especially Apollo whose priest Chryses, the father of course, was. Calchas said the Greeks would continue to accumulate defeats until Crisies, the daughter, was returned to Chryses, the father." Zeus looked like thunder and turned again to Apollo.

"You are far too young to have priests of your own. Or are you setting up a rival religion? Because, if you are, I can promise you will bitterly regret it." Apollo got up, annoyed in his turn:

"If some old guy thinks I'm worth worshipping, there isn't much I do about it, is there? Do I go down and tell him: 'hey, buster, cut it out, I haven't got my God degree yet!'" Sniggers. Zeus looked around angrily and the crowd immediately fell silent. Then I intervened. I was getting impatient.

"This is all beside the point, whether Apollo is a God in his own right." I said as loudly as I could to get their attention. "The point is that the Greek commanders believed Calchas and it was agreed that Crisies should be returned to her father, Chryses, and the matter settled." Dionysus laughed out loud:

"I bet that pissed Agamemnon off good and proper." I gave him a baleful look.

"So it did. And he, Agamemnon, stipulated that if he was to lose Crisies, then he would take Brisies, Akhilleus' girl, in her place." Now Thetis couldn't be silent any more.

"And that is what happened! Agamemnon sent his soldiers down to Akhilleus' ships, tore Brisies away and took her to Agamemnon's tents!" she cried. Then Artemis spoke:

"Did anyone actually see Brisies being taken from Akhilleus' ships or, for that matter, Brisies going into Agamemnon's tent?" I considered.

"I heard Agamemnon ordering his soldiers to do so but, no, I can't say I was an eye witness to either event." Artemis continued:'

"Did you see Crisies being taken from Agamemnon's tent and returned to her father?" I shook the noggin'.

"No, I heard Agamemnon ordering Calchas to see to it."

"So, tell me, witness, what were you actually a witness to?"

"A quarrel between Akhilleus and Agamemnon."

"And how did that end?"

"Akhilleus swore he was done with fighting for the Greeks and they could see how they got on without him. Then he walked off with Patroklos; I understand, although I was not a witness to it, that he went back to his tent to sulk." Thetis balled her fists, closed her eyes, and I was afraid she was going to go into convulsions. She threw herself at Zeus' feet:

"How can you, great Zeus, allow my son to be so dishonoured? My son and I beg you, implore you, Great Zeus, strongest and most wise, to avenge this insolent and undeserved wrong! How dare Agamemnon pull this kind of trick? The girl Brisies was Akhilleus', won by his superb efforts and sword! Great Zeus, make the Trojans strong and the Greeks weak; give Troy victories, till Greece is forced to return to my son the honours they now deny him and acknowledge their ingratitude. Insufferable boors." There was a dead silence and all the Gods and Goddesses and hangers-on kept completely still. I could read their faces like open books. No one wanted to get mixed up in this imbroglio. Then Hephaistos spoke:

"Frankly, Thetis, although I love you dearly, you have made a very weak case. Most of what we have heard is hearsay; your witness is quite open about the fact that he has no direct knowledge of most of the action, meaning we don't have an independent statement describing any of the events and therefore we cannot confirm they even took place. And, come to that, what is Akhilleus doing with the Greek Expeditionary Forces anyway? What quarrel has he with Troy? Why doesn't he just sail home and have done with it?" Then Thetis completely lost it.

"I want them dead! I want them all dead!" Ares held up his hand:

"And I really don't think there is any honour in betraying your own side because you've had a tiff over a girl." Artemis added, rather spitefully, I thought:

"And why do you come to Great Zeus, Thetis? Akhilleus feels aggrieved and comes crying to you so here you are. Supermom. Don't you think Akhilleus is old enough to settle his own quarrels without your interference?" Hera added, waiving her hands as if she'd seen a bee:

"This is too paltry an affair for Great Zeus' attention." That annoyed Zeus who frowned and started getting to his feet and start laying down the law; it didn't do to let people forget who was in charge. But Thetis screamed:

"You owe me, mighty Zeus, you owe me for giving my son only a human lifespan when he should be among the Gods!" I heard Ares whisper to Artemis:

"The way he's going, he's not going to make even that!" Artemis waggled her eyebrows. Thetis went completely wild and went on screaming:

"You, Zeus, and you, Hephaestus, have a debt of honour to me, for giving you, Zeus, aid when the other immortals plotted against you!" The immortals all looked elsewhere but at Thetis; this was not a popular memory since a lot of them had been involved. "And, Hephaestus, you I cared for when you where thrown off Olympus!" Hephaestus rose to his feet, a more serious look on his face:

"Indeed, Thetis, our debt to you we acknowledge, but I cannot see how we can repay it by injuring mortals who are in no way involved in the affairs of Olympus." Dionysus might have gone on but now Zeus rose to his feet, spread out his arms and instant silence fell over the company.

"Thetis," he began, "it does you honour to fight for your son and to wish to see his wrongs righted. And we whom you have aided do not forget. However, in the matter of this war in Troy: I have not and I hope," looking around grimly, especially at Apollo who looked nonchalant and all innocence, "none of you have in any way interfered with either Greeks or Trojans. I do not approve of this war. I find its objective trivial, frivolous and spurious. I have not sanctified it. I do not care who wins it – although I am sure that, when it does end, there will be no victor. It is always so with human wars. Furthermore, both contestants sacrifice to the same Gods and both think right is on their side and implore the Gods to stand by them.

"And I say no! I will not stand with either. And, Thetis, as I told you earlier, your son has gifts none possess but he. Let him use these to make his way in the world he inhabits. Do not come to me because he has made poor choices. And, lastly, I think the cat Gaius Marius is right: to take women as trophies in war is despicable." Brows lowered, Zeus stared fiercely at each Olympian in turn, all of whom became very busy inspecting their nails. He waggled his finger at each of them. "If I catch any of you giving aid and comfort to either Trojans or Greeks, I will personally hurl he – or she – into the darkest part of Tartarus, into the deepest pit under the earth, as far beneath Hades as heaven is high above the earth. Do not try me for you will discover I jest not. Test me not. Zeus has spoken." He said down and called out: "Get me another drink and make it a double!"

A high horrible scream came from Thetis and in a moment, she was gone. I panicked:

"Hey," I cried, "what about me? How do I get down again?"

"Don't worry," said Hermes, "I will take you." We went outside. Hermes ordered:

"Run, Gaius, run!" I didn't see the point but ran. And before I knew it, I was soaring through the sky, behind Hermes, who cried: "Don't stop, Gaius, or you'll fall!"

"Hey," I cried, "this is fun!" And I ran through the night, stars and planets all around me, and the milky way above me, until we were back on the beach.

I staggered to my tree and fell into a deep exhausted sleep. As I drifted off, a voice came to me on the breeze:

> *"Father Zeus, if ever I [Thetis] have stood aidful to thee*
> *in word or work, with this implored good requite my*
> *aid, renown my son [Akhilleus], since in so short a race*
> *[mankind] thou confined his life: an insolent disgrace*
> *done him by the king of men; he forced from him a prize*
> *won with his sword. But thou, O Zeus..."*

Homerys at work. I curled up and thought that Thetis would have been more successful in her plea to the Gods if she had had Homerys write a speech for her or if Hera hadn't been around.

2
SATURDAY

2.1 HOW SHALL I MY TRUE LOVE KNOW?

In spite of the alarums and upheavals of the night before, I slept soundly and woke up refreshed. I decided to go for a walk before breakfast, somewhere with flowers and bushes and stuff. I was tired of the sand and earth and gravel of the Greek camp, to say nothing of the stumpy trees and sparse brown grass. I knew just the spot I wanted, having seen it on a previous walk in Troy: a beautiful well-tended garden with a pond in its centre spanned by a miniature bridge. So off I went and before you could say Jack Robinson, I was on the wall. I jumped down and made straight for the pond. I was about to have my first sip of water when a head with goggle eyes came up and stared straight at me. Gave me quite a turn.

"Please, sir, don't eat me," it said. I looked again, drawing my head back for a better perspective. It was a goldfish. In fact, there were quite a few goldfish in the pond. "Or my brothers and sisters," it added as an afterthought.

"Oh, puleese," I drawled, "do I look like someone who eats raw fish for breakfast? Give me a break. And I can't cook you because, by an oversight, I forgot to bring my cooking gear!" I thought this was so funny I laughed myself almost sick. The goldfish were not amused and one said sternly:

"If you think it's funny to have your heart in your mouth every time a cat turns up, you are very callous indeed. It's very upsetting. We get palpitations and the stress is bad for our blood pressure." In the middle of all this, I heard the sound of light sandaled feet running down the path and then a female voice cried out:

"Shuuu, Shuuu, kitty. Shuu, Shuu!" I turned my head around and there was Cressida, very fetching in blue but with a look of uncertainty on her face. As the perfect gentleman, I got to my feet. She took a few steps back.

"Oh," she said for I am a largish cat, having been called a mini-ocelot. Then she picked up her courage and waved her hands at me but without moving.

"Go away, kitty, leave my goldfish alone. Shooo." Now this shoo conversation was getting tedious. I said:

"Lady, let's make a deal. You stop saying shooo and I promise not to eat your goldfish." She crossed her hands on her breast.

"Oh!" sort of a gasp.

"Deal?" She nodded uncertainly.

"I suppose so." Good. That was settled. I continued, conversationally.

"Actually, I don't eat raw fish at all. What with the pollution and acid rain, you never know what genetic changes the fish have undergone and one might catch some terrible disease!" I smiled to show this was a joke, quite a good one, I thought. Cressida smiled back weakly, as if she was scared of doing anything else, although probably she had no idea what I was talking about. I jumped up on a stone bench and indicated she should sit beside me, which she did, although rather tentatively.

"There are lots of cats in the city," she said, "but I can't remember having seen you before."

"That," I replied, "is because I am just in Troy for the weekend, as part of my holiday. My name is Gaius Marius." She put her hand to her cheek.

"Gaius Marius, that's a really strange name."

"So it is," I answered, "and that's because I come from very far away." I was going to add in time and space but that might flip her out. So I continued: "I saw you yesterday in the square." Before she could say anything about that, I continued: "I have also seen your father, Calchas, at the Greek camp. How come you got left behind?" Cressida shook her head sadly.

"When my father left, he wanted to take me with him, but the Trojans branded him a traitor and Priam refused to let me go. Why

I cannot imagine," she added bitterly, "but my father left anyway. His behaviour really shows how much he cares for me." I patted her hand with my paw.

"I wouldn't let that worry me too much," I said, "that is, about your father. Of course he wants to be on the winning side. What good is it being a seer if what you see is that you're on the wrong side and do nothing about it?" Now, I thought that was very clever but it was a bit beyond Cressida.

"What do you mean?" she asked. "Are the Trojans going to lose this war?" She stopped and chewed on her nail. "That would mean that Cassandra has been right all along." This was dicey. Of course, I knew what has been written about the outcome of the Trojan War but who knew how things had really turned out? After all, writers lie all the time. So I prevaricated.

"Your father certainly thinks so but there are imponderables, you know, different personalities and so on. Who of us can see into the future?" Cressida shivered:

"Troy is my home," she said, "I was born and grew up here. I wouldn't like to see Troy destroyed. There's so much beauty here and, when all is said and done, the common Trojans have no interest in this war at all. What's in it for them whether Helen stays or goes? They just want to live their lives in peace." Oh, dear. These words, with variations to suit the time and place, would be repeated AD NAUSEUM for the next three thousand years and still the wars will go on and on. I wanted to get into the Troilus difficulty but starting a conversation about a girl's most intimate affairs is difficult, even for a callous cat like me. However, Cressida herself broached the subject.

"If you were in the square yesterday," she said, "you must have also have seen my uncle Pandarus." I demurred but then confessed I had. "Yes," she continued with a certain bitterness in her voice, "the only relation I have left in Troy – it might be better if I had none."

"Well," I said, "he's not so bad, you know. An old guy with nothing to do. I saw him earlier on, too, before you arrived, he was with Troilus. In *The Trojan Horse*." Cressida blushed.

"It's just so embarrassing his trying to palm me off on Troilus. I'm sure there are lots of highborn girls in Troy or princesses in the neighbouring kingdoms who might take a son of king Priam's fancy.

Why does my uncle hound me with his broad hints and uncouth sidelines – as if I didn't know all about the Trojan royal family. Telling me what Helen said and wanting to make Troilus seem greater than Akhilleus. It's downright embarrassing. And where does he think it'll get us? Does he really think he can force Troilus to marry me? Me? The daughter of a traitor?" I cleared my throat a couple of times until Cressida asked me if I had swallowed a goldfish the wrong way, a remark I pretended not to hear.

"The truth is, Cressida," I said at length, "that it is not Pandarus who is trying to make Troilus take an interest in you. It's Troilus trying to make Pandarus push you into taking an interest in him, Troilus." Well, it sounded a bit convoluted but I think she got the gist of what I meant. She sat up straight and gripped the stone bench so hard her knuckles went white.

"I don't believe you," she exclaimed, "why are you being mean to me? Who told you all this nonsense – was it my uncle who set you up to it? What is he paying you?" I put on an air of haughty GRAVITAS.

"My dear young lady," I said, "if there is one lesson to be learnt in this life it's that inter-species corruption is very very rare and most difficult. What could your uncle possible offer me that I would want? A marble statue? A golden tunic? A war horse of the finest lineage?" She started to say something but I held up a paw. "I know what you are going to say: he could bribe me with your goldfish. But, you need to realize he can't do that because if I wanted to eat your goldfish, I would."

"I think you're horrid," she cried, jumping up. And then the tears started to flow. Oh, bother. Women are so difficult to talk to – I mean, what do you do with a woman in floods of tears? And of course she didn't have a pocket handkerchief and neither did I, not being that way inclined. She buried her face in her hands and sobbed away. Finally, I said wearily:

"Cressida, do sit down and stop making a spectacle of yourself. Tears are all very well; in their proper place and time and with the right audience they can be very effective indeed. But not now." She gulped a few times, sniffed, cleaned her face with the back of her hand and sat down. I continued: "To cut a long story short, Troilus is totally in love with you – can't sleep, can't eat, can't concentrate and so on. The usual thing." Embarrassing really. "But it's true,

Cressida, Troilus said so himself, in fact, he went on and on until I considered inflicting violence to make him stop. And he wants your uncle to push the affair along." Cressida opened her soft brown eyes wide, lips trembling. Really, I was not in the mood for this. "Well, say something. Either you are or are not interested in Troilus. If you aren't, there are other fish in the sea, but if you are..."

"But of course I'm in love with him," Cressida broke in, quite rudely, I thought. Her face acquired that peculiar glow of a woman in love. "How could I not be, he's so noble and handsome and brave. Ever since I was a little girl I've loved him. But he's so far above me. And there's my father..." She started biting her knuckles and a few more tears fell. I shook my head in a decided way:

"No, Cressida, he is not so far above you. Get rid of all this class thing, that he's a prince and you're a milkmaid or whatever. Why does having been born in a palace make him better than you who were born here, in this beautiful place? I bet you were better educated than he was; I've yet to see a prince with a degree in anything other than uselessness. And, as for fathers, a father who's a seer is a lot more useful than one who's a king. And, further, the question is not whether he wants you but whether you want him."

"But you wrong him," Cressida wrung her hands, looking at me anxiously as if my opinion mattered a toss. "You do indeed. He is noble, clever, empathic, merciful, a master of arms and of courtesy!" These words were spoken with an ethereal look on her face, eyes looking at the sky. Oh, give me a break. "He is a true scion of a noble line." Now, considering the mess this particular line had gotten into, this was, to say the least, debatable. But Cressida was now beyond reason. "If he is not a Hector today, he will certainly be a Hector tomorrow, doing great deeds and will go down in legend and song." Not if Homerys has anything to say about it. I lay down resting my head on my paw. This was exhausting. However...

"My dear Cressida," I said, sitting up again and tucking my tail in, "if you are so wild about the boy, why, he's yours for the taking. All you have to do is set up a meeting through your uncle Pandarus and..."

"No," cried Cressida emphatically, "I don't want uncle involved in this. He's famous for making a mess of anything he sets his mind to. And I must be careful not to seem to be too easily won. What if he should not be true, what if his intentions are base? What if he were to seduce and abandon me ..." Well, after all she said before, about the nobility and empathy, I wondered where this came from. "Remember I am a woman alone. I have no one to protect me. I have only myself..." She sat down and I thought we were in for more tears. But then she grabbed me under my armpits and lifted me up; it was all I could do to restrain myself from giving her a good scratch. I am very particular about my personal space.

"Gaius, I want you to talk to Troilus!" If she hadn't been holding me I would have fallen into the goldfish pond. "I want you to sound him out and if you think he is sincere, then you may set up a meeting between us here in this garden."

"My dear Cressida," I almost gasped, "I know you are desperate but you can't put your whole future into the paws of a cat! How should I know whether he is sincere or not! I've got no basis for comparison since in my mind a man is good if he feeds me and bad if he steps on my tail. Believe me, you're better off with your uncle Pandarus." She set me down. More wringing of hands.

"Please, Gaius, please!" Now, everyone knows that it's impossible to make head or tail of a girl caught up in this sort of dilemma. Or to make her listen. I hated to take on this responsibility but then, being a cat, if it went wrong, I wouldn't feel too bad about it as cats don't have much of a conscience. So, in the end, I agreed, albeit reluctantly. And I left a young lady in paroxysms of happiness, who would do anything for her man and was just dying to be asked ... Personally, I thought she was far too good for him. Look at the history books. Princes make lousy husbands.

2.2 OH, BE THOU MY CHARON

I wandered around Priam Square in a disconsolate sort of way, with no stomach for the task of parleying with Troilus. As I passed the east lion, I saw Hermes sitting on a bench next to someone I didn't know.

"Hi Gaius," said Hermes in his usually dry way, "this is Eros."
I stared:
"Who?" Hermes answered:

"The God of Love." I looked Eros over. He was much like Hermes except his wings were on his back and not on his feet and he didn't wear a hat. I asked:

"Where're your bow and arrows?" Eros looked at me glumly:

"One gets discouraged," he said sourly, "when one's work is not appreciated. I've tried really hard down the ages to foster true love and look what has come of it all. There was Titus and Berenice[8]. An example of love conquered by greed for power. And Tristan and Isolde: she married the wrong man by mistake and everyone was miserable[9]. And Arthur and Guinevere. She scampered off with Lancelot in spite of all the arrows I could shoot at her[10]. And what about those cases of enduring love that went wrong anyway? Abelard and Heloise, that ended in tears[11], Edward VIII and Mrs Simpson – that ended in boredom.[12]" I was perplexed.

"But all those love affairs you mention, Eros, haven't happened yet!" Eros gave me a pitying look.

"Now, I don't know how you managed to live backwards, seeing you belong in the 21st century. But you are a unique case – at least I've never heard of one before. Let me tell you that the citizens of Olympus live both forwards and backwards." I thought about this and decided it was not for me. Who wants to relive their failures over and over again? But Eros had moved on: "So many hearts I have traversed with my arrows, so many weddings I have attended and then what? Spouse abuse. Child abuse. Infidelity. Murder and mayhem. The neighbours calling the police. Lawyers making pots of money. And what have you now? Pre-nuptial agreements. So, I say:

---

[8]   Titus was the son of Vespasian, Emperor of Rome in the 1st century and Berenice a Jewish princess. Titus gave her up when he became Emperor.

[9]   Isolde was the wife of the Duke of Cornwall but who loved Tristan, the Duke's best friend. Needless to say, it all ended in tears.

[10]   Arthur, Guinevere and Lancelot are the main characters in the legend of Camelot and the knights of the round table. In this case, too, the lover, Lancelot, was the husband Arthur's best friend. This may or may not be a myth.

[11]   Abelard and Heloise were deeply in love but Abelard was a churchman and not allowed to love. This happened, I think, early in the Middle Ages.

[12]   This is 20th century romance that everyone knows all about. Personally, whether this was a case of love or self interest is open to doubt.

what's the point? I turned in the bow and arrows to Zeus. He was none too pleased but what could he do? Shoot me?" I mused on this.

"If you're no longer active, that would account for the ever increasing divorce rate. On the other hand, Anthony and Cleopatra loved each other up to the end." Eros said gloomily:

"Considering their end, that doesn't cheer me up an awful lot. I mean, come on: *A world well lost for love! Oh, puuleese!"* Hermes gave a short laugh,

"Come on, Eros, you can hardly blame either for that line – although it sounds good – considering we don't know who actually coined it." Eros sulked:

"Anyone who thinks Cleopatra incapable of shopping Mark Anthony to someone who offered her the world is off his rocker. So I say, let lovers get on with it, they are all cheats and hypocrites. And it was a boring job, anyway. Anyone who believes a lover's pledge ought to have his – or her – head examined." Hermes cut in.

"Eros insisted on meeting you to make it clear he has had nothing to do with the Troilus-Cressida imbroglio."

"Wouldn't touch it with a barge pole," said Eros firmly. "It whiffs of Romeo and Juliette still to come. One would hope Cressida has too much sense to go for the idea of eternal bliss in her situation, with the scaffold a blink of an eye away; Troilus, well, he's just an arrogant bastard, figuratively speaking, that is. Don't care what happens to him." I sat down next to them.

"No happy ending for Troilus and Cressida, then," was my comment. Eros shrugged:

"Who knows, they may be lucky and live happily ever after." I said:

"Considering the military situation, 'happily ever after' could mean the next five minutes." Hermes' comment:

"I told you he was a special cat." Eros sniffed.

"Not really, seeing that all cats are cynics from birth and for them 'happily ever after' means catching the canary and eating it." Not flattering but I wasn't going to get in a fight that I couldn't possibly win. We sat there all three looking glum.

"I suppose," I said, "you were responsible for the Paris x Helen affair and that's made you bitter against lovers. I don't think anyone would be pleased to have encouraged a love affair just to see the whole thing blow up in a war between nations." Eros laughed bitterly:

"Helen?" he said, "why, I could stick Helen as full of arrows as a pin cushion and she still wouldn't know what love was even if she fell over it in the dark. Helen is the original ice maiden." After that, I thought it time to change subjects so I told them all about my conversation with Cressida and how she had forced me to parley with Troilus.

"Well," I said at length, "I suppose, since I can't get out of seeing Troilus, I might as well get it over with. I don't suppose any of you would know where the guy is?" I really didn't feel like slogging all over Troy looking for the s.o.b. Hermes said:

"He's sitting on the bench by the north lion." I got up.

"Nice meeting you, Eros." Eros gave me a wan smile.

"If you have a special lady cat in your sight, call on me. I wouldn't mind making an exception and give you a hand." I shivered but managed not to let it show.

"Thanks a lot, Eros, but I'm a confirmed bachelor and likely to remain so."

"Wise cat." So I left them and made my way around the square to the North lion.

As predicted, Troilus was there on the bench staring gloomily at nothing in particular. I jumped up next to him and for a few moments we enjoyed the silence together. Then I opened the conversation:

"Bad day at the races?" Troilus reply was:

"Since when do cats bet on the ponies?" Me:

"Cats don't but humans do. And you look glum enough to have lost not only your shirt but your favourite warhorse." Then, of course, Troilus was, as you might say, off to the races. His face shone with that imbecile look of a man smitten and he breathed through his nose, turning on me fiercely. Oh, Lord of Cats, protect me from those in love.

"What do you know? What would you care if I told you my heart was broken." He clutched his right breast. "Was there ever such ingratitude? Was there ever a girl with a colder heart than Cressida?" He stopped. "But you don't know Cressida."

"Oh, but I do," was my answer to which he paid absolutely no attention at all.

"I worship her, I adore her," he wailed, his hand still on his heart, "I hang around her house like a lost soul on the Stygian banks who has been denied passage to the blessed shore." Well, it's actually the river Acheron not the Styx but I didn't think this was the time for lessons in Hades geography. He turned towards me, almost as a supplicant, his hands in the prayer position. He looked pitiful: "Oh, be my Charon and take me swiftly to those fields where I may wallow in the lily beds reserved for the deserving." Hey, this was starting to get pornographic. "Fetch me Eros' wings and fly with me to Cressida." I was glad Eros wasn't there, he'd be disgusted. But then I suppose Troilus was speaking figuratively. He went on, eyes turned heavenward: "I can't get anywhere near her; my only contact is through her foul uncle Pandarus and he's determined to quarrel with me." I cleared my throat

"Well," I said, "as a matter of fact, I have a message for you."

"For me?"

"Yes."

"From Pandarus?" I sighed. This was getting boring.

"No," I said crossly. "Do I look like someone who would carry messages for such a man? Get with it, fellow! From Cressida, of course." Troilus' eyes opened wide and his mouth turned into an O but he didn't say anything.

"Cressida wants to know," I said, trying to get to the heart of the matter, "whether your love for her is true, whether your intentions are honourable and whether she can look to you for the protection a young girl needs who has no male relative."

"She's got her uncle Pandarus!" was the answer. I could have brained him.

"She doesn't consider her uncle Pandarus to be a reliable guardian. Would you entrust your sister to someone like Pandarus?" Troilus stopped, thought a bit and replied:

"I don't suppose I would. One never knows quite what to make of Pandarus. Does he want a bribe? A position at court? A commission in the army?" I bristled.

"What you are saying? Is Pandarus bargaining to get the best deal possible for letting you see Cressida? That is disgusting."

"I suppose it is," said Troilus morosely, placing his hands on his knees; "I never actually thought of it that way."

"It's about time you did. Old Calchas took himself off to the Greek camp and left poor Cressida high and dry, with her stock in the marriage market at an all time low. Tell me then why she should trust herself to you, Troilus, you who have everything while she has nothing but her good name and that she would like to keep."

"Well," answered Troilus, fumbling about a bit. Evasive. Ain't that just typical. I pressed on:

"Would you honour and respect her and love her despite her father being a traitor to Troy? Would your mother accept Cressida as an honoured guest at those dinners you keep going on about?" Troilus jumped up and started walking up and down, a frown on his brow. He said:

"What's that got to do with anything?" I looked at him through cat eye slits.

"For you, nothing. For her, everything."

"This is very complicated. I need to think about all this."

"The truth is, Troilus," said I, "that you haven't got the time anymore. You should have thought of all this long ago. So, I ask you again, when you have Cressida, what will you do with her?"

"I will honour and love her above all things!" He exclaimed. Then: "I suppose I could talk mother around." My tail switched and I shook my head.

"That's not good enough, Troilus. Tell me: would you take Cressida to be your wife, love her, comfort her, honour and keep her, in sickness and in health, for richer, for poorer, for better, for worse, in sadness and in joy, to cherish and continually bestow upon her your heart's deepest devotion, forsaking all others, keep yourself only unto her as long as you both shall live?" Troilus stared at me.

"Come again?" So I repeated it all.

"Bit of a mouthful," he said, to gain time, I think. I tapped my paw on the bench.

"Well, Troilus? Come on now, the time for shilly shallying is over, the adolescents have gone to bed and the discussion is now with the grownups. What say you?" Troilus stood there bug-eyed, holding his breath then, as if taking a leap into a foaming torrent, answered:

"I would! I will! In spite of father and mother and all my brothers!" I got up. This conversation hadn't made me sanguine about Troilus but I suppose he deserved the benefit of the doubt. It can't be easy, being one of the youngest of 50 brothers.

"Right, then. I'll meet you at the orchard gate to Calchas' garden at sundown. Don't be late. Oh, and by the way, we don't want Pandarus mixed up in this. One word to him and the deal is off." And I left him.

2.3 HOW MANY GRECIAN TENTS DO STAND EMPTY

I tottered back to the beach as I hadn't had any breakfast. I was finishing the dry cat food I'd brought with me and was off to *The Greek Olive Tree* for a drink, when who should come along but Hermes.

"Hi," said he, "I remembered you were interested in why the Greeks, with all their advantages, are still not able to finish off this tin pot city." Truth to tell, after last night, I had lost interest in Greek versus Trojan but was too embarrassed to say so. Therefore, when he said: "Come along," I went. We headed for the Greek camp where I hadn't actually been yet because, even from a distance, it looked singularly unattractive. As we drew nearer, it became obvious that, after nine years as an army camp, the place was a slum. For starters, most of guards posted seemed asleep, leaning on their spears; some even curled up in the sand, snoring away; I could see no sign of officers patrolling. The whole camp seemed to say: *why bother?* It lay over a huge area inland; somehow, I had expected it to be around the city, as it would have had Troy been under siege. But Hermes told me the Greeks had given up the siege as impractical.

Coming closer, the first thing I saw where the banners, one for each Greek City State, fluttering in the breeze, most ragged and faded. The biggest banner was of course Mycenæ – black background with a golden mask in its centre – and in good condition. Next to it Sparta – Green with a golden shield. Pthia – A golden warrior on white background. Argos: white X on red background. There were many more – after all, sixty-nine City States had joined the confederation, although I gathered from Hermes some had given up and gone home and that many tents stood empty. When they first arrived, each City State had had its own demarked area but with the passing of the years, order and method – in more ways than one – had gone to the wall and the camp was all jumbled up.

Hermes took on a school masterly manner, walking with his hands behind him:

"Tell me, what do you already know about the Greeks' troubles?" I thought a bit.

"The members of the High Command are at odds with each other," was my answer. Hermes nodded.

"Exactly. Is that a cause for their failure?" I shook my head.

"No. I think they fell out because they were unsuccessful rather than the other way around." Hermes nodded again. We had now arrived at the edge of the camp where the Greeks seemed to have set up a rubbish dump. Hermes stopped and I sat down to take in the view. Chariots with one wheel; cooking pots with holes; beakers and plates and mugs all chipped to a greater or lesser extent. Ragged tents with broken poles. Broken and dented swords. Armour liberally covered in blood from which no one could possibly have emerged alive. Three, two and one legged stools and tables. Bows without string; strings without bows. Broken arrows; arrow tips galore. Shields of such peculiar shapes one wondered what the craftsman had originally intended. Wheels strewn about. Wagons without wheels. Wagons with broken shafts. Shredded clothing silently mouldering away. Broken harnesses. Worn out saddles. I looked at Hermes:

"So?" Hermes swept his hand over the whole sorry mess. "What strikes you?" he asked. I was stumped. I tried:

"It's a tip."

"That," said Hermes, "is stating the obvious. Nothing else?" I thought really hard and said, without much hope of getting it right.

"Well, a lot of this stuff could be recycled." Hermes scratched his chin.

"The word 'recycled' will only come into use thousands of years from now but the concept is older than the hills," he said. "In your world, it means plastic bottles, tin cans and so on. In the here and now, re-using items makes even more sense as the manufacturing process is so painstakingly slow and raw materials scarce. Ergo, a wagon with no wheels and four cast off wheels could, in theory, be made a usable wagon. Two wagons with a broken shaft each, a wagon with two shafts. If one of your tent poles breaks, you could in theory get a pole from another tent with only three." I said sagely:

"Waste not, want not." Hermes nodded gravely.

"So, ask yourself: why is no recycling taking place here?" I thought:

"Apathy. Disorganization. Despondency." Hermes nodded:

"And plain bad management. Come along, now." We set off again, passing through the main part of the camp. Conditions were awful. The tents were ragged and filthy. The ground was muddy although it hadn't rained for days. Someone had thrown a few planks down to make a passable path, but that hadn't done much good since a fair number of the planks were also covered in muck. The smell of decaying food was everywhere and odours too awful to identify seemed to saturate the blue sky. Soldiers were lounging about, listless, uninterested, many of them obviously sick. Hermes said:

"Dysentery. The bane of every army. Just ask Florence Nightingale during the Crimean war in about 3 000 years."

"It comes," I said snootily "from unhygienic conditions and bad food."

"Just so," agreed Hermes. We passed the field hospital. It looked hot and dirty and unsanitary. If I become sick, I pray it will be somewhere else. Stray, mangy dogs were all over but, I am happy to say, no cats. Cats know better. We came to the horses' enclosure. They looked thin and every last one needed a good bath and grooming. Many stood almost knee-deep in muck due, in part, to rotting hay and grass mixed with body waste no one had bothered to rake out. Then there were the chariots. Each and every one needed shining up; wheels caked with mud, precariously attached to their axles. I wasn't going to accept an invitation to ride in any of them. The armament tents were a picture of disorganization, heaps of swords strewn about, shields chucked any old how; someone had tried to organize the lances but had given up and probably gone off to be ill. I said:

"This is making me depressed." Hermes shook his head.

"And so it should." We came to the mess hall. I didn't know what was cooking, but it smelled revolting. A big fat man was standing at the entrance, arms akimbo, staring gloomily into space. Suddenly his face lit up, he pointed his finger at me and called over his shoulder:

"A cat! Pericles, get me the cleaver. Cat would really improve our stew. Never get much meat around here." I froze. This was not in the script. I didn't want to become stew, especially not in an unsanitary place like this. Who knew what else they'd got in the pot. Someone handed the cook the cleaver, he turned back and took a few steps forwards and then stopped. His eyes goggled. "Who got the cat? Someone's taken the cat to eat on his own. Pericles!" A frightened kitchen boy came up. He was chewing his apron in his distress and quavered:

"Honestly, Simonides, I never even saw the cat. And you were here all the time, I could never have gotten past you." But Simonides wasn't listening. He grabbed hold of Pericles and shook him until his teeth rattled.

"I don't know how you did it, but it's obvious you did. And you are going to give me that carcass..." They went back into the tent where the commotion continued. I looked at Hermes.

"What happened?" I asked bewildered, "I'm here, I've been here all the time." Hermes grinned.

"Indeed, but no one can see you. A little bit of magic, if you like; you are invisible. I think I'll keep it like that for the rest of our walk. Come along now!" I walked jauntily behind him. Invisibility was great. Not forever, of course, but in critical moments. I started day dreaming of how temporary invisibility could improve my life – at bath time or during the vet's visits...

Then we came to a smaller camp. Here, conditions were moderately better. Tears in the tents had been repaired but the result looked slovenly. The tents themselves had once been white, or so I imagined, but were now fast turning grey and brown. The clothing we saw drying in the sun must once have been gorgeous in colour but that was long ago. The furnishings were of good quality but ill kept and the bronze armour and tableware we could see looked tarnished. The whole place reeked of desolation. On the positive side, the paths were smooth, courtesy of a group of slaves gravelling in a desultory fashion, helped along by a slave driver, the only person I saw enjoying himself. Then we came to a minicamp up the slope of a hill, away from all the rest. I wouldn't say everything looked pristine but an overall vast improvement with regard to the lower camp. Two standards fluttered in the breeze above it. I said:

"Someone doesn't want to be affected by the doom and gloom," Hermes looked at me.

"This is Odysseus and Nestor's camps." We walked up and saw that everything was different here; although as old and battered as elsewhere, an effort had been made to keep tents in decent repair and armaments in the best condition possible. The soldiers looked as healthy as could be expected and the servants worked without supervision not, mind you, singing and laughing, but at least quietly. The horses browsed free on the hillside, watched by a number of lads.

Hermes stopped and waved his hand further inland.

"Over there, you can just glimpse it, is where the camp followers live." I looked.

"I don't see any tents," I said. Hermes shrugged.

"Since when do assorted army suppliers, prostitutes, cleaners and so on warrant tents? They must bring their own. Do you want to go and have a look?" I looked anxiously at Hermes.

"Do I have to? I didn't sign up for it when I bought the package tour." Hermes smiled:

"Suppose I can let you off." We sat down; the whole camp lay before us. I said:

"It seems unlikely that the Gods are responsible for the condition in the camps."

"Undoubtedly," replied Hermes. "You have to be human to get yourself into such a deplorable state. So," he continued, "why don't the Trojans take the opportunity to sweep the lot of them into the sea and have done with it? The Greeks will never be more vulnerable than they are right now." I thought about this for a bit.

"Hermes, the Greeks being stupid don't make the Trojans smart. I think the Trojans are lulled into a sense of false security behind their strong and unbreeched walls. They are, shall we say, CHEZ EUX. At home. They sleep in their own beds, eat at their own tables, fight with their wives and slap their kids around. OK, they can't leave the city, but still, Priam Square is busy with its cafés and market stalls; the Trojans meet friends for a drink, and there is always the hope the Greeks will get fed up and go home." I chewed on this a bit further. "I don't know the conditions of their hospitals but so far there is no sign of disease in the city. Perhaps they just leave their fallen outside the walls. I know that sounds awful but then, why take the chance of bringing plague into the city? The no man left behind theory is all very well. But at what cost?" Hermes laughed silently, the first time I'd seen it.

"Gaius, you are so right."

"One for all and all for one," I went on, "the needs of the many or the needs of the few?" I held up a paw. "Also: the Trojans have Hector who is brave and so on and so forth, loved and respected by all. But remember he must serve as Commander-in-chief as well as being their most able warrior. The Greeks have Akhilleus, a great hero far superior to Hector but what a loose cannon! At least Akhilleus is not Commander-in-Chief; there's Agamemnon to do all the bullying. In the field of strategy, Troy doesn't seem to have any. But then neither do the Greeks. I think that Odysseus could possibly dream up something the Trojans wouldn't like; however, his time doesn't seem to have come yet." Hermes got up.

"There you are, Gaius, all in a nutshell. This has been both enjoyable and profitable. At times, I like to get the layman's view, if you know what I mean." On another subject, I said:

"I thought you were going to shop Aphrodite for having been involved in the Paris fiasco yesterday." Hermes grinned and shook his head.

"Secrets are only useful if they remain secrets. Aphrodite knows I know. That gives me a hold over her for later use. If I told Zeus, there'd be hell to pay for her but what would be in it for me? No, no. This sort of advantage must be used carefully and strategically." I looked at Hermes. He would have made a good cat.

2.4 OF SNAKES AND FLEDGLINGS

Then, all of a sudden, from being a ghost town, every part of the Greek camp came alive. Everyone seemed to be on the move. Heralds, some carrying pennants, some blowing trumpets, junior officers and common soldiers were gathering under their City's flags. This sudden change needed looking into, so we came off the hill and closer to the scene of the action. Not knowing whether I was still invisible, I didn't want to get too close and kept a sharp lookout for Simonides and his cleaver. We found a convenient hillock that gave us a splendid view while keeping us away from the crowd. At the point where the commanders' tents met the general camp, a platform had been set up and who should be standing on it but Agamemnon. He held up his hands for silence and, surprisingly enough, got it.

"Soldiers of the Greek City States, Comrades and allies, hear me for my cause and be silent that you may hear; believe me for mine honour and respect mine honour so that you may believe." There was something familiar about these words, but for the moment I couldn't put my finger on it.[13] Agamemnon went on: "For nine years we have laboured at a just war to which, however, there appears to be no end. In spite of our superior manpower, training, equipment and strategy, Troy continues behind its mighty walls and their allies from the inland kingdoms have made it possible for them to withstand our siege and cancelled out our superiority on the battlefield. So perhaps we should take stock and decide whether it is in our best interests to continue this war. Look at our once proud ships with their rotting hulls; our arms are rusty; our wives and children long for our return and our homelands need us. Yet the task we set ourselves nine years ago is still unfinished." He stopped for a moment and looked around.

"Men, the time has come to face the fact that we may not be able to accomplish our task should we stay twice as long. Therefore, it is my decision that we abandon this hopeless enterprise and return to our homes over the sea. For, do what we may, it seems the Gods have decided we shall never take Troy!" I was aghast. Agamemnon was giving up. But the multitude loved it. Cheers rang out, men hugged each other, jumping up and down in their excitement. Agamemnon held up his arms: "Comrades, let's to our ships and sail away from these accursed shores back to our lands, our homes and our families!" The pandemonium was unbelievable, and who could blame the common man, dragooned into a war for no purpose but the glory of the upper classes, for being eager to be gone.

"Would you believe this!" said Hermes. "Look at Odysseus and Nestor, just behind Agamemnon; they do not look pleased."

---

[13]   *Julius Caesar*, William Shakespeare, Act III, Scene II

"I don't see why," I replied, "since they have little to gain from this imbroglio. Odysseus, as far as I can gather, isn't into glory and Nestor is way beyond glory."

"Ahh," was Hermes' comment, "you forget booty, loot. The riches of Troy, one of the most splendid cities in the known world." I asked:

"What about Helen?" Hermes gave an unexpected laugh.

"Helen? Who's Helen?" I was about to make a fool of myself when I saw his point. I turned my attention back to the scene before us. By this time, the multitude was in full swing, swarming all over the place, getting their belongings together, clearing channels so they could push rowboats into the sea, and hammering at the stays that held up a number of beached vessels. Odysseus now got up on the platform and held up his arms, calling for silence. Blasts from Ithaca's trumpeters finally got everyone to pay attention.

"My friends and fellow Greeks, you have forgotten the pledge we took when we set out that none should return till the city of Troy was no more and Greece's honour restored. And now you would set off homeward, your task undone. I can understand you feel you have had much toil with little to show for it and are disheartened. Even the sailor at sea for a single month longs for the comfort of his home and family and no longer be at the mercy of wind and waves. We have been kept here for nine long years; how can I blame you for becoming restive. But, think, my compatriots, will we not be shamed if we return after so long a stay with empty hands? Therefore, my friends, I entreat you to remain a little longer."

"Why?" shouted a voice in the crowd. "What do you think we'll achieve by staying, as you say, 'a little longer', that we haven't over the past nine years?" A voice I knew well spoke up. Thersites, the blabbermouth:

"May I ask the Greek High Command what more you want when your tents are crammed with gold and fair women. How can you, the Greek High Command, wish to extend the misery to its soldiers except in the hope of more gain and profit?" Thersites jumped up, turned his back to the platform and roared: "Let us sail home, leaving these arrogant bastards to pursue honour and glory but, first and foremost, wealth and riches; why, they might even discover they have no need for us at all!" This all went down a treat with the common herd and the applause was immense. I even think Thersites would have swung the mood away from Odysseus if something extraordinary had not happened.

At the back of the camp, where the plain started to rise to meet the plateau was a fine plane-tree with a stream of pure water welling up from its roots. There, to the horror of all, a fearful serpent slid out of the opening, enormous, massif, its scales like blood-red stains. Taking its time, it slid up the tree, fearsome coil embracing the trunk round and round, until it reached the upper branches. On one branch, a nest of young sparrows, newly hatched, chirped, watched by their mother. In a twinkling of an eye, the serpent swallowed the nest, chicks and, with the least of efforts, caught the mother in its jaws. It then sedately descended the tree and returned to its lair under the earth. There was a communal gasp from all the spectators, even from me. Hermes remarked:

"What are you so surprised at, you of all species? Cats stalk and eat birds all the time. It's in their genes." I answered with dignity:

"Personally, I would hate to get my mouth full of feathers and have blood dripping from my jaws. Disgusting!" Hermes' comment:

"Curious. You must be a new breed of cat. Evolution, I suppose." I did not dignify this with an answer. In the meantime, on the platform, Agamemnon and Nestor stood petrified while Odysseus shouted for someone to go and get Calchas who came with slow dignity onto the platform, most probably thinking up likely explanations. At last he spoke, opening his arms as if to embrace the universe:

"Why, my fearless Greeks, are you speechless and surprised? It is obvious that Zeus, God of Gods, has sent us this sign to guide us in our choice. The serpent swallowed the eight chicks and then their mother, a total of nine. How do we interpret this? My friends, for nine years you have fought to conquer Troy; and, in this, the tenth year, the City shall fall to you." Lowering his arms, he concluded: "This is the will of Great Zeus, God of Gods: that the city of Priam shall fall to the Greeks." I turned to Hermes:

"Well, what do you say to that?"

"I say," was the reply, "that Calchas is worth every drachma the Greeks pay him." There was a long moment of silence. Then Agamemnon cried:

"As always, the Gods know the minds of men. We, the Greeks, have been wasting our time on petty quarrels. In the quarrel between Akhilleus and myself, I readily admit I was the first to offend; once we are all reconciled, our differences behind us, the Trojans will not stave off destruction for one day. Our course is now clear. Troy will be ours and that very soon! My worthy Greeks, let us now crush the Trojans. Whet your spears; see to the worthiness of your shields; feed and groom your horses, and look carefully to your chariots, make sure the wheels are secure, the shafts tight, the reins unbroken. We will fight the Trojans without rest until Troy is ours or is no more!" The Greeks raised a shout, till the camp rang out with praises for Agamemnon. My comment was:

"About five minutes ago, they were all set to go home. Now, they are all set to fight to the death. What happened?" Hermes looked straight ahead.

"Human nature, that's what happened. Changeable as the wind, treacherous and ever shifting. Come on, they're going to start their disgusting sacrifices and barbecues."

"The least you can do," I said as we walked along, "is to let me have the inside story of that awful snake we just saw." Hermes raised his eyebrows.

"What do you mean? It was a snake having its breakfast."

"It wasn't conjured up by Zeus or someone?" Hermes looked offended.

"Of course not! Do you really think Zeus goes in for those cheap parlour tricks? If he wanted the Greeks to sit up and listen, he would have sent a thunderbolt or two." I thought about this for a bit.

"We only have Calchas' word for there being eight fledglings," I said thoughtfully, "making nine with the mama bird. And, of course, seeing the Greeks have already been here for nine years, it's hardly rocket science to predict the war will be over in the tenth. You know what, I wouldn't be surprised if this was all a scheme of Odysseus'." Hermes waggled his eyebrows. It seemed we were done with this subject. Hermes disappeared in his usual manner . But, Homerys was there, creating a tremendous fuss.

"All wrong," he cried, "all wrong! I alone know the truth, it's all in my epic; the snake and the fledglings appeared in Aulis, in Aulis! Not here in Troy!" I quickened my steps, knowing what was to follow:

> *... when in Aulis[14] all our fleet assembled with a freight*
> *of ills to Ilion and her friends ... a dragon with a bloody*
> *scale, horrid to sight ... the plane tree climbed and*
> *ruthless crashed to death a sparrow's young in number*
> *eight ...the dam, the ninth, ... devoured her too..."*

I snickered. Sorry, Homerys, can't have it all your own way, you know.

2.5 HERE IS GOOD BROKEN MUSIC

Of course I headed straight for *The Trojan Horse*. I decided I'd earned another cream tea, to hell with the calories. Marianne was not there but the old duffer in the white spotty apron willingly got me my tea. I was concentrating on not losing my whiskers in the clotted cream when a young fellow came in, with another four fellows behind him , each carrying an instrument: lyre, flute, drum and something that looked like a guitar but not quite. The leader addressed the old guy – I couldn't hear what they said but it got into quite a hassle. The I grasped that the young guy wanted a dais for his musicians. The old guy shook his head, spread his arms – his meaning was clear – we ain't got no dais. The other guy buried his fist in his other palm and went outside, while the musicians just stood there like so many wax figures. The guy came back with two others, navvies by the look of them.

"Crates," the first guy shouted, "I want crates! I want eight crates and I want them now!" The navvies hurried off and before you could say Jiminy Cricket, they were back with the crates. The boss guy ordered:

"There," pointing at a sort of bay window, "set them up there! Four along, two deep! Waiter," turning to the old guy who'd gone back to his newspaper, "Two table clothes!" Muttering and holding his back, the waiter went off and came back with two tablecloths that, if I might guess, came out of the washing hamper. These were laid over the crates and four chairs were set on them. The leader of the

---

14   Port in central Greece, north of Athens, where the Greeks assembled their
      fleet before leaving for Troy

group pointed at the musicians and ordered: "Up!" The guy with the flute looked at the set up:

"Doesn't look all that safe," he complained. The leader turned on him like a tiger and the four carefully stepped up and gingerly sat down and started tuning their instruments. I found this unnerving, it sounded so much like four bad tempered cats having a quarrel. In the meantime, the young fellow got into another argument with the waiter. He waved his arms around and pointed at the tablecloth on the nearest table, "That tablecloth," he shouted, "is not clean! Get a fresh one!" Well, it did have a few spots on it from previous customers. The old duffer argued a bit but then threw his hands up and got out another that was just a mite cleaner than the first. He then laid the table for tea, and if the china was not exactly Wedgewood, it was slightly better than what I had been given. The quartet now seemed to have tormented the cats enough and started playing something recognizable as music. The street door opened and I heard a smarmy well known voice. Pandarus came through the door, all smiles and bonhomie and addressed the guy:

"Timon, isn't it? A follower of Paris, if I am not mistaken?" Timon was not amused and snarled:

"I follow Paris if he happens to be walking in front of me." I inspected the ceiling. A stand up comedian. I thought it rather funny and sniggered but Pandarus was not amused. He said with dignity:

"I mean, my dear fellow, you are on Paris' staff?" Timon answered in an offhand manner:

"If I am, what business is that of yours?" Pandarus tried another tack.

"You work for a noble fellow. I cannot praise him enough."

"The Lord be praised," answered Timon smartly. Stalemate. But Pandarus either was the densest fellow around or had the skin of a rhinoceros for he wouldn't let go:

"You know me, do you not?" He asked, rather grandly.

"I've seen you around," was the answer.

"My young friend, I'm the nobleman, Pandarus."

"Good for you." I could have told Pandarus he was wasting his time. But he ploughed right on. He looked at the musicians.

"What sweet music. For whom do they play?"

"For whoever is around to listen." Timon must have guessed what Pandarus wanted but wasn't about to give it to him. Pandarus persevered:

"And who asked them to play?"

"I did." Pandarus finally understood that to get the answer he wanted, he'd have to ask a direct question. He said in his most condescending manner:

"Dear Timon, we seem to be at cross purposes. I'm being too polite and you are being too cunning. So, let us try again. Who wishes to hear music?"

"Well," answered Timon, "if that's what you wanted to know, why didn't you ask? Paris, of course. Since he's my boss, d'you think I'd be running around making arrangements for anyone else? He's on his way here with the mortal Venus, the very essence of beauty, love's invisible soul…" Timon showed he too could be pompous. Pandarus raised his eyebrows:

"You mean my cousin Cressida?" Timon sneered.

"Who on earth is Cressida? Oh, the traitor's daughter. And what would Paris be doing with Cressida, your cousin or not? Any idiot would know I mean Helen." Pandarus appeared deeply offended.

"It's obvious, my young friend, you have not yet seen my cousin Cressida." Timon rolled his eyes. "I have come to speak to Paris. I have a special message from his brother, Troilus."

At that moment, Paris and Helen arrived and Timon made good his escape. I could see that Helen's mood hadn't improved since I saw her on the battlements. In fact, I wouldn't have crossed her for a tin of cat food. And I would only have commandeered a thousand ships if they guaranteed to take her away and not bring her back, ever. As my Greek pal the drunk said, there are other women. Paris was hobbling on a stick, one arm in a sling and bandages around his head. Pandarus of course pretended not to notice either Helen's filthy mood or Paris' aches and pains. He said, at his most flowery:

"What a fair day this is, my good Paris, and how much fairer your presence and that of the fair Queen Helen make it." Helen answered sourly:

"And who might you be?" That would have sent me scuttling down the alley but Pandarus was made of sterner stuff. He smirked:

"I am Pandarus, the nobleman, dear lady, at your service." Helen looked away from him, as if he'd suddenly vanished:

"Of course. Brother to the Traitor Calchas." That was a nasty one but Pandarus rallied, turning to Paris:

"My dear prince, what exquisite music." Paris was not made of the same mettle as Helen and did not have the guts to tell Pandarus to get lost. Also, with Helen in her present mood, he may have thought Pandarus could help cooling things down. Paris turned to Helen:

"My dear, our friend here is full of harmony." Pandarus looked coy:

"Oh, no, no indeed. I know very little about music, my knowledge is really very limited."

"See, my fair beauty, how modest our friend is," applauded Paris. Pandarus went on:

"My fair Queen," in a voice dripping with honey or so he thought. "I have business with the prince." Turning to Paris: "Will you give me a few moments of your time?" Helen frowned:

"I don't see what business anyone could have with Paris that the whole world couldn't know about. I certainly don't care what it is and am not moving from my tea." She waved her hands at them. "Why don't you two run along and exchange whatever secrets you have in the men's room." She clapped her hands. "Waiter, another scone, some more clotted cream and jam." The waiter, old as he was, jumped to it. Pandarus tried to rally:

"You are too good, my queen." He turned to Paris and tried again. "I have a message for you, Prince, from your brother Troilus..." Helen cut in.

"Troilus. Another wastrel. What good is he to anyone? It's like the more sons Priam had, the more useless they became. Selfish and cowardly. One might have hoped Troilus was the last in that line but Hecuba seems not to be able to stop breeding." Pandarus was aghast:

"Oh, my dear Queen, I'm sure you don't mean that." He continued, to Paris: "Your brother sends his greetings and ..." But Helen was at it again.

"Try me," was her reply. Then she leant back in her chair and continued: "Now, since you are here and there seems no way of getting rid of you, you will amuse me by singing a song. Come along now, I'm waiting." She called for more tea. You had to admire the lady. I started to grasp how she got those thousand ships launched. Pandarus was no match for her. Nor was Paris, or Menelaus, I'll be bound. Pandarus had now run out of words. Score one for Helen. All he could say was:

"Sweet queen, my sweet queen, my very sweet queen," looking aghast.

"Oh, really," drawled Helen, "I am your sweet queen, is that so? And Calchas is your sweet brother? And Cressida your sweet niece, sweet Calchas' daughter?" There was a menace in these words that must have struck at Pandarus' innermost heart. He turned to Paris and said in a rush. "Troilus has asked you to give his excuses to the king and queen, your parents, and say he will not be able to come to dinner tonight..."

"Is that so?" was Helen's comment. "I think a little bird told me that your oh so lovely Cressida has her eye set on Troilus, a fool but still a prince of the blood. How quaint! A prince of the blood and a traitor's daughter." Worse and worse. Pandarus almost gagged but managed to say:

"Oh, you are quite mistaken, my poor cousin is unwell and is to keeping to her bed. As for love affairs, dear me, Cressida is far too young."

Paris asked:

"So, my dear Pandarus, why was my brother Troilus so late arriving at the field today?" Helen chimed in:

"You might also ask why Paris was so early in leaving it." Pandarus squeaked:

"I don't know, I swear," his eyes popping out of his head, adding: "I have just remembered an important engagement, and must leave you. Farewell." And he fairly ran, with Helen calling after him:

"Give my love to your sweet niece." But Pandarus was gone. Paris snarled, all his good humour gone.

"If I were king, he would not live long!" he said. Helen raised her eyebrows:

"If I were king, you would not live long." Paris turned on her:

"Helen, this is too much."

"Is it?" she answered. "Do have some tea."

"You shouldn't taunt me in public like that."

"We shouldn't be in public, making spectacles of ourselves. You should be hiding under your bed. In fact, can I ask, just as a curiosity, where you got the guts to sail all the way to Sparta to abduct me – and my possessions, as I continually hear. What were you high on? Ecstasy? Mescaline? Or good old fashioned crack?"

"You can't talk to me like that," Paris raged.

"Really? And what are you going to do to stop me?" Listening to all this, I couldn't help thinking that, had Paris sinned, he had surely paid – and over ten years the cost tended to add up. Paris called wearily for a whisky and soda. Before he had taken the first swallow, Hector came in, still covered in dust and bits of blood, wearing his armour and carrying his sword. He looked balefully at Paris. Oh, oh, I thought, someone else who has it is in for our Paris. I almost felt sorry for the poor soul. What had started out as a schoolboy prank had very definitely turned sour. But first Hector turned to Helen.

"Helen," he said, "as always, I am glad to see you. But astonished to find you here, out in public."

"Hi, Hector, my brother, at least in misfortune. I don't particularly want to be here but my lord Paris insisted we get out of the house. And he has arranged it beautifully, has he not, musicians and all." I couldn't make up my mind whether I liked Helen least when she was being rude or sarcastic. Hector turned to his brother, who was staring straight ahead.

"My brother, you would have done better to have hidden away in our father's palace than parading about in Priam Square. Don't you know that our people and our allies are dying fighting for this town? Why, I can only imagine your reaction had you seen a common soldier shirk his duty on the battlefield as you did." Paris answered:

"My brother, what you say is very true; why don't you go on to the field and I'll follow you directly I've put on my greaves and armour and picked up my weapons." Helen let out a short bitter laugh:

"Bit late in the day, my fine fellow. What you should have done you did not do – allow my husband Menelaus to slaughter you. That would have been the honourable way out. Now, how will you salve what is left of your honour? Believe me when I say it is irretrievably lost."

"Helen," said Hector gently, "you are being too harsh. A moment's panic..." Helen looked straight at him.

"A moment's panic, indeed! Tell me, Hector, have you ever had a moment's panic? Has Helenus or Troilus or Agamemnon or even my past and, who knows, future husband, Menelaus? Warriors do not have moments of panic, my dear, as well you know. Why not say it out loud? Paris is a poltroon and a coward." Helen stopped but she wasn't done yet. "This fellow is not to be depended on and I, as the Gods are my witnesses, am reaping what he has sown and so will many innocents." Paris looked affronted, picked up his crutch and said:

"Wait for me in the field. I shall be there directly!" He stomped out. Helen said:

"My brother Hector, sit down and let me get you something to drink. The whole burden of the defence of your homeland falls on your shoulders for a cause you do not even believe in. Forget Paris. He can neither be shamed by dishonour or men's evil speeches. And, once you have rested, you and I will go up to the tower and you will throw me down and this whole matter will be settled." Hector smiled sadly:

"My dear Helen, I cannot stay for all the goodwill you bear me. I must rejoin the Trojans, who need me to lead them. As for Paris, who knows, Helen, one day he may perform a feat that will cleanse his name and give him back his honour. Now, I must go to see my wife and my little son, for who knows if I shall ever return to them." And so he went, leaving Helen alone with the musicians who had stopped playing long ago and where taking in the action.

"Get out," she screamed at them, and they did, as fast as ever they could. Helen followed at a more leisurely but still firm pace. She looked at me. "And what are you staring at, you stupid cat? And when did cats start drinking tea?" She was gone.

So I sat on my own until who should come in but Pandarus, followed by Troilus. Lord of Cats, give me strength. Pandarus seemed to have recovered from his drubbing by Helen or perhaps he was passing it on. He spat angrily at Troilus:

"Well, have you seen Cressida?" This set Troilus off down the well trodden path we'd been on before.

"Ok," answered Pandarus, stemming the flow. "I'll go and find her." He stomped off. Troilus was about to return to his moaning, when he felt a well placed claw in the fleshy part of his thigh. He howled and jumped up, more or less at the same time. I hissed at him, my hackles raised, ears laid back, for I was now in a bitch of a temper.

"What did I tell, you, dunderhead? No more conversations with Pandarus or you and Cressida are through before you begin."

"What did you have to claw me for? What did I do to you?" I glared:

"Because I am pissed, brother, and the next time I see you with Pandarus, I'll go for the jugular. Now, get lost. I don't want to see you again before we meet at Calchas' garden gate." Troilus ran out, limping a bit. Of course Pandarus had to come back.

"I couldn't find her," he started out, "she's probably prettying herself up, you know what girls are like ..." He looked around bewildered. "Where's he gone?"

"How should I know and why should I care?" I growled, laying my ears back and swishing my tail. "And if you had any sense, you'd let this whole matter alone. You'll end up getting yourself and Cressida accused of treason the way you go on." I got up, stuck my tail in the air and left.

Whom should I see just outside *The Trojan Horse* but Homerys, his voice ringing:

> *"And was thy [Paris] cowardice such (so conquered) to*
> *be seen alive? O would to god thy life had perished by his*
> *[Menelaus] worthy hand, to whom I first was wife. Before*
> *this, though wouldst glorify thy valour and thy lance and*
> *past my first love's boast them far: go once more, and*
> *advance thy braves against his single power: this foil*
> *might fall by chance. Poor conquered man [Paris]: 'twas*
> *such a chance as I would not advice thy valour should*
> *provoke again: shun him, thou most unwise lest next, thy*
> *spirit sent to hell, thy body to be his prize."*

I shook my head. Good lines but I could really not imagine Helen saying them.

2.6 AS TRUE AS TROILUS, AS FALSE AS CRESSIDA

Calchas' garden gate was set in an archway and at the time agreed upon, I was lying on top of the arch, enjoying the last rays of the sun. Troilus was there, too, about half an hour before the time set, and started boring me stiff the minute he turned up. His voice was rapturous, his hands clasped and he was looking heavenward.

"Oh, she will come! I know she will come! My love! My own!" Hey, pal, don't get ahead of yourself. "It makes me dizzy just to think of it. My mind's in a whirl." I never thought I'd hear that outside a Hollywood musical. "I think I'll die of joy, I'll be so overcome just to see her!" I snarled

"Will you settle down! She'll be here. She just needs to get ready." Well, that could take a while if I knew anything about ladies, female or feline. I added some advice for good measure. "Mind that you show her your best side. Be witty, romantic, heave a few sighs and groan as if you were about to die. Girls like that." As usual, Troilus wasn't listening but continued on his own theme, hands to his breast, eyes to the sky:

"My heart is beating as if it were about to burst. I'm sure my pulse rate is up, too. My eyes are misting over. How can I even look at her? She's so far above me." At that moment, the garden gate opened and there stood Cressida before I expected her. But then, with the fuss Troilus was making in the middle of the street, she probably didn't want the whole neighbourhood involved.

"Well, Troilus," said Cressida cool as a cucumber and intent on keeping the upper hand. "I understand you wished to see me. And here I am." He entered the garden and shut the gate behind him. Cressida looked extremely fetching; she had obviously made an effort at her toilette. Pale blue dress and an oriental shawl with gold fringes, her hair carefully arranged, partly held up by a golden ribbon, partly hanging around her face. She sat down on the bench and Troilus joined her there. He was speechless which made a nice change. As all highborn ladies, Cressida was adept at small talk.

"Lovely evening, don't you think? And I hear there will be a full moon." Troilus found his tongue:

"Oh, Cressida, sweet Cressida," but then trailed off again. He shook himself and started again: "Your presence has left me speechless." Another pause and then ... "Oh, Cressida, how I've longed for this moment and imagined how it would be."

"Wished, my Prince?" says Cressida, in a slightly aloof manner girls adopt with their swains. "The Gods grant that ..." Troilus interrupted her, he couldn't help it, it was in his nature.

"What, my darling? Can you not see that my love is like a clear fountain? Why do you insist on seeing the weeds and not the lily pads?" He pointed at the fishpond. My friend the goldfish stuck his head out, a worried look on his face. I mouthed to him. 'Don't worry, it's all hyperbole!' If Troilus was one of those who think ladies can be won through of their ears, he was sure working at it. But Cressida was not so easily had. She knew a thing or two about the perfidiousness of men.

"I too wish for clear water," was her answer. "Alas, I fear it will not be so easy to get rid of the weeds!" Troilus had a ready answer to that. He looked at her earnestly:

"Fear makes devils out of angels. Fear clouds the senses and intrudes upon happiness." Cressida straightened herself and smoothed her dress: She said haughtily:

"Blind fear based on reason is safer than blind reason alone. If you expect the worst even without knowing why, things often turn out not to be so bad after all. If you do not, frequently there is nothing but disappointment." Troilus was about to interrupt but Cressida raised a finger: "But often fear is based on reality, on intangible knowledge, on intuition just beyond the conscious mind. And that fear, my dear Troilus, should be taken seriously." But Troilus wasn't about to go all Freudian.

"My beloved, there is no reason for fear; there are no snakes in our garden of love." Snakes, is it? They've always had a bad press. The goldfish looked around, a worried look on his face. Poor guy. For him the world was full of menace. Cressida raised her eyebrows:

"Is there nothing akin to snakes in our garden?" Troilus was right there with an answer. Glib, that's the word for him.

"The only monster, my sweet, is that desire is boundless while action has boundaries." Cressida replied, getting to her feet and heading for the pond:

"They say lovers swear to what they cannot or will not deliver. Lovers have the voices of lions and the courage of rabbits." Hey, leave out the animal kingdom. People are trouble enough. Troilus was on it:

"Not us, oh, not us, sweet Cressida, I assure you. Praise the wine after you have tasted it; judge me upon the evidence of my actions. There shall never be a truer lover than Troilus." Rotten sentence. "I swear this by the moon that shines on us tonight." Dusk was now falling. Cressida walked upon and down, wringing her hands.

"So whatever folly I commit, I must dedicate to the moon. But why swear by the moon which is ever changing? Will you too have phases? Bright one day, then waning to dark, then gone?" Good point, Cressida. But Troilus was having none of it. He flung himself on his knees before her:

"Oh, my love. Change! I will never change! If not the moon, I will then swear by the sun that is forever constant. Be true to your Troilus, my love, for no one will ever love you more." He rose and put both hands on her shoulders. She turned her face away and said slowly:

"Yes, the sun rises in the East and sets in the West and that never changes. But sometimes, my prince, the sun may be covered by clouds and not seen for many days." She turned and now they stood facing each other. She looked into his face and said almost in a pleading tone:

"So, tell me true, Troilus, what do you want of me?"

"I want to be your one true love. To cherish you forever. To protect you and share my life with you till death do us part." Their hands entwined and their lips almost touched. And, at last, she said the words he longed to hear:

"Troilus, I have loved you night and day for many weary months." Of course, Troilus replied:

"But, Cressida, my own Cressida, why then were you so hard to win?" She turned away, hands clasped:

"I was won when you first looked at me. But had I confessed it then, you would have played the tyrant. I love you now; but not till now so much that I could not have mastered my love." Then she turned away again, and buried her face in her hands. "I lie: my thoughts have been running wild, out of control for many days. Love has become my god and I am its servant." She seemed on the point of tears. "Why am I saying all this? Who will be true to me if I am not true to myself and cannot keep my own secrets?" She then calmed down and returned to the bench, head bowed. "But though I did love you, I would not woo you. How I longed to be a man or that a woman had a man's privilege of being the first to speak of love." Honey, being a woman sucks, we all know that. "Oh, why don't you stop me from babbling? I'm sure I have said too much. See, you say nothing although you've drawn out my innermost soul."

"Why should I speak," said Troilus gently, sitting down beside her. "When I hear such sweet music from you?" He took her in his arms and she clung to him. They kissed, a kiss that seemed to go on for a long time. Suddenly, Cressida freed herself from him. She started to moan.

"I'm sorry, I'm sorry. I wasn't begging for a kiss! What have I done? I have lost myself. You must go." Troilus but his arms back around her.

"But , my darling Cressida? How have I offended you?"

"You have not, but I have. There seem to be two of me, a faithful and trusting lover who wants you to stay, and a prudent woman who wishes you to leave." The she raised her hands to heaven. "Oh, but I'm losing my mind," she cried. "I don't know what I'm saying." Troilus said gently, stroking her locks:

"Cressida, you make perfect sense to me." But Cressida wasn't so easily consoled. Her self-esteem and confidence seemed to have hit rock bottom. She cried:

"Who knows, perhaps I am more cunning than I am in love; perhaps I have said so much to make you tell me your secrets. And perhaps you don't love me at all – no one can both love and be wise." Troilus answered:

"Oh, if only I could be sure a woman would remain constant to her vows even as she outlives her youth and beauty, her mind renewing itself as her body weakens. Or that I could believe that my integrity and love would be met by equal purity. This, as I see it, is the heart of a woman: keeping the flame of her love alight, remaining true to her promise, faithful to her vows. How happy I should then be! I am a simple man: my truth is a simple truth." What a me-guy he is. Of course, Cressida objected. There was too much in this for men and not much for women.

"Then I must disagree with you."

"What a war this will be!" exclaimed Troilus. "Right against right, who will be proven most right?" He became lyrical. "In times to come, lovers will swear to be as *true as steel, as sun to day, as dove to her mate, as iron to the magnate, as earth to centre.* And when they run out of the usual oaths and comparisons, they will say *as true as Troilus,* and that will prove their love beyond all doubt." Humm, ok, we'll take it at face value. Cressida agreed enthusiastically, heaven knows why.

"Oh, yes," she said, with her arms around his neck. "And if ever you find me false or evasive, even when time is old and has forgotten itself and Troy has turned to dust, let it be remembered: when women are false to their lovers, *as air to water, wind or sandy earth, as fox to lamb, as wolf to heifer's calf, leopard to the hind or stepmother to stepson,* then let them say *as false as Cressida.*"

Oh, dear. If you're good, you're Troilus, if you're bad, you're Cressida. I didn't like the sound of this. Cressida turned to me on my place on the arch:

"Gaius, you will be witness to this bargain." I really didn't want to be dragged into it; as a contract, no court would uphold it. I said carefully:

"I have witnessed your agreement. You have pledged to be true to one another. If either of you prove false, I will be the judge." But this was not enough for Cressida. Having given in, she threw all her chips on the table and said:

"Let all constant men be Troiluses and all false women Cressidas." As usual, the men were getting the best deal. I sniffed and said:

"To that, I will only agree with a codicil: Let all constant women be Cressidas if she proves true and all false men Troiluses if he does. And if you do, Troilus, she'll sue you for breach of promise. I'll see to that." But the lovers were now beyond any sort of common sense. With their arms around each other, they passed into the house. I felt a tingle along my spine. This was not going to end well. In fact, it had all the ingredients of a perfect disaster. The goldfish and I exchange looks and I jumped off the archway.

It was a pensive Gaius Marius who made his way to the bolthole at Antenorides and from there to his bed under the tree by the beach. I was uneasy. And finding Hermes and Eros waiting for me didn't improve my mood.

"Well," asked Hermes, "how did it go?" I started to hate myself for being a part to it all. I should have left it to Pandarus.

"Oh, it was a love feast," I answered, "which makes me wonder why I feel so lousy." Eros sniggered.

"Elementary, my dear Gaius. All those lies do something to your insides. I've felt it myself. And it hurts most when, at that moment in time, both sides couldn't be more sincere. Which one is going to crack first?" For a minute, I felt quite bewildered.

"Oh, sorry, you almost lost me. Troilus, of course."

"You think so?" Hermes raised his eyebrows.

"But naturally, my dear friend. Troilus has most to lose. Which means there will be more opportunities, reasons and excuses available to him. Cressida, poor thing, has only her life."

"You're so right," Eros nodded sagely. "You've only missed that Troilus is one of the youngest in a huge family so he will most certainly be everyone's darling boy. He will have been indulged and cosseted and spoilt beyond reason. So, when push comes to shove or, for that matter, when the going gets tough and the tough need to get going, don't count on seeing Troilus in the front rank." Hermes sighed:

"You're right. That sort of upbringing doesn't give you a spine." The three of us sat there gloomily. Luckily, Eros had brought a hip flask and we each took a strengthening nip.

2.7 THAT ONE MEETS HECTOR

After they had gone, I decided I needed a nightcap so off I went to *The Greek Olive Tree*. The Greek High Command was all there, each man intent on his drink and peace reigned. The entry of a staff officer made them all sit up. The man went up to Agamemnon.

"Visitor from Troy," he announced. The Greeks looked at each other. Social calls from one camp to the other were not common occurrences. The staff officer gave way to Æneas, who'd had a bath and changed since Hermes and I saw him coming off the field, and was now all done up in golden greaves and armour, bronze helmet, red cloak with matching tassels. He bowed in the general direction of the Greeks and said:

"I am Æneas, a prince and herald of Troy. I come in peace with a message to the High Greek Command." Agamemnon said:

"My good Æneas, the Greek High Command receives you and in peace awaits the message you bring. Eurybates, a refreshment for our guest." Æneas received the mug gratefully and took a refreshing sip. Placing his mug on a nearby table and taking a roll of parchment from under his cloak, he said:

"Hector, prince of Troy, sends this message," unrolling the parchment. Now, I could tell you exactly what Hector wrote but Homerys just did it so much better so I will use his version. Hector, I am afraid, would never write the great Trojan novel.

"Hear ... ye well-armed, Greeks, what my strong mind ...
commands me speak; the Gods hath not used their
promised favour for our truce, but studying both our ills,
will never cease till ye ruin Troy, or we consume your
mighty sea-borne fleet.
...amongst you all, whose breast includes the most
impulsive mind,
Let him stand forth as combatant, by all the rest
designed to witness our strife:
if he with home-thrust iron can reach the exposure of my
life,
spoiling my arms, let him at will convey them to his tent,
but let my body be returned, that Troy's... descent
may waste it in the funeral pile; if I can slaughter him,
I'll spoil his conquered limb
and bear his arms to Ilion, where ...
I'll hang them, as my trophies due; his body I'll resign

to be disposed by his friends in flamy funerals
and honoured with erected tomb, where Hellespont falls
into the Ægean, and doth reach even to your naval road,
that when our beings in the earth shall hide their period,
survivors sailing the black sea may thus his name renew:
'this is his monument, whose blood long since did fates
imbrue
whom passing far in fortitude, illustrious Hector slew';
this shall posterity report, and my fame never die."

Æneas rolled up the scroll. There was a stunned silence and for a moment no one spoke. Then Menelaus got up, red faced and took a few menacing steps towards Æneas.

"Is this some kind of a joke?" he shouted. "We've just been through all that – with your champion, Paris." Æneas answered stoically:

"Paris is not our champion. Hector is our champion."

"Maybe so," sneered Menelaus, "but Paris is for sure your fastest runner. The utter gall of this lot. To all effect and purposes, I," and he banged on his chest, "won the single combat by default as my opponent abandoned the field." Agamemnon got up, put an arm around his brother and got him back to his seat. Then he turned to Æneas:

"We accept your offer, Herald; your message shall be spread throughout our camp calling for a champion to come forward. If no one takes up the challenge, I myself will meet Hector." Æneas bowed slightly:

"Great king, I will take your message back to Troy." Then Agamemnon put an arm around Æneas' shoulder, saying:

"We will lead you to our pavilions and the Greeks shall hear your message tent by tent. You will feast with us before you leave and behold the welcome of a noble foe." Æneas did not look pleased but sighed and accepted his fate with as good a grace as possible. They all trooped off, and not before I was ready for it. I felt quite exhausted. Homerys's world was truly a complicated one. Eurybates' brought me another drink and tuna snaquettes.

Then I noticed that Nestor and Odysseus had stayed behind. Odysseus was rubbing his chin thoughtfully. He called for fresh drinks for himself and Nestor.

"Stick it on the High Command's tab," he said, winking at Eurybates. Then he turned to Nestor: "So," he said slowly, "what is Hector's game? Does he want to erase his brother's foolishness and wipe away his shame? Does he know Akhilleus will not fight and that there is no other Greek to equal him? Hector wins. End of stalemate, keep the lady and her goods. The Greeks go home. End of story." He looked at Nestor. "Not a bad plan and I'm surprised Hector had the brains for it. Not bad at all. But still, I can't quite get a handle on it." Nestor said nothing but stared at Odysseus, all attention. "Now," continued Odysseus. "we return to the matter of Akhilleus; he is a pain but also by far our best warrior." Nestor nodded. "But if he is to be of any use to us, he needs to be under control and that means taking him down a peg or two."

"And how do you propose to do that?" good question, Nestor.

"You'll agree that this challenge from Hector is for Akhilleus and Akhilleus alone."

"True," Nestor nodded, "even Akhilleus can figure that out."

"So, Akhilleus will be ready with his answer, strutting around like a cock on a dung heap."

"Of course," said Nestor, "but will he forget his disagreement with Agamemnon and come out as our champion? Won't he just stay in his tent sulking?" Odysseus waved his hands about as if he were swatting flies.

"My friend, that little affair will all be forgotten when Akhilleus' pride comes into play. Nevertheless, a lot will ride on the outcome of this challenge, not so much as regards how this war will end but rather on our own standing and credibility, both with the Trojans and our own troops."

"I see," said Nestor thoughtfully, "and it's up to the High Command to decide who will be the Greek champion. We need to make it clear that our choice will not go to the best but the most deserving; someone who has shown loyalty and done his share for the war effort. At least," he added, "that is how it should sound."

"To put it all in a nutshell," Odysseus summed up. "Akhilleus must not meet Hector's challenge for two reasons." He rocked forwards and backwards on the back legs of his stool. "First because, if he wins, he'll become unbearably arrogant and he's already insolent enough; second, if he loses, we'll have no one to fall back on, having shot our best bolt. I think," he continued, "we must look at it this way: if we lose, we can always say: 'oh, if only Akhilleus had been here'." He took a deep swig from his mug. "So," he was now all business. "We'll have a lottery and make sure Ajax' name is drawn."

"But that's cheating," protested Nestor. Odysseus ignored this paltry detail and ploughed on.

"The High Command will express its pleasure at Ajax's selection. Akhilleus will be as sick as mud. Of course he thinks himself far superior to Ajax and so he is, but that's exactly the point. Win or lose, with Ajax in the field, it'll be a win-win situation for us." Nestor was impressed. "Akhilleus will hate Ajax for it. Wonderful idea. Let's go and tell Agamemnon."

Well pleased with themselves, they went off.

Eurybates' and I looked at each other bemused. Then Eurybates' started polishing his mugs with special vigour. Right you are, pal, you're better off keeping a low profile. Even a cat needs to watch out with this lot. After all, nine lives only go so far.

Just as I felt peace had been restored, Akhilleus stomped in followed by Patroklos taking a corner table, calling for wine and be quick about it. Eurybates was not thrilled, he wanted to close up shop and go to bed. In the time honoured tradition of waiters, he wiped the table in a marked manner, banged down two mugs and a jug of watered wine without a word and went back to the bar. Akhilleus stared at him, then said:

"Have I become poor all of a sudden?" Eurybates said nothing but continued with his polishing. Akhilleus sat up straight saying with all the arrogance he could muster. "Don't you realize that I am Akhilleus, the greatest warrior in Greece?" Eurybates raised his eyebrows:

"Really, sir? I heard you haven't taken to the field these many days!" That left Akhilleus nonplussed and he buried his noise in the mug trying, I suppose, to come up with a clever answer. A faint breeze touched my fur; I looked around and there was Hermes, leaning on the bar. I called out for watered wine from Eurybates who gave it to me, no questions asked, and for a few minutes Hermes drank in a pensive sort of way. Then he said.

"If a great man falls out of favour with fortune, other men will immediately shun him; in fact, he will be able see his fall reflected in their eyes. Men, like butterflies, open their wings to catch the warmth of the sun. Let the sun set and so will they." Sounded good. But butterflies. As if reading my thought, Hermes resumed. "It's a metaphor, Gaius. Tell me, how does a man achieve greatness?" It was my turn to be nonplussed. This question was perhaps a bit above my pay grade. But I gave it a try.

"Well, if a man is pushy and greedy and ruthless, I suppose he can achieve greatness." Hermes waggled his finger indicating a negative.

"No, Gaius. A man is only great if he is considered great either by his peers or his subjects. You cannot be great all by yourself." My head throbbed. I said:

"What about tyrants? What makes them great?" Hermes answered:

"Their fellow humans who are ready to carry out their orders and who think a bit of the greatness will rub off on them for doing so." By this time, Hermes' mug was empty and I nodded to Eurybates that more was needed. A new mug slid before me. I said to Eurybates in a low voice:

"Put it on Agamemnon's bill." Eurybates waggled his eyebrows in a conspiratorial kind of way. Hermes had a snort and continued:

"A man's honour," he said, "depends on factors beyond himself and over which he sometimes has little control, such as rank and friends in high places. Riches and high office are more often gained through connections and very seldom on merit. A man who falls from high rank may drag others down with him; therefore, that man's friends disappear at the first inkling of trouble." I mulled on this. Meritocracy was way in the future – even my future. I said:

"I see what you mean; there are many examples in history, Hitler and Stalin of course come to mind. Hitler dragged his cohorts – those that hadn't had time to off themselves or get away to Argentina – all the way to the Nuremberg trials. And Stalin's death – possible a murder – ended with his pals in the Gulag or in front of a firing squad." Hermes nodded:

"One could of course go on and on. The formula is set in stone and never varies. Humans are such predictable creatures." I thought for a moment then said slowly:

"What you are telling me is: if a man wants to measure his own greatness, he must look into others' eyes." Hermes nodded but before he could answer, our erudite conversation was interrupted by Akhilleus who bellowed:

"What do you mean, Eurybates, 'a man must see his greatness in others' eyes'!" Eurybates raised his eyebrows.

"Wasn't me," he answered concentrating on his mugs. Akhilleus stormed:

"Since there are only the three of us here and it sure as hell wasn't Patroklos, it can only have been you!" Eurybates nodded his head towards my corner.

"Cat," he said. Akhilleus laughed scornfully.

"Cat! Tell me another!" Then he looked at me, I waved a paw.

"One can't have an argument with a cat!" Akhilleus exclaimed. "You're putting me on." Hermes sighed:

"What a jerk-o! I'll leave you to it, mate." And disappeared. But now Patroklos had become so confused he couldn't tell one thing from another. His excited and high-pitched voice wailed:

"Is that what you think of me?" he said, almost chocking on his own words, "that I would ever doubt your greatness or that I am the type who abandons a friend in need? I will never forsake you, no, no matter what happens to you. Never! Never!" Oh, dear. Eurybates and I exchanged looks. I thought we were in for another lover's lament. But Akhilleus cut the evil off at the root by saying, in irritation:

"Of course I wasn't referring to you, Patroklos. You've gotta stop taking everything personal." So Akhilleus had been meandering along the same points as Hermes and his thoughts had dovetailed with my last remark. Well, I saw Akhilleus' point. Having gone to his tent to sulk, he had turned himself into a sort of pariah with little standing with the Greek High Command or the war. However, as in most cases, reality checks are unpleasant and best forgotten. So, having said it was, Akhilleus decided it was not. "But that's not my case!" he cried, banging his mug on the table. "I am still Akhilleus and I have no equal. I will die Akhilleus and my name will ring down the ages." Yes, I thought. If you are a good boy and fawn on Homerys. Without Homerys, you are just so much dead meat. Hermes may have vanished, but my nose told me his place had been taken by another old friend. Akhilleus noticed it too and shouted:

"Thersites, what are you hiding for? Or better, how do you think you can hide at all? I can smell you a mile away. Be a man and show yourself!" Thersites crawled forward in a fawning sort of way – reminding me of Hermes' description of tyrants and fawners:

"Are you going to buy me a drink?" He whined. That was the cost of Thersites' fidelity. A free drink. Akhilleus waved his hand around.

"And why not? I am sure you don't deserve it." And laughed heartily while Patroklos sniggered. Thersites snatched the mug from Eurybates. I watched through slits in my eyes. Nothing good was going to come of this. Thersites said in a servile tone:

"My dear Akhilleus, may I have the presumption of telling you that skulking in one's tent has its drawbacks? You may well piss off Agamemnon but you also don't know what's going on." Akhilleus frowned.

"What have I missed that would do me any good to know?"

"Well," continued Thersites, "do you know about the snake and the birds and Calchas' predictions?" Akhilleus looked displeased.

"I would not allow any of my Myrmidons to mingle with that rabble and become part of Odysseus' and Agamemnon's odious little schemes."

"Great Akhilleus," said Thersites snidely, "Calchas says the war will be over by Christmas. That's not too far in the future and it may well happen, although I hardly dare say it, you will be left out of the last act. What would then become of you should Troy fall while you were, shall we say, busy indoors?" Akhilleus looked miffed. If Troy fell, he, the great Akhilleus, wanted most of the glory – to say nothing of the loot. And you don't get either from inside your tent. "Further," continued Thersites, "Hector has sent a new challenge for a one-to-onecombat with a Greek champion that is supposed to end the war!" Akhilleus jumped out of his chair.

"What? Why wasn't I told? Who has been chosen?" Thersites smirked horribly, plainly enjoying himself.

"They've decided, since you are not available, to have a lottery!"

"A lottery!" sneered Akhilleus, "they want a lottery with the world's greatest warrior in their camp!" Thersites wrung his hands in mock anguish:

"But, great Akhilleus, you were so emphatic that you wouldn't fight for the Greeks anymore. And they have no one else of your calibre. Can I have another drink?" Akhilleus waved his hand as this was of no importance, which Eurybates took as a yes and Thersites got his top up.

"But you can't participate in their lottery," squeaked Patroklos, "you'd lose face if you were not chosen."

"To Hades with it," shouted Akhilleus, "what if someone else clobbers Hector? I'll look like a damn fool, a has been!"

"But, Akhilleus," panted Patroklos, "no one can beat Hector except you or perhaps... " diffidently", "Ajax." Akhilleus turned in fury at Patroklos.

"I," and he beat his breast, "I am the only one who can bring Hector down." His eyes became wild. "They should have come and begged me to defend the honour of Greece." He stopped, then continued thoughtfully: "Perhaps they are waiting for me at my tent this minute. Come on, Patroklos, don't dawdle." And he stormed out, Patroklos running after him. I looked at Thersites.

"You," I said, "are a piece of work." Thersites sniggered.

"Ain't I just? You might say I put the cat among the pigeons, so you might. Eurybates, this deserves one for the road – and put it on Akhilleus' tab."

"Right," said Eurybates, "one for the road. Then get lost. It's late and I need to get my beauty sleep. You can stay there if you like, Gaius." But I preferred my tree on the beach. As I was leaving, I heard Thersites say:

"Are you going to participate in the lottery, Eurybates?" I didn't hear Eurybates' answer but I could imagine what it would be.

3
SUNDAY

3.1 NO, MAKE A LOTTERY

Breakfast. I had mine under my favourite tree by the beach. I gauged the weather. If we were all lucky, there'd be a thunderstorm, which would put paid to this afternoon's insane antics. But the Gods were not with me. Another perfect day; even the woolly clouds were gone, leaving the sky a clear and matchless blue and the sun in charge, no contest. The odd seagull was winging and diving and riding the air currents. There were already some Greeks disporting themselves in the water; the perfect day for it.

I considered how I'd spend my time until the single combat event. Lounging about doing nothing seemed like a good idea and I was just settling down to do so when Homerys and his boy passed my tree. The boy looked excited.

"Aren't you going to the lottery drawing," he asked me. "Homerys and I are; I just can't wait to know who will fight Hector." I sighed. Such innocence is so touching and I hadn't the heart to tell the lad that the whole thing was rigged. "I bet," the kid continued, "it will be Akhilleus. Boy, that will be exciting. I've got his autograph." I raised my eyebrows. Did Akhilleus know how to write? Did Homerys's boy know how to read? Better not ask. Homerys waved his arms around.

"Come along, Gaius Marius," he said, looking for me the wrong way. "It will be an education for you." So I joined the party and we set off. Before I knew where I was, Hermes had joined our little band of brothers.

"So," I asked, "what are you looking forward to? Do you think Akhilleus will win the lottery?" Hermes half grinned.

"If he did, that would really be exciting. Would he come out of his tent? Would he forget his sulks? Or Brisies?" I snarled.

"Gotta be kidding. He's forgotten all about her long ago. He may still be mad at Agamemnon, though. Be interesting to see how he would get around that." Hermes looked at me knowingly, waggling his finger:

"But we know, don't we, that there is no chance of that."

"Hermes," I said severely, "you've been eavesdropping. Now that is natural for a cat but you, as a God, should have higher standards."

"Get off it, Gaius," scoffed Hermes. "What good would being a God be if you can't indulge yourself in a bit of wiretapping?" We were now at the Greek camp so our conversation had to end. We found Homerys a nice stone to sit on, the kid ran off and Hermes and I sat at Homerys's feet. All the Greek princes were gathered in a circle. Nestor stood up.

"My fellow Greeks, we are here to choose the champion who will take up Hector's challenge. Since we know that each one of you would gladly volunteer, it has been decided to draw lots so no one has a fair advantage." Was there an edge of sarcasm in Nestor's voice? The princes looked at each other but no one had anything to add. Hermes and I looked at each other. Hermes said:

"I wouldn't really call them cowards; they're just not in the mood."

"I know someone who is," I answered, as Akhilleus and Patroklos turned up. Akhilleus looked like thunder. It seemed an easy bet that no one had been around begging. The two sat down. But Nestor was not done.

"You have each been given a shard of pottery. Make your mark indicating your choice for champion and place it in the helmet the soldier over there is holding." Then he turned and said deferentially: "Akhilleus, I didn't know you would be joining us. You are most welcome. We need all the help we can get if we are to take down Hector." Agamemnon then deposited his shard of pottery, followed by Menelaus, Akhilleus, Diomedes, Ajax, Idomeneus and so on. I think Patroklos wanted to add his own mark but somehow he couldn't reach the soldier with the helmet. Nestor then took the helmet, mixed the shards around with his hands, shook the helmet, closed his eyes and picked out one of the shards and held it up. Homerys, of course, had to shove his oar in. With arms spread wide and face towards heaven, he cried:

Again Nestor spake: "Let lots be drawn by all; his hand
shall help the well-armed Greeks to whom the lot doth fall,
and to his wish shall he be helped, if he escape with life the
harmful danger breathing fit of his adventurous life."

Nestor looked discomfited as he hadn't said anything of the kind. Hermes snickered, commenting:

"Frightening, isn't it? Not knowing how you'll turn out in Homerys's book. Verily, as the man said, truth is in the eye of the beholder." Nestor decided to ignore Homerys's broadside and drew out a shard from the helmet. "Who's is this mark?" he cried, holding up the one he had selected. There was a short silence as everyone craned their necks to see. Then there was a loud shout:

"Mine, mine, it's mine," cried Ajax, jumping up and down and grinning all over his face. "It's mine! I'm the champion!" He danced about. Akhilleus stalked off, his face like a thundercloud, followed by Patroklos, while everyone else crowded around Ajax, slapping him on the back and saying what a good lad he was and how happy they were for him. Homerys rose again, lifted his arms again and chanted:

"Father Zeus that rulest from Ida, vouchsafe victory to
Ajax, and let him win great glory; but if you wish well to
Hector also and would protect him, grant to each equal
fame and prowess"

There was great cheering and clapping at this, after which the crowd started to disperse. I said glumly:

"I can't understand why everyone applauded old Homerys since he didn't say who would win." Hermes sneered,

"Don't try and be funny, Gaius. Do you really think anyone understood – or even listened?" There was much truth in this so I dropped the subject.

The Greek High Command was still hanging around and at that moment Calchas went up to Agamemnon. That surprised me since these two were not bosom pals. However, Calchas was there for a purpose as I discovered when he addressed himself to Agamemnon.

"My Lord Agamemnon," he said, bowing. "I abandoned Troy, my family and people to join the Greek side. I've been branded a traitor by my countrymen, exposed myself to all sorts of innuendos to live in a world that is not my own, where I am, for all your kindness, a stranger in a strange land. All this I have done in obedience of the will of the Gods and because I believe the Greek cause to be fair. For all these reasons, I now ask you to grant me my just reward for my services to you." Agamemnon looked at him magnanimously, putting an arm around Calchas' shoulder. He had it seems forgotten their former tiffs.

"And what will that be? State your terms, my invaluable Trojan friend." Calchas continued:

"You have a prisoner, Adrestus, a great warrior whom Troy can hardly afford to lose. I know you've often asked for my daughter Cressida in exchange for a Trojan prisoner but so far Troy has refused to let her go." Well, well, perhaps Calchas was not such a deadbeat dad after all. "So, I ask you to offer to exchange Adrestus for my daughter. This time, I do not think the Trojans will refuse. If you return my daughter to me, I will consider myself sufficiently rewarded for my services."

Agamemnon nodded affably. "Certainly, my good Calchas, this is no more than fair although we would be allowing Adrestus to fight again. What say the other Greek commanders?" There being no dissenting voices, Agamemnon went on: "Diomedes, go and get this sorted. Say we want..." He stopped and turned to Calchas. "Sorry, what was her name again? Oh, of course, Cressida, if they want Adrestus back."

"I'm on it," says Diomedes. I shivered. This did not bode well for the lovebirds. I said to Hermes:

"Now we will see what metal our Troilus is made of." Hermes nodded.

"So let's be off to Troy. We don't want to miss this prisoner exchange."

"Right," was my answer, "let's hightail it to Troy."

3.2 NO SOONER GOT BUT LOST

Hermes and I headed up the hill and passed into Troy. We went straight to *The Trojan Horse* as this was a good place to start our operations when, PARBLEU, there, at a corner table, were the lovebirds themselves, Troilus and Cressida, billing and cooing. They seemed to have it all figured out now. Cressida said languidly:

"The night was all too short." Right. But let's keep it clean, shall we? She continued: "That's the trouble with nights. Some drag on and on until you feel dawn will never come. But when you're with the one you love, time flies quicker than thought, and before you know where you are, it's morning – long before you're ready for it." They giggled and prodded each other as lovers have done for time immemorial and will do as long as humans infest the earth. Hey, kids, get a room. Then Pandarus arrived. What joy! The lovers didn't look thrilled. At first, Pandarus looked surprised at seeing the twosome, since he hadn't been privy to last night's activities. But of course he saw at once what was going on and asked Troilus, ignoring Cressida:

"Well, young Troilus, where's my niece Cressida?" Oh, he was a riot. Cressida giggled some more:

"Oh, you mocking uncle! Make yourself useful and go drown yourself in the fountain in Priam Square." Now there was a sentiment I could share. "You egged me on and now you make sport of me." Pandarus pretended to be hurt:

"Egged you on? It doesn't seem to me you needed any 'egging on'! Ha, ha, ha," he became hysterical at his own wit, an occupational hazard, it would seem, with both Trojans and Greeks. "Do I sense Troilus didn't get much beauty sleep last night? And why not, may one ask? And, my dear niece, did he keep you up, too?" He almost rolled about, holding his sides and laughing himself sick. Cressida smiled; she seemed to love the whole world, even uncle Pandarus, which showed it could be done. She gave Troilus another prod:

"What did I tell you? He truly is my wicked uncle." Oh, it was a love feast this meeting of the mutual admiration society, the birds twittered, the sun shone and all was joy. Pandarus took himself off, soon followed by the amorous couple.

Hermes and I were on our second cup of tea – Marianne having become used to bringing two cups – no questions asked – when we heard the tramp of feet in the street outside and, almost immediately, a whole cortège came in: the Trojans Æneas, Paris and Deiphobus, the Greek Diomedes followed by the Trojan Adrestus. Oh, oh. Things were moving. Suddenly, I felt a presence next to me and there was Eros. He sat down.

"So our Troilus' backbone is to be tested right off," was his comment; Hermes added:

"How about a little flutter? Gaius, what will you put on Troilus as a staunch defender of his true love?" I raised my eyebrows and looked at the two sideways:

"Are you kidding? Will you take ten to one that Troilus will collapse like a house of cards?" But neither of them took me up on this. Meanwhile, Æneas was making small talk:

"After all," he said somewhat obscurely, "we all know each other so well." Eros sneered:

"Of course they do, Gods give me patience. They've been neighbours for nine years."

"Besides which," added Hermes, "they're mostly related by blood. There's been a lot of intermarriage between Troy and the Greek City States." Diomedes, however, was not in the mood for all this CAMADERIE and answered sourly:

"Indeed we do and I hope we may soon become total strangers for even longer." Hermes, Eros and I looked at each other. Cousinly love was conspicuous for its absence. Paris drew himself up: "There's no need to be so bitter," he said huffily. "After all, this is official business." Diomedes replied:

"So, let's get on with it, shall we? I have Adrestus, you have Calchas' daughter, whatever her name is. The exchange was agreed at the highest level." Adrestus twiddled his thumbs and tried not to look like the fool he was for falling into the Greeks' hands. He said in a jovial tone addressing Paris and Æneas:

"Hi, guys. Sorry to put you to all this trouble. I got jumped by three Greeks, or it might have been five. Fair cop, you know." He got himself a cup of coffee from Marianne. Æneas nodded:

"It's a fair trade. I'll just pop along to Calchas' house and get the lady." And off he went. As they waited for him to return, Paris said to Diomedes, showing just what a lousy diplomat he was.

"Well, Diomedes, tell me: who in your opinion deserves Helen: me or Menelaus?"

"Omigosh," remarked Eros, "Not the most tactful of fellows, our Paris." Diomedes gave Paris a long look. I wonder what Diomedes would have thought had he seen Helen and Paris at tea yesterday. He finally answered, putting his finger to his chin:

"Well, let's see: between Menelaus, her husband, who has come to claim her, although she's now definitely damaged goods, at a price to be paid by all the Greek City States; or you, Paris, who dishonoured her and is now trying to hang on to her whatever the cost to your kin and countrymen? Not much to choose between you." Paris looked affronted and offended. What had he expected?

"You are bitter about your countrywoman," he said sternly. Diomedes shrugged:

"She has been a bitter draught to her country. For every drop of blood in her whorish veins, a Greek's life has been lost; for every ounce of flesh on her body, a Trojan has died. Since she learned to speak, she has not uttered as many words as the number of Greeks and Trojans who have given their lives for her." Paris tried to talk him down.

"My friend, you degrade what you wish to buy. We, on the other hand, defend what we are not prepared to sell. That is the path we have chosen, the path of honour." Diomedes didn't bother answering but turned away and stared into space.

"I think," said Hermes, "I've had just about enough of this place. And I came here for a rest, can you imagine? A plague on both their houses, I say."

"Hear, hear!" Eros and I both agreed. Then I had a thought:

"Eros," I said, "instead of dealing in love and lovemaking how about if you used your powers to end wars? I mean, the principle is the same, isn't it? Say you pierce the hearts of Paris and Menelaus or Priam and Agamemnon or Akhilleus and Hector? Then they would love each other like brothers and the war would be over."

"Oh, yeah?" asked Eros in a nasty voice I didn't quite like, "and what about Helen?" That was a difficulty I hadn't quite figured out yet.

"Perhaps they could share," I said but I knew it was weak. Eros snorted then became pensive. "On the other hand," he said, "if the menfolk came to love each other, Helen might become irrelevant." That was something to chew on. Hermes changed the subject:

"Tell me, Gaius, what if this whole situation occurred in your day? What would happen?" I thought for a bit. Offhand, I couldn't remember a war over a woman but then the causes of wars are complex and not always as straightforward as the powers-that-be would like the masses to think. I said slowly:

"Well, the two sides would first throw out each other's embassy staff; then they'd negotiate, get nowhere, call a meeting of the United Nations who would set up a committee that would take two years to issue a White Paper; during this time, each of the antagonists would try to bribe, threaten or cajole other UN members to join their side, there'd be talk of sanctions, usually economic ones; there would then be a vote in the UN General Assembly on a resolution so bland as to make it meaningless and then there would be war. I suppose!"

"Plus ça change," said Hermes, "plus c'est la meme chose."

Æneas came back, looking discomfited.

"She wasn't there, you know," he said, perplexed. Why he should expect Cressida to spend twenty-four hours of every day inside her house I could not fathom. After all, there'd be household shopping to do and elevenses with her friends in Priam Square. Then Pandarus turned up, huffing and puffing.

"What's all this about? I hear you've been to my brother's house. What is it you want?" Then he saw Æneas and Paris and became his usual subservient self: "Prince Paris – and Æneas. I hardly recognized you, it's so early and I take a bit of time getting going in the morning. Age tells, you know." He tittered but no one else did. Paris said:

"We're looking for your niece, Pandarus. We're doing a prisoner exchange – Cressida for Adrestus." Adrestus waggled a finger at Pandarus:

"Pandarus, my old friend. How's the boy?" He continued cheerful as well he might who'd been in danger of remaining interred with the Greeks for the duration. Pandarus' eyes goggled. This he had not foreseen and, for the first time, he seemed lost for words. And then Troilus came rushing in.

"What's going on?" he asked breathlessly. "I hear you've been to Calchas' house looking for Cressida." Paris raised his eyebrows:

"And why should you care, little brother?" Æneas took over in his usual smooth way:

"My dear Troilus, surely you must have heard that there's going to be an exchange of prisoners – Adrestus for Cressida, Calchas' daughter. It has all been agreed between your father and Agamemnon. The Greek Diomedes has brought Adrestus and is now waiting to take Cressida back to the Greek camp." Troilus says in a low voice:

"So it's a done deal." He asked Paris:

"And why wasn't I told?" Paris almost sneered:

"Little brother," which must have irritated the hell out of Troilus, "you haven't seemed much interested of late in the management of the war. And, frankly, negotiations for prisoner exchange is a mite above your pay grade." Troilus sizzled but kept quiet. Pandarus had moved into a corner where he was muttering to himself:

"I can't believe it. No sooner got but lost. The devil take Adrestus, the plague take Adrestus. Why didn't the Greeks break his neck when they had the chance?" I felt quite sorry for him – Cressida was the only card he held – but then, you gotta be able to take the rough with the smooth. Pandarus went on: "I wish there was a hole in the ground I could crawl in to."

And then Cressida arrived. Her first glance was to Troilus and her face lit up. But then she became aware of all the others and it clouded over. Something was obviously wrong. Æneas turned to her courteously.

"My dear Cressida, how fortunate you should come in. We have wonderful news for you. You are to be reunited with your father. Diomedes has come to take you back to the Greek camp." Cressida's face was a study of horror mingled with so many other emotions I couldn't start to enumerate them.

"My father," she whispered, "the Greek camp." Her eyes went from one man to the other and then she sat down, curled herself up, her hands holding her head and a keening wail came from her – and she went on and on, a terrible sound like the agony of a dozen souls in Hades. None of the men said or did anything. No man ever knows what to do with a hysterical woman. They just find her an embarrassment and wish she'd stop. At last Cressida found her voice:

"O, uncle Pandarus, O you immortal gods, I will not go!" Pandarus answered weakly, his eyes moist too:

"You have no choice, my dear. You must leave Troy and return to your father." Cressida sobbed hysterically:

"No, no! My father! I have no father, no kin but Troilus!" and threw herself on the floor. "Oh, you Gods, may Cressida's name be the very essence of falsehood if she leaves Troilus. Time, force and death, do to me what you want, I will be supported by my love, the very centre of my existence!" She raised herself to her knees, the very image of despair. "Tear out my bright hair, scratch my cheeks, crack my voice and break my heart! I will not leave Troy." Oh, dear. This was terrible. I looked at Hermes and Eros.

"You two are supposed to be gods of a sort! Can't you do anything?"

"I could shoot my arrows at Cressida and Diomedes," answered Eros slowly. I shook my head in anger.

"Of all the lousy plans, that's gotta be the worst I've heard so far." Æneas was now catching on that there were waves within waves.

"Troilus," he said and turned towards that gentleman, "what have you got to do with all this?" Troilus was standing quite close to me, petrified, and I sank my claws into his shoulder, whispering in his ear:

"This is your hour, Troilus, just don't stand there like a Grecian urn. Come on, man! Do something! Say something! Anything!" Troilus was so far gone he didn't even feel my claws or see the blood seeping through his sleeve. He remained stock-still and it was Pandarus who tried to raise the sobbing Cressida, saying:

"Calm down, now, control yourself, there's a good girl." A lousy line, but then men will be men. Cressida cried out, allthe world's despair in her voice:

"Why should I be calm? How can I control myself? This grief is perfect and full and I taste it as strongly as I feel it. If I could dampen my love or wring forth a weaker and colder version of it, then I might control myself. But I can't, I can't. Oh, how am I to bear this?" She finally got up and flung herself into Troilus' arms. "Oh, Troilus, Troilus." And then Pandarus started crying and tried to embrace them both.

"Oh, my lambs!" At last Troilus found his voice. He embraced her, and with his hand put her head on his shoulder:

"Cressida, I love you so much and with a love so pure that the blessed Gods have become envious of my devotion and are taking you from me." Right, Troilus, it's all about you, isn't it? Find someone else to blame. Why wasn't I surprised? What a cretin. Cressida seemed to get the general idea, too. She moved away from him and said in a very small voice.

"Then it's true that I must leave Troy!" Troilus nodded his head. He got some more claw treatment. I hissed:

"Remember your oath in Priam Square, Troilus. It wasn't 24-hours ago and already you've broken it. I'm ashamed of you." Troilus said through his teeth:

"Shut up, can't you? What would you have me do?" My reply:

"You were going to burn Troy to the ground for Helen. So burn Troy to the ground for Cressida." Troilus whispered:

"Don't be ridiculous! It's not the same thing at all!" I was now getting very angry and an angry cat is a dangerous thing. I hissed:

"Is it not? Then I must be very dense for it seems the same thing to me." Eros said:

"Don't waste your breath, Gaius. This guy is just a lilly livered poltroon. And you can't make a silk purse out of a sow's ear." Æneas interrupted all this undercover chat:

"Well, Troilus, your brother and I are waiting for an explanation." Troilus said sheepishly:

"I love Cressida with all my heart!" Æneas raised his eyebrows. "And?"

"Cressida loves me." Now Paris intervened:

"Well, I am sure that's all very well but it has nothing to do with the matter in hand, does it? Cressida has been exchanged for Adrestus so Cressida goes to the Greeks." I stretched out my paw as far as I could but it was impossible to reach Paris' jugular. What a hypocrite! A small voice – Cressida's – said:

"And leave Troilus?" Troilus nodded.

"Leave Troy and Troilus. Such is your fate, my love. I am sorry!" Cressida sat down again. She had stopped crying and was now beyond tears.

"I can't believe it." Troilus suddenly found his tongue. He held her at arm's length and said, sorrowfully:

"My dear, you must believe it. Fortune has abandoned us. We must now take our leave of each other with such words as we can find; embrace as we can while frozen with grief; repeat our vows if our strangled voices allow it. We two, bought with hundreds of sighs and promises, must be sold for so much less amidst abundant tears and few kisses." Yeah, Troilus, words, words are cheap and, to paraphrase Pandarus, don't accumulate debt. Pandarus had returned to his corner, wringing his hands in anguish and continuing his lamentations. Cressida then stepped back from Troilus and said in a voice devoid of emotion:

"So, I must go to the Greek camp." Troilus answered:

"I don't see any other way."

"An unhappy Cressida among all those merry Greeks," she continued. Well, I didn't quite follow that. If there were merry Greeks, I hadn't met many, except for Thersites in his unique way. Cressida continued: "When shall we see each other again?" Troilus' answered, trying to reach out for her but she avoided his touch:

"Hear me, love, be true to me, not that I doubt you, not at all, but be true and I will see you again. I will bribe the Greek guards." Well, that shouldn't be hard. "And, if possible, come to you every night." Cressida seemed truly distressed:

"Why do you keep repeating 'be true'? Do you doubt me?" Troilus continued, damn him:

"I'm afraid, Cressida, of the influence the Greeks may on you; they're handsome, easy of manner, good at flattery and they'll be round you all the time. You will love one of them and forget me." What a brute the guy was. Simply being forgotten was too good for him.

Cressida responded horrified:

"You don't love me," she cried. Of course he didn't. Take my advice, lady, and move on. Men just aren't worth the bother, be they Trojans or Greeks. Troilus ploughed on:

"But, dearest, I don't doubt you at all, and if I do, let me die a villain." Pal, no one disputes your right to that title. "But with so many temptations around you, who knows what may happen."

"So that's what you think of me," Cressida answered sadly, her head bowed.

"Of course not. But we humans are mere reeds who bend as the wind blows, frail beings not beyond temptation." Before Cressida could answer, Æneas broke in:

"Sorry, my love birds, but we need to finish this." Troilus said to Cressida:

"Come, give me a kiss and let us part." This was cold comfort for Cressida. She asked:

"Will you be true?" Reasonable question. Troilus would have laughed but this wasn't the moment.

"Alas," he cried, "that is my vice, my fault. I can't be anything but true. My motto is 'plain and true'. That's who I am." Well, well, methinks the gentleman doeth protest too much. Or maybe she'd already served her turn and it was Troilus who was moving on. Horrid thought, even for a cat. Having nothing further to say to Cressida, Troilus turned to Diomedes who had followed all this leaning against the door jamb. "Friend Diomedes, here then is the lady you want. May I ask you, as a gentleman, to treat her with the respect she deserves? If you do and are ever at the mercy of my sword, just say 'Cressida' and your life will be as safe as Priam in his palace." Diomedes ignored Troilus and turned to Cressida:

"Lady, I am entirely at your service. If you are ready, let us go." He held out his arm to her. Troilus of course was offended; let someone pick up what he has thrown away and there would be hell to pay. He spat angrily at Diomedes:

"Greek, is this the way you answer me? Let me tell you, she is so far above you that you would be unworthy of calling yourself her servant." Yeah, Troilus, make friends and influence people. "I demand that you treat her with respect; if not, I swear by Pluto I will cut your throat even if the great Akhilleus himself were to protect you." Troilus still didn't know what was going on in the Greek camp. Much good he would be for the coming battles. Diomedes now held up his hands in a gesture of peace.

"Trojan, don't take that tone with me. As a member of and messenger from the Greek High Command, I have the privilege to speak freely. When I am back with the Greek army, I can assure you

Cressida will be treated as a lady and honoured as Calchas' daughter, to whom all Greeks stand in debt." Bitter indeed in Trojan ears. "Don't tell us what we can or cannot, should or should not, do. You do not command the Greeks." Troilus became incensed.

"Diomedes, you will live to regret your words." Diomedes shrugged. After this scene, I was afraid he would take Cressida at Troilus' valuation – less than Helen but perhaps a bit above poor Brisies. Then Cressida took Diomedes offered arm while Pandarus took her other arm under his. Paris called after them:

"Pandarus! You are not to leave Troy! Adrestus, go with them and make sure Pandarus goes no further than the gate."

"For Crissake, Paris," Æneas said angrily, "what hold do you think we have over Calchas by keeping Pandarus?" Paris turned his back on Æneas. Sort of *I am a Prince and you are not.* The more I saw of Paris, the more of an idiot he became. There had to be another explanation for Helen's infatuation with this moron.

Troilus called us back to the present by kicking a few table legs. So macho. Paris sneered:

"So, young Troilus, you have been pricked by Eros' arrow? But not too deeply, I gather." With one furious look at Paris, Troilus turned and walked out. Eros got up, fire in his eyes, but Hermes held him back.

"Eros, what do you think you're doing?"

"I will not let my name be taken in vain," he said through gritted teeth, "I am, so to speak, a demi-God."

"Come on," retorted Hermes, "we'll sort this guy out later." Eros sat down again, snarling:

"Oh, I'll get him, see if I don't." Hermes held out his hand:

"Get out the hip flask." Eros replied sadly:

"It's empty. How many crises do you think one can get through with just one hip flask?" Rats!

And so, the heavy cross beams of Antenorides gate were raised, the great bolts shot back, the ancient double gates creaked open and Cressida left Troy.

3.3 BEFORE THE MATCH

We were all in bad tempers so we split up to sulk, each in his own fashion. I had decided to give the combat between Ajax and Hector a miss but, of course, when the time came, I couldn't keep away. There was little enough to do in Troy at the best of times. I wandered towards the Greek camp. On the way, I had to pass Calchas' tent, placed slightly away from the main encampment. Wise of Calchas; he had less noise, less smell and got some peace and quiet. I saw Calchas and Cressida sitting close together on a bench, Cressida's face still swollen from all those tears although they had now dried up to the occasional hiccough. Calchas had his arms around her shoulder. I decided to eavesdrop, succumbing to the cat's ever-present desire to snoop.

"Oh, father," wailed Cressida, "won't you, won't you please let me go back to Troy to be with him?" Calchas stroked her softly.

"My dear child," he said gently, "if he let you go, I am not too sure he will welcome you back."

"But he would, he would," she cried sitting up and gripping his hand, "it was the others, the others who forced me to leave." She lowered her eyes to her hands in her lap and played with the fringe of her shawl. Then she looked up hopefully: "Perhaps he will send for me." Calchas shook his head sadly.

"Even if he did, I would not allow you to go back." Cressida grabbed hold of his shoulders and looked into his eyes.

"But why not? If my whole happiness depends on my being with him? To stay with him in Troy?"

"My dear, Troy is finished." Her hands flew to her mouth.

"What? They will lose the war? Have the Gods told you that?" she cried. Calchas' shook his head:

"I don't need the Gods to tell me what is obvious to my own eyes. A seer is nothing very special; his talent is to look at the present and from it foretell the future. I do not know whether Greeks or Trojans will win; even if Trojans do..." He swept him arm around. "Look about you, Cressida. What do you see?"

"Why," she cried in surprise, "what should I see? I see the camp of the Greek army."

"Before the Greeks arrived, this was a fertile plain. It was scattered with small holdings, people who raised crops and tended their animals. And where are they now?" Cressida looked bewildered:

"The Greeks drove them away."

"True, and destroyed the fields and made a wasteland around Troy. Do you think, once the Greeks are gone, the land will become fertile again or that the peasants will return?" Cressida answered in a small voice

"Return to what? Mud and stones?" Calchas nodded and patted her hand.

"The city depended on its herders and farmers".

"But," said Cressida, "the city is not yet starving."

"Because, my dear, the kingdoms inland have supplied Troy – not out of charity or friendship but because while Troy stands they themselves are safe from the Greek army. And, my child, what of the city itself? How many houses are now empty, how many young men have died?"

"But if the Trojan are victorious ..."

"Even so, there is a decay within that has nothing to do with the Greeks. Priam is an old man; he is way past his prime and should have turned power over to the younger generation long ago. And yet, had he done so, Hector would be king. And Hector, although a formidable warrior and a good and merciful man, would be a weak ruler. He has not the stomach to wield power." Cressida shivered:

"Decay, father, that is a strong word." He nodded:

"Yet only decay or decadence explains how Paris was allowed – no, encouraged – to sail for Sparta, abduct Helen and welcomed with wild enthusiasm when he returned. Troy was doomed, Cressida, from the moment Helen set foot in Troy." I didn't think I wanted to hear any more. It was all too depressing, especially because Calchas was probably right.

It was a thoughtful Gaius Marius who finally arrived at the site chosen for the combat. For a moment, I felt quite confused. It looked like a village fête. There were refreshment tents at either end, one for the Greeks, one for the Trojans, their respective standards floating in the breeze. Little tables were set up outside each tent. Makeshift benches had been set up on either side to accommodate spectators.

These were, except for the front row, filled to capacity, the front row I believed reserved for the higher ups. I decided to go to the Greek refreshment tent. If nothing else, I was sure not to run into Troilus there. *The Greek Olive Tree* had closed for the afternoon and Eurybates and his team were flitting about with drinkables and edibles. A lady I took to be Eurybates' wife was dishing out tea, cucumber sandwiches and currant cake. Eurybates kindly brought me some water and snacks outside the tent so I could sit in the sun.

The flower of Greek chivalry was gathered at the outside tables, gorging themselves: Agamemnon, Menelaus, Odysseus, Nestor, Diomedes and Idomeneus. Akhilleus and Patroklos were at a separate table, perhaps to emphasize Akhilleus' superiority. The lesser lights kept to the refreshment tent, as close to the bar as possible.

Then Menelaus pointed down the field and said:

"Look, there's Calchas. And the girl must be his daughter." Agamemnon turned to Diomedes:

"So, got the girl, did you?" Diomedes nodded:

"Yep." He fidgeted with his hands. 'There was a bit of a dust-up," he confessed. "In fact, I found the whole procedure quite embarrassing." The others turned to him.

"Well," asked Nestor, "so what happened?" Diomedes scratched his ear.

"Seems," he said, "that Cressida was having a love affair with Troilus, you know..." Odysseus interrupted:

"One of Priam's brood." Diomedes nodded.

"The girl made a terrible fuss. She didn't want to come with me, wept and had hysterics. It was quite embarrassing." Agamemnon:

"Why didn't you just leave her there? We could have taken gold for Adrestus."

"That's the point," explained Diomedes, "none of the Trojans suggested that. Nobody tried to negotiate or find another solution so the girl could stay. Not even the boyfriend. So what could I do? I couldn't very well sort out their problems for them. So I just took the girl as I was told to. She had to be half carried; me on one side and her uncle Pandarus on the other. Oh, and they wouldn't let old Pandarus go."

"Thank Gods for that," breathed Odysseus, "we have enough trouble as it is without that old codger." Then he added: "But don't forget, it was not really our call whether the girl came or stayed. It was Calchas'." The rest nodded. That closed the subject. I was flabbergasted. It seemed the Greeks had more heart than the Trojans – as for Troilus, seeing how easily he could have negotiated Cressida's staying, his behaviour was contemptible. And Paris must feel that the only love affair allowed in Troy was his. But I wouldn't bet a jar of catfood of his making it to his 10th wedding anniversary. I suddenly caught Odysseus' eye. He turned away. But not before I had seen a pensive look in it.

At that moment, Calchas and Cressida came up. Cressida had washed her face, her hair organized and looked quite pretty and stylish in her blue dress and colourful shawl. Calchas stopped in front Agamemnon:

"Great king, let me introduce my daughter Cressida, who has been returned to me through your good offices." Agamemnon beamed. He always was one for the ladies. It would literally be the death of him.

"Lady," he said with a courtly bow, "you are welcome to the Greek camp." Cressida gave a short curtsey and answered, her eyes modestly downcast:

"Thank you, Sir, and thank you for reuniting me with my father."

"Let me introduce you to the other kings of Greece," he swept him arm around grandly. "Diomedes you already know." Diomedes and Cressida bowed to each other. General introductions followed, to all of which Cressida responded prettily. I could see she would be a great favourite. After all, the Greeks hadn't seen a decent looking woman for a long time. Diomedes came up to Calchas and Cressida.

"Lady," he said, "let me take you into the refreshment tent." Cressida nodded with a small smile and the two went off. Calchas turned back to Agamemnon; Nestor said approvingly:

"A lady of style and sense," and everyone agreed, except for Odysseus who said nothing; he seemed to be steeped in thought. I looked at him through slit eyes. This was the boy to watch and not to trust. He was up to no good.

"My Lord, one thing more I have to ask of you."

"Speak," answered Agamemnon grandly. Calchas continued:

"I ask for passage for myself and my daughter on the next vessel sailing for Greece." Agamemnon looked a bit discomfited; makes you think, if your best fortune-teller suddenly wants to leave the scene of the action. Agamemnon cleared his throat. Calchas must have divined his thoughts because he continued: "Great King, my work here is done. The end of the war is near and the fate of all of you sealed. Therefore, you no longer have need of my services." Calchas threw a quick glance at Odysseus. I interpreted that the outcome of this particular war rested with him. Agamemnon cleared his throat again:

"Of course, Calchas, your wish is granted!" Keeping a seer around who wanted to leave might lead to dangerous consequences. Calchas bowed.

Then Ajax arrived, suited and booted, wearing his best armour, greaves, the latest word in helmets, sword, war axe, spear and shield bright and gleaming like the sun, to the wild delight of the Greek spectators. Ajax waved at the crowd and the cheers grew louder. He was primed, able, ready and willing to go; in fact, it seemed he could hardly wait. Agamemnon came up and gave him a slap on the shoulder in a bonhomie sort of fashion.

"Looks like you're all set, my friend, and in fine fettle. Courage high, eh? Good. So, have your herald blow his trumpet to call your adversary to the field." Ajax turned to the trumpeter, a little guy with a squint, and handed him some silver coins, ordering grandly:

"Ho, trumpeter, crack your lungs and split your windpipe, blow until your cheeks are about to burst, fill your chest and let your eyes spout blood. You are Ajax' voice." Well, it seemed an awful lot to ask for a few silver coins. The trumpeter thought so too. He blew on his trumpet in the usual manner. All listened. Total silence. After a few minutes, Odysseus commented, raising his eyebrows:

"No answer." Akhilleus looked at his nails and said:

"It's early days yet," somehow indicating that Hector was not about to jump at the chance of meeting Ajax and letting Ajax wait was not the same as if it was Akhilleus waiting. Ajax swung his sword about:

"Perhaps," he said, "Hector's had second thoughts about facing ME in single combat!" I could see the capital letters. Akhilleus laughed out loud:

"You wish!" he sneered. "Rather, Hector has decided not to waste his time fighting a third rater." Ajax eyes bulged and he raised his sword in preparation to striking Akhilleus. But Odysseus jumped between them.

"O.K., you guys, cut it out. Akhilleus, why don't you just go back to your tent and sulk. I really don't know why you are here at all."

"I'm here," raged Akhilleus, "because I'M the Greek champion, not that mongrel upstart." More capital letters. Ajax fumed:

"What do you mean by that? Never mind, I'll just skewer you and have done with it."

"Are we Greeks never going to stop fighting each other and start fighting the Trojans?" shouted Odysseus and stamped his foot. "This is getting to be a habit and it's not doing us any good. Agamemnon, you're the leader of this expedition. Do something!" Agamemnon cleared his throat.

"Odysseus is right, boys, this is not the time or place." Then he brightened. "Tell you what, Akhilleus, you can have Brisies back – how about that?" and he gazed benignly at Akhilleus, who turned his back and said in an absent way:

"Brisies, who the hell is that?" The other Greeks looked at each other, eyes wide, while Odysseus mouthed: I told you so.

At last, a trumpet call was heard from across the field. Hector had arrived. Everyone streamed out of the refreshment tents. I saw Hermes and Eros sitting on the front bench on the Greek side, having tea and wolfing down currant cake and sandwiches. I went and sat next to them.

"How," I asked, "did you get hold of the edibles without giving anyone heart failure?" Hermes scratched his head.

"To tell you the truth," he answered," the lady behind the tea urn did look a tad strange as we walked out." Why was that not surprising? As we waited to be entertained, I kept thinking of Odysseus. I told Hermes and Eros what had occurred.

"Weird," I said, "Odysseus only saw her for two minutes. What happened to make him so thoughtful?" Eros shrugged:

"Odysseus' mind is full of plots and stratagems; only his mother could love him." Hermes added:

"Mark my words, he's already thinking how he can use Cressida to make trouble and sow dissent." I looked at him in surprise:

"In Troy or among the Greeks?" Hermes shrugged:

"Doesn't matter," he answered, "it's all gist to Odysseus' mill." Seeing I was about to disagree, he added: "Don't argue! You'll see soon enough." And with that I had to be content and we turned out attention back to the field. Then Homerys and his boy arrived, and squeezed into the front row also, although I would have thought there was not enough room left for an infant fly. But, on the contrary, we all fitted in nicely.

3.4 HECTOR FOR TROY, AJAX FOR GREECE

Greeks and Trojans met in the centre of the field and Æneas called out:

"Hail, men of Greece." And, turning to Agamemnon: "How do the two sides wish to leave the field once there is a winner? All together or Trojans to one side and Greeks to the other?" Agamemnon answered, waiving his arm in a magnanimous sort of way:

"Doesn't matter to us. We will leave that to Hector." Æneas answered:

"Hector has no preferences." Akhilleus, who was standing just in front of us said, and I heard bitterness in his voice:

"That's Hector all over. Reasonable and full of modesty." Æneas turned towards Akhilleus and said pleasantly:

"Akhilleus. Always pleased to see you. Hector was much surprised when he heard he was to meet Ajax rather than yourself." Akhilleus answered sourly:

"The decision was not mine to make." Hermes said:

"It's very boring to sulk in your tent where no one can see you. Much more fun to sulk outside where you can bother everyone." Eros and I sniggered. Æneas continued, pleasantly enough.

"Akhilleus, valour and pride are intrinsic to Hector's nature. The first, almost infinite; the second, totally absent. Weigh him carefully; what you mistake for pride is courtesy." He turned to Ajax: "You, Ajax, share half of Hector's blood and that half of Hector has stayed in Troy. Half a heart, half a hand, half a Hector has come to seek you who are half Trojan, half Greek."

Agamemnon then said:

"Idomeneus. You will act as a second for Ajax as Æneas does for Hector. The two of you will agree on the base rules." He looked around at Greeks and Trojans alike. "Remember our compact: this single combat will determine the outcome of our quarrels. There can be only one winner, the survivor. These two men represent every Trojan and every Greek. That was our covenant." He looked around frowning. Right. I'd almost forgotten the purpose of this whole thing. We pays our money and we wants our blood. I couldn't show any enthusiasm for this. I don't like blood. There's such a horrible finality about it, it runs one way only - out. However, before getting down to it, the two sides stood at attention, facing each other, and sang their national anthems, the Trojans, as the challengers, first.

Gods love our land of Troy
Long live our noble Troy
Gods save our Troy
Make Troy victorious
Happy and glorious
Long may it provide refuge over us
Gods save out land.

Then the Greeks:

Oh, say can you see by the dawn's early light
What so proudly we hail'd at the twilight's last
gleaming?
Whose blue sky and bright stars through the perilous night,
O'er the Greek City States were gallantly streaming?
In the fire's red glare,
O'er the Acropolis there,
Gives proof that our flags are still flying out there.
O, say do those star spangled banners yet wave
O'er the land of the Greeks and the Greek City States!

Funny, there was something familiar about both tunes and lyrics but I couldn't place either.

This ceremony over, Hector and Ajax shook hands and prepared for combat, Æneas and Idomeneus standing slightly behind them,

Agamemnon off to one side, to umpire, I suppose. Now, I must confess I know absolutely nothing about human combat. Humans don't have natural weapons as cats do – claws and incisors. When cats fight, you hardly see them move, just fur flying. Humans jump about a lot, sometimes using their swords as axes, chopping, or as a knife, thrusting. To me, it seemed a lot of wasted energy. Eros told me there were also certain rules: how you may or may not kill (or where you may or may not maim) your opponent. The basic rule seemed to be: no biting; that would have taken me out of the running immediately.

Before the game got going, I heard Agamemnon whisper to Odysseus:

"Who is that angry looking Trojan over there?" Odysseus answered:

"That's one of Priam's brood, Troilus. You remember, Cressida's lover. Promising, they say, as a warrior; not given much to speech but rather to deeds; says what he means and means what he says. He is as manly as Hector but more dangerous, as Hector's anger is always tempered by mercy, while Troilus tends towards the vindictive. Æneas says he may be a second Hector and Æneas ought to know."

"How the heck," exclaimed Hermes, "does Odysseus know so much about Troilus?"

"He's making most of it up," I sneered. "Anyone who says Troilus is silent has never been to tea with him." We all laughed but at the same time there was an undercurrent to Odysseus' eulogy that made me feel uneasy. Odysseus never did or said anything without a motive. He was lean and mean; such men are dangerous. However, now everyone's attention was on the combatants in the field.

Ajax was a large lad. He wore a grim smile as he strode forward, brandishing his long spear. The Greeks cheered themselves hoarse, waving little flags. The Trojans were not so pleased and even Hector seemed wary. He may have preferred Akhilleus after all. Too late now. Ajax held his shield in front of him like a wall – Hermes said that, besides the bronze plate, it had seven folds of ox hide. Ajax cried out:

"Hector, you shall now learn that the Greeks have other champions besides Akhilleus who, let me assure you, is more bluster than brawn. It may be to your misfortune that my name, and not his, was drawn in the lottery. You may find that I, Ajax, am greater and more fearsome that Akhilleus." Akhilleus, who was sitting on the front bench with Patroklos, ground his teeth. But Hector was not to be bullied or put down.

"Don't sell me short, noble Ajax. I have been deep in the blood and butcheries of battle since you were a boy. I am a master in using my leather shield either on the right or left. I am a master of horses and can charge anywhere among chariots and horsemen; in hand-to-hand fighting, no one equals me. I would consider it beneath me to take a man as you off his guard – I will smite you openly." Eros rolled his eyes.

"This part," he said, "is a bit like opposing cats puffing out their tails to make themselves look bigger." I pretended not to hear. Hector now poised his spear high and hurled it; it went through six of Ajax' shield's layers but could not penetrate the seventh or the layer of bronze. Then it was Ajax' turn; his spear struck Hector's round gleaming shield, piercing right through it, but he managed to swerve and this saved his life.

Then they fell upon each other like creatures of great strength and endurance: Hector struck the middle of Ajax's shield, but the bronze did not break and the point of his spear turned. Ajax then pierced Hector's shield once more; the spear went through it as he tried to spring forward to attack. Hector staggered back, giving ground, then seized a stone, rugged and huge, and with it struck the center of Ajax' shield so the hard bronze rang. Ajax in turn caught up a far larger stone, swung it aloft and hurled it with prodigious force. It hit and broke Hector's shield, throwing him on his back, the shield crushing him. However, Hector managed to get to his feet.

Then a diversion occurred. A chariot came up at top speed and everyone turned towards it, the combat for the moment forgotten. And who should alight but Priam, leaning heavily on his stick and supported by Antenor. I gasped. All the spectators gasped. The Greeks on the field looked miffed.

"Truce," cried Priam, "I call for a truce. My friends, night is falling and combat should cease." Priam staggered towards Hector and embraced him, getting Hector's blood all over himself. This pissed Ajax off:

"What is this? Hector, fight or I will brand you a coward. There is enough light yet that I may kill you before the moon comes out." He sprang into position but Hector was still encumbered with his aged parent. Priam cried out:

"Hector, my son, the mainstay of both myself and Troy, do not, do not, continue with this madness." Priam turned from Hector and faced Akhilleus.

"My Lord Akhilleus…but why are you not garbed for battle? You are the champion of the Greeks, the only one worthy of facing my son in combat!" Akhilleus sneered:

"Not today, old man. Greece has found another champion and turned Priam to face Ajax. The old man started and then held out his arms to Ajax, who looked daggers at him.

"Ajax…Ajax my nephew, the son of my beloved wife's sister! But surely you are our ally! What are you doing in the Greek Camp?" But before Ajax could reach for his axes and cut the old man in half, Hector intervened, standing next to his father. He echoed Priam:

"I will not fight to the death with you, flesh of my flesh, blood of my blood…"

"You said that before," shrieked Ajax. "You're just using it as an excuse to get out of this, of being killed by Ajax! And you've plotted with this old codger to do me out of my rights!" He stamped around while Diomedes and Nestor tried to calm him down, Diomedes saying soothingly:

"You can't kill him from behind, you know. So put up and be a brave boy!" Ajax sneered. Hector continued in a most flowery way:

"My father is right. How could I shed the blood of my mother's sister, my aunt, may the Gods keep her." Then he faced Ajax: "You have lusty arms and Hector would have them fall upon his, thus," and he caught Ajax in a bear hug that Ajax did his best not to return, saying instead:

"I came to kill you, cousin Hector, and bear back the glory and honour I would have achieved through you death. Damn and blast!" He threw down his seven-layered shield and shouted: "Well, then, if it has to end in a stalemate, let it be known that Hector backed down for I would not." Well, Ajax might not be the sharpest knife in the kitchen drawer but he sure had guts. Hector cried out:

"Ajax, you are one of the strongest men I have ever encountered; your handling of the spear excels that of all other Greeks. We will fight again another day till heaven gives victory to one or to the other. Let it be said among the Greeks and Trojans: 'They fought valiantly, but were reconciled and parted in friendship'." Ajax stalked off with a look of disgust. Now, as a whole, the Greeks looked slightly sandbagged. I mean, there they were and their guy was doing great and suddenly the guy who is losing says: 'Sorry, can't go on, I've got night blindness.' But Menelaus wasn't having it:

"Agamemnon," he jumped to his feet and cried out: "You cannot allow this. The challenge, sent by Hector, was that the dispute between the Trojans and Greeks were to be settled by the death of one of the combatants. But now Hector is turning and running, with the excuse that it's getting dark. I say he be branded a coward!" Hector was not thrilled with this attitude and replied coldly:

"I will not be branded a coward. I have stated my reasons and I believe they should be respected."

"All well and fine," shouted Menelaus, "you withdrew when you saw Ajax was about to overcome you. If you cannot kill your kinsman, I will take his place. I am not your kinsman and you can kill me with impunity." But, to be honest, Hector had been given such a drubbing by Ajax he couldn't have fought even me with a paw tied behind my back. However, Agamemnon saw this was going nowhere and even if Menelaus killed Hector, the Trojans would not concede. Priam then threw himself at Agamemnon feet and cried out:

"My friends, let us put a stop to this. Spare my son either victory over his kin or his death under the hands of a warrior not worthy to be his adversary!" Agamemnon finally found his tongue:

"My good Priam, we had thought Hector would honour the outcome of this combat as signifying the end of our differences. However, he has reneged under your influence and we will remain as before!" Hector looked daggers at him. "Be content, go back to Troy and Hector will join you shortly." Priam hobbled off with Adrestus holding him up.

"This is a bit thick," I said to my companions. "You send out a challenge for combat to the death, get your opposite number all steamed up and for what? No one wins and everything is exactly as before?" But my friends both shrugged:

"You mustn't take war in ancient cultures too seriously, Gaius," admonished Eros. "Most of the time it isn't about killing but getting hostages for money or to trade."

"Real war, with blood everywhere and guts spilling out," continued Hermes, "is only for the lower orders." Then Odysseus intervened for the first time, calling out to Calchas who was standing on the side:

"Calchas, what say you to this dispute?" Calchas bowed his head then said:

"The fate of this war is set and will not change. This combat, whatever its outcome, would have altered nothing." Odysseus turned to Agamemnon.

"Call this a draw and let's put the whole thing to sleep." And Agamemnon did so but with little enthusiasm in his voice.

Hector started leaving the field, but Agamemnon called him back:

"Hector, now that we are done with the main part of the business, I would invite you join me in the Greek camp so we may meet with you in friendship." Odysseus said:

"Your brother, Troilus, too, is welcome. And you, Æneas." Hector considered, and answered:

"Very well, I accept and thank you for your courtesy." To Æneas: "Have Troilus join me; the other Trojans may return to the city."

Homerys seemed to have shut out the real world for a bit, and was busy with his verse-making. There was no way we could escape his version of events:

Then had they [Ajax and Hector] laid on wounds with
swords, in use of closer fight,
Unless the heralds (messengers of gods and
godlike men),
The one from Troy [Talthybius] , the other Greece
[Idæus], had held betwixt them then
Imperial sceptres then the one, Idæus, grave and wise,
Said to them: "Now no more, my sons; the sovereign of
the skies
Doth love you both; both soldiers are, all witness with
good right,

*But now night lays her mace on earth; 'tis good to obey
the night."*

I looked at my two companions:

"Heralds? Idæus? Talthybius? Who are these guys? Has Homerys gone mad or is he both blind and hard of hearing." Eros patted me kindly:

"Now, Gaius, don't take on so. Homerys knows what his audience wants. And, of course, if you repeat fiction long enough, it will become fact. Done all the time." I had to agree with him and with that be content.

The whole party adjourned to the *Greek Olive Tree*. Eros, Hermes and myself in tow. I took up my position on the end of the bar, Eros and Hermes on stools next to me. Curiously, no one tried to sit on them. I got a nasty look from Agamemnon.

"That cat follows me about. I don't like him. Will someone please drown him." Surprisingly, it was Odysseus who interfered:

"Leave the cat alone, Agamemnon. It's bad luck to kill a cat."

"Yeah," drawled Hermes, "in Egypt, you'd get the death penalty."

"They're going to be pretty popular in Rome, too," added Eros. "It's the late Middle Ages you'll have to look out for."

"Thanks," I replied, "I have no intention of being around in the Middle Ages, late or otherwise." After everyone had been served, I signalled Eurybates for some water and carafe of wine. He just brought them over, together with two mugs. I take it he had been speaking to his wife about the incidents in the tearoom. As we quaffed away, I said:

"When all is said and done, what is the difference between a Geek and a Trojan? They look the same, dress the same, speak the same language and worship the same Gods. What they need is more integration or perhaps multiculturalism. Exchange students; reciprocal trade agreements; joint health projects. The more I see of this war, the less I understand it." Eros and Hermes looked bored as if I were stating the obvious. I continued: "I'm starting to agree with Homerys: the Gods should come down from Olympus and shake some sense into the whole lot." Eros leaned his head back and spoke around Hermes:

"Really, Gaius, you of all creatures should know that like fights like."

"Yes, yes," sneered Hermes. "It comes down to the fact that humans love wars. Why, even in the 21st century, with TV and movies, reality contests and amateur music contests, they still can't give up a good war. It's an addiction." There was no way of countering Hermes' arguments, not that I wanted to defend humanity in any way or form, so I turned my attention back to the present. Everyone now had a mug and the snacks were disappearing as if by magic.

"Hector, I, commander of the Greek Expeditionary forces, greet you and bid you welcome." That, of course, was Agamemnon blowing his own trumpet. Hector smiled and replied, perhaps none too tactfully:

"The greatest of all except, perhaps, for Akhilleus." Agamemnon looked none too pleased but tried to hide it. He continued:

"My worthy opponent, what is past we cannot change and what is to come we cannot see. So, again, Hector, welcome." He turned to Troilus who had taken up a position quite close to me, and said: "And you, sir, are also welcome." Troilus scowled. Menelaus did not join in this mutual admiration society but stood apart at the bar, brooding. He turned and was about to say something when Nestor went up to Hector and put an arm around his shoulders:

"My dear Hector, I have seen you often on the field, surrounded by the best of Greek warriors. I knew your grandfather, Laomedon, and fought with him once. He too was a great warrior, but not to be compared with you. Let an old man embrace you." Hector looked wary as well he might for, if Nestor comes, can Odysseus be far behind? However, he returned Nestor's embrace:

"I greet you, Nestor, who has walked side by side with time for so long." Then Odysseus broke in – I just knew it would come:

"I wonder how Troy continues to stand when her sustaining pillar is here with us." Now, that didn't sound good for Hector. Odysseus might be up to something. Assassination? Kidnapping? Ransom? But Hector had by this time mellowed, what with the wine and the bonhomie and had gone all sentimental:

"Indeed, there is many a Greek and Trojan dead since I first met you and Diomedes as the Greek envoys to Troy." Odysseus stroked his chin; he had memories of his own:

"You might also remember what I said then: that one day Troy's tower, that now almost touches the clouds, may lie crumbled at the city's feet." Hector gave an embarrassed laugh:

"I do remember, my good Odysseus, yet the tower still stands, does it not? And let me now predict that it will continue to stand; but if it is to fall, each stone will have cost a drop of Grecian blood." Then, seeing that this remark was not particular popular and that he was, after all, surrounded by Greeks, tried to lighten the tone so he might leave *The Greek Olive Tree* in one piece. "But one day Troy and Greece will have become dust and forgotten; and all our problems meaningless."

"True, my good Hector," I whispered, "but for that to happen, I advise you that killing Homerys should be the next item on your agenda." Eros and Hermes nodded.

"If Homerys survives," said Hermes, "the world will never be rid of the Trojan War." Odysseus closed this dangerous albeit interesting discussion.

"As you say, my friend, time heals all wounds." Everyone toasted Hector. And then Agamemnon.

Akhilleus appeared with Patroklos behind him. It's difficult to sulk in your tent if all the action is taking place elsewhere. Of course, his diplomatic nature emerged immediately. He spread his hands towards the sky and his face, too.

"Tell me, oh Gods, through which part of Hector's body shall I destroy him? Shall it be there, there or there?" pointing to various spots on Hector's anatomy. The more I saw of Akhilleus, the less I liked him. He continued: "From which wound will Hector's spirit fly out? Answer me, Gods!" He raised his arms heavenwards. This was turning ugly. I imagine Hector wished he'd gone to Happy Hour at *The Trojan Horse*. He looked black as he answered:

"Well, now, Akhilleus, that's hardly a fair question to put to the Gods. Do you really think it's so easy to kill me that you can plan what part of my body would best serve?" He stared at Akhilleus and in turn pointed at various bits of Akhilleus' anatomy. "My enemy, I'm not planning to kill you there, or there, or there. I'm going kill you everywhere, over and over again." He suddenly seemed to remember that he and Akhilleus were not alone. He turned to the rest of the party who were drinking it all in while pretending to be engaged elsewhere.

"Forgive me, my friends, I seem to have forgotten my party manners, but your Akhilleus is too insolent." He turned to Akhilleus again: "I haven't seen you in the field this many a day. Perhaps, when you actually turn up, we'll see who's the better man." There was an awkward pause. Surprisingly, Ajax jumped into the breach, putting his arm around Hector's shoulders:

"Cousin, don't listen to that braggart. And you, Akhilleus, how about showing up or shutting up."

"We may have misjudged poor Ajax," murmured Hermes. By this time, Akhilleus had lost his cool. Being ticked off by Hector was bad enough, but by Ajax was not to be endured. He snarled:

"I'll meet you on the field tomorrow, Hector, and then we shall see who is the better man." Hector did not answer but nodded slowly. Agamemnon then opened his arms wide as if to embrace the whole company.

"My friends, it's time for dinner." Everyone followed him on to the terrace where Eurybates had arranged trestle tables. Everybody, that is, except Diomedes, who seemed to have disappeared. I looked around. Nowhere. In fact, he hadn't been anywhere for ages.

3.5 AS TRUE AS CRESSIDA, AS FALSE AS TROILUS

As Odysseus prepared to follow the rest, Troilus plucked at his sleeve:

"My good Odysseus, could you please direct me to Calchas' tent?" Odysseus looked at him cunningly. I had a feeling he had been waiting for this moment but how on earth did he know it would come? Odysseus answered courteously:

"I'll take you there myself." Well, there was no way I was going to miss what was going to happen next so I slid down from the bar and followed, keeping to the shadows. Hermes and Eros were right behind me. You can't see a cat in the dark no matter what colour he is in the daytime so I was as invisible as my two companions. It didn't take long for Odysseus to put whatever scheme he had into action. He asked in an offhand manner, as if making polite conversation:

"So tell me, Troilus, what kind of reputation did Calchas' daughter Cressida have in Troy? Did she leave a boyfriend there? Pretty girl like that?" Troilus turned scarlet to the roots of his hair. Poor lad, no guile at all.

"Sir, she was loved and did love." Odysseus raised his eyebrows but said no more.

We arrived at Calchas' tent. Cressida was outside, sitting on a rug that she was busily trying to unravel. However, she was not alone. Her companion, the missing Diomedes, sat crossed legged facing her, plucking at the grass. Odysseus pulled Troilus into the shadows of the trees. And we three, me, Hermes and Eros, sat down on the grass behind them. Unaware that they were being watched, Cressida and Diomedes were silent and did not look at each other. Cressida was dabbing at her eyes and blowing her nose. At last, she said:

"If you are a gentleman, you will not speak to me of this again." No prizes for knowing what this was. Diomedes answered:

"I will not if you ask me. But you should think of it. There is no reason to dwell on what has gone wrong and cannot be righted." More sniffs from Cressida; then she seemed to pull herself together. She said, trying to sound playful but not succeeding very well:

"So, my lord protector. What would you have of me?" Diomedes answered:

"For now, your regard. Later, your friendship, and one day, perhaps, when it is yours to give, your love." In true woman's fashion, Cressida bowed her head slightly, turning her eyes upwards to look at Diomedes.

"My regard? That you have. My friendship? It is yours. My love? Ah, my lord, that would be taking liberties with a poor friendless and unprotected girl." She lowered her eyes. I could hear Troilus grinding his teeth. Diomedes raised Cressida's face with his hand under her chin; they looked directly into each other's eye.

"There may come a time when your heart will be free ... will you remember me then?" Cressida whispered:

"Remember? I remember you now, as I will tomorrow and all my days after. I will remember you were my friend in my time of need when I had no other." Troilus whispered to Odysseus and I'm surprised the whole place didn't hear him:

"She swore, she swore her heart would never be free!" Odysseus put his hand on Troilus' shoulder:

"Keep silent and listen."

"For my kindness, why, Cressida, any gentleman would have done no more and I do not wish to be remembered with gratitude. But as one who could be worthy of your love." Cressida pushed his hand away and lay down on her side, resting on her elbow, her eyes on the fringes of her shawl. Considering how long she'd been picking at them, I was surprised there were any left. She said in a low voice:

"Oh, you Greek with your honey tongue, don't tempt a vulnerable girl into folly." Diomedes laughed and answered:

"Folly? Why, I am as serious as Nestor!" His keen glance looked at her. "But how serious are you?" Cressida cried out:

"Serious?" She looked at him in all innocence: "In what way should I be serious?" Diomedes demanded:

"By giving me a token to seal your promise." Cressida said nothing. Considering Cressida had brought nothing from Troy but the clothes she stood in, that was understandable. At last she said sadly:

"Alas, even if I would, I have none to give."

"Cressida," said Diomedes, laughing gently: "I need no token to remember you by as your image will be forever engraved on my heart." Odysseus had his hands full in keeping Troilus back. Eros said sadly:

"Have you ever heard such tosh? It doesn't even make sense." Hermes answered from the shadows

"Ahh, my friend, that is the language of love." Eros countered:

"I can't believe my arrows bring out this rubbish in people. Never again, Zeus, hear me, never again." Our attention went back to the scene before us. Both Diomedes and Cressida were now standing up, facing each other. Diomedes had taken a token pin from his cloak and handed it to Cressida.

"Since you have no token to give me, take mine and wear it not only in memory of me; but to guard you against any man, whether Greek or Trojan, who would do you harm. You are under the protection of Diomedes. No one will dare touch you." Cressida pinned it to her dress.

"Diomedes, I thank you. As a girl alone out here, it will make me feel safer."

"Fear nothing. And now I must go." Cressida grabbed at his arm:

"To the wars! Do not, oh do not." Gently, Diomedes removed her hand from his arm.

"War is my destiny. But now I know I will survive. I will return and see you tomorrow." There were now tears in Cressida's voice.

"Alone. I shall be all alone." Diomedes looked around him.

"Look," he said, "there's a cat there. Isn't it the one you said was your friend?" Rats! I'd been spotted. Well, there was nothing to it so I walked forward and faced them. Cressida murmured:

"Oh, Gaius, I'm so glad to see you. Will you stay with me?" I nodded:

"I will!" Better with me than these conniving humans. Diomedes turned to leave:

"Lady, goodnight," he said. "And to you, cat, whatever your name is." Well, if he couldn't remember it, I wasn't about to give him the satisfaction of repeating it. Cressida still clung to him:

"He loved me once," and the tears brimmed in her eyes.

"Move on, Cressida," Diomedes counselled. "Move on." So Diomedes left, back to the blood and gore. No matter how sweet the lady, a juicy war will always take precedence. As he went Cressida buried her face in her hands and murmured:

"Farewell, Troilus. Half my heart is still yours, but I'm afraid the other half is looking elsewhere. Frailty, thy name is woman." And she slipped into the tent.

Diomedes now being out of earshot, it seemed Troilus had just about had enough. He stood stock still as if turned to stone. Then he cried out:

"This is madness! She swore to be eternally faithful! And now, one day, one little day!" Odysseus took him by the arm to lead him away:

"I think you've seen enough. Come, my friend, before you do something you might later regret. This place is dangerous and the time deadly." Well, for sure, Troilus wouldn't want to be caught in the Greek camp at such a moment. But he would have none of it and wrenched himself away from Odysseus.

"No, leave me be!" Odysseus held him in an iron grip.

"Quiet! Or I'll drag you off."

Odysseus ... I wondered about Odysseus. And so did Hermes who said:

"Curious. I can't figure Odysseus out. Why should he take an interest in this banal affair? A mere lovers' quarrel?" Eros said:

"One thing's for sure, Troilus is not going to be of much use on the battlefield tomorrow. Or am I out-Machiavelleing Odysseus?" I shook my head. I could now see it all. Odysseus had just put another nail in Troy's coffin, albeit a small one. But all is fair in love and war.

In the meantime, Troilus seemed to have gotten a grip on himself and said to Odysseus, head held low:

"Let me stay a minute so my soul can record every syllable I heard tonight. Was it really she? Something deep inside me tells me it was all a dream, that I cannot trust my ears or eyes, that my senses have led me astray. Surely she was not here"

"Well, my friend," sighed Odysseus, "if I could undo it all with one word, I would. But that is not in my power." The hypocrite. Troilus groaned:

"I suppose I need to accept it, then. The other way leads only to madness." He paused, then went on: "I would not believe a woman could act like this. Are all women alike? What about our mothers? Can we condemn the whole sex on Cressida's behaviour?" Odysseus raised his eyebrows and glowered. This was not a popular sentiment.

"I don't think you should get our mothers mixed up in this," he said. But Troilus was not listening. Did he ever? The commotion had brought Cressida out of the tent. She stopped and stared in horror at Troilus. He saw her the same moment, turned towards her in fury and ranted, pointing his finger at her:

"This was not my Cressida. This is Diomedes' Cressida. If beauty has a soul, this is not she; if souls make promises, if promises are sacred and are the delight of the Gods, if a person is one indivisible unit, this was not Cressida. Cressida is mine," he continued, "tied to me by bonds of heaven. And now those bonds are broken and what is left of her faith has gone to Diomedes."

Then, in his characteristic way, he started wailing: "O, Cressida, o false Cressida, false, false, false. Let all liars be compared to you and they will all seem wonderfully truthful." He turned his back on the tent and started into the darkness. Cressida buried her face in her hands, sobbing, and cried:

"Oh, Troilus, you have misunderstood. Indeed you have."

"I don't think so," he answered, venom in his voice. "As changeable as the wind is she, with promises and vows of eternal love to me while her caresses and kisses go to another."

Who said that love and hate are two sides of the same coin? Troilus might even have loved Cressida but he didn't, as sure as Hades, like her. He stomped off, when suddenly he let out a yell and fell to his knees. Not surprising, since ten sharp claws had torn into his calf muscles. I was getting ready to spring for the jugular when I found myself yanked off the ground, held by the scruff of the neck, with all four paws tearing at the air.

"Let me down," I yelled at Eros, for he was the one holding me in this undignified position. "I'm going to tear out his eyes. False, lying bastard!" Troilus' eyes were as big as saucers as he looked at this enraged screaming feline in mid-air. "What price your troth, Troilus," I yelled, "when you promised to *love her above all else* and then betrayed her at the first sign of trouble?" Troilus held out his hand.

"I couldn't help it," he lamented, "Adrestus ..."

"Adrestus?" I screamed, struggling to get free of Eros. "What do you care about Adrestus? Did you promise to love Adrestus above all else?"

"And there was my family ..."

"Your family? Does your family come before the woman you love? For Helen, you would see everyone in Troy dead, what would you do to for Cressida? Leave Adrestus with the Greeks? Face Ma and Pa? Marry her there and then, that's what you should have done. You are a faithless coward! May you rot in Hades!" And suddenly I was on the ground.

But before I could take any action, a bright light glowed beside me. I looked at Eros. He was glowing, surrounded by a golden light, and seemed to have grown taller. And Troilus could see him, too; he cowered on the ground, holding up a hand to shade his eyes from the brightness. Eros pointed a finger at Troilus.

"Troilus," and his voice was deep and stern, "you have been tried in the art of love and found wanting. And here is your doom: for as long as you shall live, no woman shall love you and you shall love no woman." Troilus gave a cry and staggered away. Eros turned back to his normal self.

"Well," I said, "I'm amazed, Eros. That was some show." Eros ground his teeth.

"Dirty bastard," he said in deep disgust. "I'm sick of these Trojans and of the Greeks, too. Hermes, let's go. Goodbye, Gaius, see you around. Oh, and Gaius, don't worry about the curse. It won't last very long." I waved a paw, too shocked to do much else but think that Eros had just told me Troilus wasn't long for this world. Hermes winked at me and they were gone. I was still paralytic when Æneas came running past me, followed by a none too pleased Ajax.

"Where has that boy gone?" Ajax complained. "Does he think I have all night to nursemaid him and make sure he's not gutted by one of his own guards?"

"Look" cried Æneas. "I think I can see him up ahead." And the two blundered on. I continued sitting there, feeling shattered. At last I moved and crept into the tent. Cressida was lying on the rug, sobbing. She looked up at me.

"Oh, Gaius," she wailed, "what have I done? I'm cursed as a faithless woman. What have I got to live for now except my shame?" I nuzzled close to her.

"Shame, the shame belongs to Troilus who abandoned you in your hour of need." And to Diomedes, I might have added, who took advantage of that moment. "Don't cry, Cressida, they just aren't worth it. None of them." And how often will this sentence be repeated down the ages? And much good has it ever done. I curled up and lay listening to Cressida's sobs; eventually, we both drifted into sleep.

3.6 A SUMMER NIGHT'S DREAM

I sleep badly. This is almost unheard of in felines who also don't often dream but I do and my paws and tail switch like mad. I seem to have plunged into a world of blood and fire, the night dark, with no moon (although there was one when I went into Cressida's tent).

I feel myself suspended in the air, hovering high above the Dardan plain. Even in the gloom of night, my feline eyes see furious figures galloping: I see Agamemnon leading the Greeks, Hector, the Trojans. The two forces clash and the head-on collision sends men, horses and chariots flying everywhere, anywhere. Both armies battle fiercely; the tide has turned against the Greeks and the Trojans – I can tell the difference by their helmet crests, horsehair versus plumes – are herding the Greeks towards the sea and the beached Greek vessels. I squirm in my sleep; I don't like battles; the Greeks' situation has gone from bad to worse. I twist and turn in. Then I see someone running, running towards the Greek tents. I seem to have fallen into Homerys's epic:

> *[At] which martial sight, when great Akhilleus views,*
> *a little his desire of fight renews*
> *and forth sends his friend [Patroklos] to bring him word*
> *from a wounded lord from the skirmish brought.*

I am in a corner of Akhilleus' tent. Patroklos has come in and Nestor is with him. The news is all bad. Nestor and Patroklos try to convince that Akhilleus must support the Greeks if they are not to be annihilated. If he, Akhilleus, will not go, he, Patroklos, will take his place. Homerys verses float on the wind:

> *.... Nestor then besought*
> *he could persuade his [Akhilleus] friend [Patroklos] to*
> *wreak their harms*
> *or come himself [Akhilleus] decked in his dreadful arms.*

Nestor then leaves; Patroklos continues urging Akhilleus to action but he still demurs – should he climb down from his high horse and fight or keep his haughty mien and sulk and let the consequences be what they may – another candidate to inherit the wind. He struggles. But, in the end, vanity wins over valour. This sends Patroklos into a frenzy insisting he, Patroklos, must take his, Akhilleus, place. At first, Akhilleus scoffs but Patroklos makes such a scene it wears down even Akhilleus. Patroklos harangues him:

"If you will not go," he shouts, "let me wear your armour so the Trojans may think you are back. This could demoralize them and give the Greeks some breathing space and a chance to regroup." Incredibly, Akhilleus starts going on about how Agamemnon cheated him. He walks up and down in his tent, checking his grievances off on his fingers as if Patroklos has not heard all of them a hundred times. Patroklos is ready to burst with frustration. At last, Akhilleus reaches the end of his list. He says, with airy nonchalance and in grandiose terms:

"Still, let bygones be bygones. No man may nurture his anger for ever; I said I would relent when battle and the cry of war reached my own ships as they now have; nevertheless, I do have my pride and, since you are so insistent, yes, put on my armour and lead my Myrmidons to battle." He swaggers around, well pleased.

"Troy has taken heart because they have not yet espied the gleam of my helmet. When they do, the plain will be strewn with their dead as they flee from the idea of ME. And so it would have been, if only Agamemnon had dealt fairly by me." He puts his arm around his friend's shoulder: "So, Patroklos, go and save the fleet before the Trojans burn the lot and we get stranded here forever. When you have done that," and he rubs his hands together, "then perhaps I will get the many riches that are my due." Homerys's verses sang out:

Akhilleus, at Patroklos' suit doth yield
his arms and Myrmidons; which, brought to the field
the Trojans fly.

Akhilleus goes on, spouting instructions: "When the ships are safe, come back here; don't fight the Trojans further in my absence or you will rob me of glory that should be mine alone." Patroklos scrambles into Akhilleus' armour, helped by a squire of sorts: greaves with silver ankle-clasps; cuirass, richly inlaid and studded; a silver-studded sword of bronze, the mighty shield; the helmet with its crest of horse-hair; two spears that suit Patroklos' hands, rather than Akhilleus' own spear, so stout and heavy no one but Akhilleus can wield it.

And so Patroklos goes forth into the night. Akhilleus' chariot, with Automedon, Akhilleus' charioteer, holding the reins of the immortal horses, Xanthuius and Balius, who are ready and waiting. The Myrmidons are falling in. I hear the names of their commanders – Sperchius, Borus, Eudorus, Alcimedon. Before they leave, Akhilleus speaks to them:

"I know," he says, "that for these past days you have blamed me for not allowing you to join the battles and that you have thought of mutiny and threatened to sail home." Homerys sang:

> *"Now, then you [Myrmidons] you may bathe in sweat of these great works ye wished; now he that can employ a generous heart, go fight, and fright the bragging sons of Troy."*

Loud cheers and much waving of weapons. The Myrmidons, bloodthirsty and savage, are like hounds on a leash. To my horror, I find myself in the chariot as Patroklos climbs aboard and Automedon sets of at a violent pace, flying across the plain, the men running behind him at a furious rate. I hang on for dear life, clinging to Automedon's left leg who, surprisingly, seems to feel nothing.

Then I find myself by the beached ships, cowering behind Ajax, still proud, self-centred and arrogant but who now is finding it difficult to hold his ground against the Trojans' javelins; his shield arm is numb, he finds it difficult to breathe but still the Trojans cannot make him give ground. Then Hector is upon him on his great steed and, with his sword, splits Ajax' ashen spear in half, and Ajax has no option but to withdraw even further, leaving the beached vessels open to Trojan attack. The Trojans, storming in behind Hector, cast flaming torches upon the ships and at once the fire catches and spreads. The Greeks panic although Ajax manages to keep them in some kind of order.

Suddenly, I am back in Akhilleus' chariot – Patroklos has arrived at the head of the Myrmidons and assail the Trojans from the rear; the air now rings with Greek battle cries. As soon as the Trojans see what they believe to be the mighty Akhilleus, they are thrown into confusion and the heart goes out of them. Patroklos and the Myrmidons manage to drive the Trojans from the ships, allowing the Greeks breathing space to quench the blazing fires.

Now the Trojans are driven back, with the Greeks pouring across the plain behind them, Patroklos at their head. The Trojans have become a disorganized rabble, they scatter, and the battle becomes man against man. Hector arrives upon the scene once more and, seeing that the fortunes of the day have turned, stands his ground and attempts to get his comrades to regroup. In vain; the Trojans continue their flight.

In the meanwhile, Patroklos gives chase, calling on the Greeks to follow him, full of fury against the Trojans who, in their despair, fill the night air with their cries of panic and rout; the sky darkens as running feet of men, chariot wheels and horses raise clouds of dust.

Patroklos espies Hector and becomes intent on pursuing him, but Hector's swift horses disappear into the darkness. However, Patroklos cannot let go and continues the chase in the pride and foolishness of his heart, Akhilleus' admonitions forgotten. His quarry momentarily out of sight, Patroklos rushes on, Of course, Homerys has to stick is oar in:

> *Draw back, Patroklos, it is not your destiny to sack the city*
> *of Troy, or even that of Akhilleus, a far better man than you.*

Patroklos, naturally, is not listening. He thrice charges the walls of Troy near the Chetan gate, each time thrown back by defenders on the ramparts. Patroklos is now beyond the point of no return and comes in for a fourth try.

Now Hector, from the shadows of the gate, sees his chance, and urges his steeds forward, straight at Patroklos, his spear at the ready. The force of Hector's charge sends Patroklos sprawling onto the ground. Jumping from his chariot, Hector draws his sword but not before Patroklos manages to regain his footing and retrieve his own. For some little time, they circle each other until a Trojan throws Hector a bronze-shod spear that Hector, with great skill, drives right through the lower part of Patroklos' abdomen; Patroklos, now mortally wounded, collapses. Hector kneels and removes his enemy's helmet;

he, and the Trojans about him, gasp in amazement. It is not Akhilleus. Hector kneels by him and says sorrowfully:

"Patroklos, you thought wearing Akhilleus' armour you would become Akhilleus. Poor wretch! Your reward will be to be devoured by vultures before the gates of Troy." Then, as life ebbs away, Patroklos answers:

"Hector, you too shall live but a little season before death and doom close upon you; you shall be laid low by the great Akhilleus." And so Patroklos dies. Hector shakes his head sadly:

"Poor fool. I took you for your better."

I awake with a jump.

"He's dead, he's dead," I cry. Cressida wakes up too and, eyes wide, asked:

"Who, Gaius, who's dead?" I look at her blankly.

"I don't know," I answer foolishly, "it must have been something I dreamt."

4
MONDAY

4.1 THE DAY AFTER THE NIGHT BEFORE

When I left Cressida the next morning she was in a calmer frame of mind and doing housewifely things around her father's tent. As I walked towards Troy, I met up with Homerys and his boy. There was a bit of a friction because the boy claimed that, as I was there, he, the boy, could stay on the beach and I could look after Homerys. However, I had to dash cold water on this plan, seeing that I was vertical while Homerys was horizontal and, besides, since he couldn't see me, how was the thing to be done? The boy suggested I wear my leash so Homerys could hang on to that. As my leash was not available, that was a washout. Homerys said that, had I been a lion, he could have hung on to my mane. Now, I'd love to be a lion to please Homerys. But the fact remains: I'm a – I hate to use the word – domestic cat, albeit large for my kind.

So there we were, all three trudging towards the Chetan gate that was standing wide open. Trojan Warriors streamed out towards the plain below. And on, the plain, the Greeks were busy 'warming up', I suppose you could say. After the meeting of the mutual admiration society the night before, we seemed to be back to business as usual. Deciding wars by single combat has always been a popular notion, but I have never heard it being taken seriously.

On our way to Priam Square, we passed the steps leading up to the royal palace. Hector was coming down, fully equipped for battle, followed by two females, one of them holding the hand of a little boy. Homerys said:

"Is that Hector coming down the stairs? Let's sit and rest here for a bit; I might get some good copy." So we sat down on the bottom step. Well, Homerys may be blind but I've never known anyone with better hearing. The boy, of course, ran off at once, heading, no doubt, for the fountain and mischief. One of the ladies I knew; Cassandra. The other had to be Andromache, Hector's wife and the kid his son, Astyanax. As they reached the road, Andromache threw her arms around Hector and clung to him:

"Hector," she cried, "please listen to me. Don't go to the field today. I dreamt all night of wars and battles and the shape and form of slaughter. This day will not end well." Hector looked at her, somewhat coldly, I thought.

"My dear, you give me no choice but not to listen to you. You know I must go. So be a true wife, wish me well and return to your domestic duties." Cassandra joined Andromache in her pleadings:

"My brother, this will not your day. Hear me, my brother, be wise, not brave. There is no glory or honour in bringing about your own destruction." Andromache took Hector's hand in her own and said as the tears rolling down her cheeks.

"Dear husband, think of our small son, and of my helpless self, soon to be your widow. If I lose you, I would be better dead and buried, for I shall have nothing left to comfort me save sorrow. I have neither father nor mother or other kin. You, Hector, you must be father, mother and brother to me. Have mercy upon me; make not your child fatherless and your wife a widow."

"Wife," replied Hector sorrowfully, "don't think I haven't gone through all this. But how would I face our people if I were to shirk my duty like a coward? That, I cannot do. To fight bravely at the head of my troops is what I was born for and my destiny follows the will of the Gods." Cassandra wrung her hands and wept copiously:

"My brother, when you are no longer here, Troy shall be unprotected and how long will it then be before our city is destroyed and our people with it? And what of the women of Troy, you mother, wife, sisters and kinswomen who will lose their freedom forever to become slaves in Greek households. Because that will be our fate, those of us who survive the slaughter!"

Of course, she hit it right on the nose but, as usual, no one was listening. Amazing how men's duties always align themselves directly with their own wishes. Hector stretched his arms towards Astyanax but the child, frightened by Hector's full armour, shied away and tried to hide behind Cassandra. Both parents laughed although personally I didn't see the joke. Hector took off his plumed helmet and took the boy in his arms, kissed and dandled him. Then he cried out, holding Astyanax aloft:

"Zeus, grant that this child may be, even as myself, chief among the Trojans; let him be not less excellent in strength as ruler of Troy so it may be said of him: 'The son is better than the father'." He put Astyanax down, embraced his wife and sister and said: "Now, let me go and we will meet again in a happier time." I looked at Homerys to see how he was taking this. He was nodding away, saying:

"Very right and proper. Thus should heroes behave." I murmured:

"The only good hero is a dead hero," and Homerys squawked:

"What did you say?" As so many other humans I have met, Homerys only hears what he wants to hear. I let it go. By this time, Andromache was asking Cassandra to get old Priam to see what he could do. As Cassandra ran up the steps to the palace, who should come down but Troilus, booted and suited, helmet under his arm. I could see one leg was bandaged and he walked with a slight limp. I was pleased with this positive result of my handiwork. Hector greeted him:

"Come, brother. Come, cast off your implements of war. I'd rather you stayed behind; let your muscles grow stronger before you take to the field. I'll stand today for you and myself and Troy." Had Hector known what had been going on in Troilus' life, he wouldn't have come up with such a foolish proposition. Troilus was out for blood, anyone's, even his own. No way he would be staying home. He answered curtly:

"My dear brother, you have too much milk of human kindness in your blood. I've seen you many a time, a Greek helpless at your feet, give him a hands up, pat on the back, telling him to go home." Hector pooh poohed this.

"That's merely fair play, you know. Code of honour and all that. Don't hit a man when he's down." Troilus:

"Fair play? I call it fool's play, I do, by Olympus. Let's leave pity and mercy to our women. When we're armed for war, brother, and our swords dipped in poison, cast out pity. Then it's no quarter and no surrender." Hector frowned. He repeated:

"Little brother, I'd rather you didn't fight today." Troilus answered, working himself into a fury:

"And why not? Who's to stop me? Not if my mother and father fell at my feet, tears streaming down their cheeks, nor any brother, with drawn sword, will stop me. I go to the battle, come Hades or high water." At that moment, Cassandra returned, Priam, hanging on her arm, and pleading:

"Father, keep Hector here. He is our pillar of strength; if he falls so do you and so does Troy." The old man laid his hand on Hector's arm:

"Come, Hector, let's go home. Your wife and your mother have had disturbing dreams and Cassandra has seen that this is not your day. And I, too, feel uneasy. Come back. Leave the fighting to others today." But of course Hector refused and the more they all begged, the more stubborn he became. Perhaps, thinks I, if they had all insisted that he go and kill every single Greek, he would be back in the palace two steps at a time. Hector said impatiently:

"Æneas is already in the field and I have pledged myself to meet a number of Greeks this morning." Great. Look, Dad, I promised I'd go out to kill or be killed. "Do you wish me to be false to my word? Am I to break my faith and lose face?" Well, sounded good to me. Troilus frowned at Cassandra.

"It's all the doing of this foolish superstitious girl and her idiotic prophecies!" He cried. "Come, brother, leave the women to their needles." This unlooked and uncalled for attack sent Cassandra round the bend and she started crying and screaming:

"Hector, Hector, I see you dying; look how your eyes turn pale; look how you bleed from your many wounds! Hear Troy lamenting, Hecuba weeping and Andromache inconsolable." Her arms reached towards heaven. "Distraction, frenzy and amazement take possession of the citizens of Troy. Hector! Hector's dead! O Hector." Bowed down by grief, Cassandra sank to the ground. Well, that would for sure have kept me at home. Cup of tea, comfy chair and a good book. Troilus, of course, sneered at her and said to Hector:

"Come, let's go." But Cassandra wasn't done yet. Flinging herself on Hector, she cried:

"Farewell, my dear brother, I take my leave of you. You deceive both yourself and all of Troy." Hector turned to Priam, looking somewhat distracted himself:

"Come, my good father, we all know Cassandra and her frenzies. Go among the crowds and give them hope while we do mighty deeds. We'll talk about all this in the evening." Homerys shook his head sadly.

"HUBRIS! But it must be so. The Gods wish it." He sighed and I could see his brain working: 'Pity about Hector but what a wonderful ending to my book.'

Meanwhile, Troilus was muttering to himself. Perhaps there's something truly wrong with Priam's children; Troilus seemed about as mad as Cassandra although there was method in her madness but none in his. He growled between his teeth:

"Diomedes, Diomedes! Just you wait, Diomedes!" Then more sons of Priam's turned up plus the main Trojan aristocrats, all ready for another day at the races. I was sick of all their battles and killings and mauling and maiming and I had no intention of spending any more time on the tower battlements. I left Homerys to his hexameters or whatever and decided to go and relax in Cressida's abandoned garden.

4.2 THE SERPENT'S TOOTH

Cressida's garden was all peace and quiet. There was a soft breeze under the late summer sky and diverse butterflies and bumblebees and other bees where going about their legitimate business among the flowers. I lay down on the bridge that crossed the pond, put my head on my front paws and closed my eyes.

"By the way, we were never introduced," said a voice. I opened my eyes reluctantly; no peace for the wicked, but how I had been wicked I couldn't seem to remember. There was no one on either side of me, in front or back, so I looked down. There was the pop-eyed goldfish. He continued: "I'm Claude." I waved a paw.

"I'm Gaius Marius," and hoped that would be the end of the conversation. But of course it wasn't. I suppose one forgets how much conversation went on in the days before radio and TV when there were few forms of amusement. Claude said:

"She's not coming back, is she?" I shook my head.

"No, she isn't." Claude looked crestfallen.

"So who's going to look after us?" Typical. Self, self and self. I answered nastily:

"Perhaps a cat will come along and eat you. That should take care of all your troubles." Claude frowned:

"That wasn't a very nice thing to say!" and, with an offended look, returned to the pond depths. I wasn't about to miss him. I had a bit of a wash, a good stretch and went back to sleep.

And so the morning passed and the afternoon hours wore away. No sounds of battle or other upheavals reached Cressida's garden. Instead, sounds restricted themselves to humming, chirping and buzzing. But of course it couldn't last. What garden does not have a serpent? This serpent took the form of Pandarus, looking much the worse for wear, indulging in a sea of self-pity. After crashing open the gate, he sank down on the garden bench where Troilus and Cressida had so lately sworn eternal love. He said to no one in particular:

"I've got this awful cough I can't get rid of. What with one thing and another, I don't think I'm long for this world; my eyes are rheumy, my back hurts. I think I'm the sickest man in Troy." I said nothing, hoping he wouldn't see me. In fact he didn't for some little time, just sat there sniffing and dabbing at his eyes with a non-too-clean handkerchief he also used to blow his nose. I closed my eyes. Cats cannot stand anything unhygienic. It made me wonder how our species got through medieval times. Of course, nothing is perfect and soon Pandarus caught sight of me. He pointed, as if a cat was something new in his world experience.

"You," he said, "you were Cressida's cat!" I yawned. Lord of Cats, give me strength! I looked at him with my blue eyes.

"I am no one's cat," was my answer. But Pandarus had already lost interest in that part of the conversation.

"I met Troilus leaving for the battlefield. I wanted to wish him luck but he turned on me like a tiger, literally like a tiger and literally spat at me: 'Get lost, you damned go-between. May ignominy follow you for the rest of your life and shame live forever in your name'." I toot-tooted. Sounded a bit extreme; after all what was Pandarus' real crime? I will agree no one loves a busybody but, then, it was Troilus who had hung onto Pandarus, begging, pleading... Now, in true Troilus fashion, he had shifted the blame for all his faults and mistakes onto whoever was nearest. Pandarus started sobbing. I said:

"I wouldn't worry if I were you, Pandarus. Troilus is a rag a tag and a hank of hair." Of course, he didn't listen; people who want to air their grievances don't want advice so I let Pandarus continue:

"These are my wages for being selfless and putting others first. How good were my intentions; and the result has been that now I am despised!" He sobbed some more. "Why was it all my fault? I meant it for the best." Yeah, the world had not been fair on poor Pandarus. In fact, had he but known it, I was probably more to blame than he was. But then cats don't care if they get blamed. I did what I did; didn't work out? Too bad. Move on. But Pandarus wasn't moving on. In between more sobs, he cried: "Weep, weep, all of you who have tried to unite true lovers. Weep for Pandarus or, if you can't weep, a few groans will do. May you reach a happier end than poor Pandarus." There was no way I could comfort Pandarus so I lay down, closed my eyes and murmured:

"How sharper than a serpent's tooth it is to have a thankless child!" Cressida – or Troilus for that matter – weren't Pandarus' children but I suppose at the end of the day nieces and nephews come to the same thing. So we stayed in the garden, Pandarus sobbed, I snoozed, and Claude came back up. I murmured to him:

"Perhaps Pandarus can take care of you!" Claude instantly disappeared into the depths, never to re-appear. As I was leaving, I heard Pandarus half-singing to himself:

> *Full merrily the humble-bee doth sing,*
> *Till he hath lost his honey and his sting;*
> *And being once subdued in armed tail,*
> *Sweet honey and sweet notes together fail.*

If it's not one thing it's another in Troy. Either there is Homerys lurking about with his endless epic; if one manages to escape him, there're always pitiful old fools around wallowing in self-pity and regrets.

4.3 PROFIT AND LOSS

I made my way to *The Greek Olive Tree*. There were few people there, just soldiers unfit for combat, having been mauled earlier on. Most of them were on the terrace. The bigwigs must have been laying it on still. Eurybates brought me my designer water and tuna snacks. I snoozed a bit after that, enjoying the peace and quiet. A long time seemed to pass, a trickle of wounded turning up, leaning on comrades or dragging themselves along. Eurybates was right: this was the only game in town. Then who should turn up but Thersites, dirtier than ever, smellier than ever. And all excited.

"I was there; I saw the whole thing." He looks at me knowingly. I signalled Eurybates to give him a drink. Thersites took a long swig and began: "Of course Troilus and Diomedes clashed, but that was a washout. I was hoping they'd kill each other." He cackled. "But, as the man says, you can't have everything." I just loved Thersites' style and class. He continued: "Then Ajax, he had a bad time of it down at the ships and I enjoyed every minute of that. Boy, was he mad when he found he'd fought Patroklos thinking it was Akhilleus. So that's him taken down a peg or two. He sure was pissed; all that effort and nothing to show for it. Then they sent me, me, to tell Akhilleus about Patroklos. I ran all the way." I bet. Bringing bad news was what Thersites liked doing best. I asked:

"How did Akhilleus take it?" Thersites leaned back with an air of utter contentment.

"Very badly, very very badly. He raved and cried and carried on, swore up and down he'd get Hector if it was the last thing he did."

"Truth to tell," I said, "it was in part his fault for sulking and stewing about all his wrongs. If he'd gone, Patroklos would still be alive. And Patroklos did well, you know, at the ships." Thersites looked at me curiously.

"Were you there?" I cleared my throat.

"Well, not really," and left it at that. He turned his beaker upside down to show it was empty. I said sarcastically:

"Have another?" Irony was lost on Thersites and he replied:

"Don't mind if I do." Eurybates tipped him up and Thersites look a long draught then swirled what was left around. "I met Hector, too." He snickered. "Hector actually thought I was a warrior. Needs glasses, he does. But he soon saw his mistake and was off. Wasn't going to waste his energy on the likes of me." I had some watered raki – you can't handle Thersites on designer water. And, of course, he wasn't done:

"Did I tell you I saw Paris and Menelaus? They weren't fighting, just trading insults." He scratched his head. "Something else happened – oh, yes, this Trojan jumped me. I asked: 'who are you?' He: 'a bastard son of Priam's'. I said: 'I love bastards. I'm a bastard too, born, in mind, in valour, in fact, in every way illegitimate. One bastard shouldn't fight another bastard, it's unethical.' And I ran away." Lord of cats, give me patience.

It was past teatime when the Greek higher-ups started arriving. They had taken time to get more or less cleaned up with fresh tunics, washed the mud off their feet and put on clean sandals. I looked around and took stock of who was there.

Agamemnon and Menelaus were at a table by themselves, deeply engaged in discussions and writing things down on a piece of parchment. Menelaus looked up at the assembled survivors.

"I hope, gentlemen, that you have done a head count of your trips and have handed in your lists of casualties. We don't care about the wounded, not just now, not before we draw our plans for the next battle." Everyone nodded and I suddenly realized Agamemnon was making a list of the Greek losses, like some macabre accountant. Diomedes was entertaining Odysseus and Nestor with his exploits:

"I found Troilus, you know, knocked him off his horse," he said arrogantly. "Fellow vanished into the dark." Odysseus looked at him slyly:

"I thought I saw you trying to brain Æneas with a boulder," he said in an offhand manner. "Is this a new way of waging war in Argos?" Diomedes had the grace to blush.

"Well, it seemed a good idea at the time since my lance broke when I speared him and he was down." Agamemnon looked up and frowned:

"My dear Diomedes, boulders as personal weapons were ruled out of the Mesopotamia Convention. I hope you have a copy – if not, my chief clerk shall get you one." Diomedes waved his hand about:

I agree – and I have a copy of the convention, thank you very much, somewhere around. Anyway, I got nowhere boulder or no boulder, and Æneas is still in the best of health, bar for a broken hip bone. My aim must have been way off."

Odysseus and Nestor exchanged glances. Agamemnon went back to his list.

"So we can't put Æneas on our list," he said. "Pity. But Menon, Epistrophus, Cedius, Polyxenes and Acamas are dead." Idomeneus interrupted him:

"Acamas is a Trojan, Agamemnon," he said quietly. "In fact, I killed him myself." Menelaus looked up:

"So he is. We'll have to take him off our list, Agamemnon."

"I'll slip him into the Profit column," answered Agamemnon without missing a beat. Idomeneus :

"Slot in Erymas, too. Took some killing, that lad. Had to run him down – and through." Agamemnon nodded:

"Right. Quite a balanced statement, we have. What about Patroklos, is he taken or dead." Nestor broke in:

"Don't you know Patroklos is dead? I tried to get Akhilleus into the field but he was still miffed. So Patroklos put on Akhilleus' armour and went to battle. He drove the Trojans from our beached ships and just in time, too; Akhilleus couldn't have done better. However, success went to his head and Patroklos thought he could tackle Hector. Hector, of course, saw Akhilleus' armour, chariot and weapons and that was the end of poor Patroklos. We had his body carried back to Akhilleus' tent." Odysseus said scornfully:

"That should have woken our super hero up right proper." Agamemnon stopped writing his list.

"I didn't know." He seemed more upset by the effect this might have on his balance sheet than losing Patroklos. Can't say I blame him. Patroklos had had one blazing moment of glory but now he was just a statistic. Agamemnon went on: "If we go on in this way, there won't be enough Greeks left to sail the fleet home." He took a swig of wine. Odysseus took up Nestor's tale.

"You should have seen Akhilleus when he saw Patroklos' corpse. He wept, cursed and swore vengeance. He took about a thousand oaths he would send Hector to Hades." Odysseus pondered a bit. "We should have concentrated on Patroklos long ago. That would have been the way to get at Akhilleus." Perhaps, but the difficulty would have been in finding a Trojan to take the trouble of killing Patroklos. He had never been high on anyone's shit list. Nestor said thoughtfully:

"Troilus was full of beans, here, there and everywhere. Engaging and redeeming himself with such careless force and forceless care as if luck bade him win all. That must have been after his meeting with you, Diomedes." He continued: "Hector outperformed Hector. He was all over the field. First in his chariot, then on his horse, then on foot. Greeks strewn all around him. It seemed impossible that one man alone should be able to create such havoc."

Agamemnon sighed:

"It explains why we didn't do too well, what with Hector giving us the run-around and our best fighters bent on personal vendettas." Gimlet look at Diomedes. For sure, all this settling of personal scores must be vexing for a commander-in-chief. The whole thing was becoming surreal. A war like no other. Menelaus said:

"That kid Pandarus tried to shoot me," he said conversationally. Diomedes looked up:

"Pandarus? Pandarus is Calchas' brother and must be sixty if he is a day." Odysseus shook his head.

"There is more than one Pandarus in Troy, my friend. This one is a whipper-snapper from the foothills of Mount Ida. For some reason, those people consider themselves to be Trojans." He stopped for a moment and concluded: "He is supposed to have been trained by Apollo himself, strange as it may seem, since his shot went right past me." I thought back to my visit to Olympus and Zeus' comments about Apollo's archery. Perhaps not so strange after all. Homerys, of course, would claim that some deity or other had protected Menelaus. Homerys does not recognize incompetence. Then Diomedes exclaimed:

"Oh, the Mount Ida Pandarus. I killed him myself later in the day. Æneas had him primed and they were coming at me like bats out of Hades. I shot Pandarus but Æneas got away – a second time. Of all the blasted luck."

Agamemnon put down his stylus:

"Well, brother, so that's it." Menelaus nodded and signalled for a footslogger to take the accounts away. "I make it 300 Greeks killed against 316 Trojans." Agamemnon rubbed his hands in satisfaction. "So we still have an edge. Not a significant one, but still an edge." Odysseus buried his face in his hands and Nestor sighed, a deep and sincerely felt sigh. Agamemnon would have made a great Wall Street analyst. Mind you, I was not about to hand him my portfolio.

4.4 HECTOR, MASTER OF HORSES

After that, I made my way into Troy and *The Trojan Horse*. A bit more civilized morning than the Greek gang. The *Trojan Horse* was pretty empty; it was early and I supposed the warriors were getting their eight hours. Marianne brought my tea and tuna without being asked. I sat alone for a bit, musing over this and that. Peace was shattered when Homerys's boy came in, trailing Homerys, whom he ensconced at my table without so much as by your leave and immediately took off. I waved frantically at Marianne. Tea, bread and cheese for Homerys. Saved us from 200 hexameters. Marianne complied, being as fully away of the danger as I was. Homerys was all wound up:

"What's all this Troilus and Cressida stuff? Who on earth is Cressida? Is she Crisies? Is she Brisies? And, as I told you before, Gaius, Troilus is dead before my epic even starts." I looked to heaven. This habit of Homerys's repeating himself was getting annoying. Homerys went on: "Now I've just met a stupid old man called Pandarus. Why, in my epic Pandarus was a great warrior and archer, son of Lycaon, and he led the men from the lowest spurs of Mt. Ida, who were Trojan by blood. This other Pandarus, I disown him." So that settled Pandarus' hash as far as Homerys was concerned. Under the bus with Pandarus.

Homerys fell into silence, concentrating on his breakfast. I considered telling him all about how his stories had evolved and changed to meet the demands of other eras, especially in Medieval times when troubadours, tournaments and gentlemen's chaste love for unreachable or unsuitable ladies reached a peak and gave us *Le Roman de Troie* and later Chaucer's *Troilys and Chreysid*. But it would be too much of a bother and anyway I didn't think I could make a good job of it. So I held my peace. We ate our food in silence, each deep in his own thoughts.

Suddenly, Homerys held up his hand:

"Listen," he said, "listen." I listened and countered:

"Can't hear a thing." In fact, all had become hushed and still. The ordinary bustle of daily life had ceased. There was no clanking of soldiers coming and going. No women with rowdy children on their way to market. No vendors shouting the excellence of their wares. No birds twittering, no dogs barking. Even the wind had dropped. It was as if a blanket had smothered the city of Troy and the plain beyond. Then, uncannily and suddenly, somewhere in the city a thin wailing sound arose, for all the world like a damned soul in Hades. Another voice joined in, then another and another. Homerys's boy came rushing in, his eyes the size of saucers.

"Hector," he panted, "Hector is dead." More and more voices took up the wailing, until the whole of Troy seemed to have joined in.

"Hector is dead!" I breathed uneasily. Even though I knew about it, I was still shocked because there's always a chance it won't. Trojans started trickling in to the café in dribs and drabs. Marianne and the waiter got busy, but she was so upset and cried so much she couldn't figure out the orders and just started flinging mugs and placing jars on the bar so people could help themselves. Æneas was the first of the higher echelon to turn up, still dirty and covered in blood. He'd lost his helmet and his shield had an enormous gash in it.

"Boys, we mustn't be disheartened. After all, the day was ours," he said to no one in particular. Troilus joined him, Adrestus and others. Troilus was bitter.

"Hector dead! How did it happen?" Æneas sighed:

"Akhilleus!" he answered. Adrestus exclaimed:

"Akhilleus? But Hector killed Akhilleus by the Chetan gate last night!" Æneas shook his head sadly.

"No, that was Patroklos, wearing Akhilleus' armour and riding his chariot." Although I had heard this last night at the Greek Happy Hours, I had a spasm as last night's dream came flooding back to me.

"Patroklos is dead," I whispered. "I saw it happen!" He died a hero's death but who would remember except Akhilleus? Here in Troy, sadly Patroklos had already been forgotten. Troilus continued bitterly:

"And Hector is now being dragged around the walls of Troy at the tail of his killer's chariot." Homerys stood up and declaimed in a loud voice:

*...when he [Akhilleus] saw dawn breaking over beach
and sea, he yoked his horses to his chariot, and bound
the body of Hector behind it that he might drag it about.
Thrice did he drag it round ..., and then went back into
his tent, leaving the body on the ground full length and
with its face downwards. But Apollo would not suffer it
[the body of Hector] to be disfigured ...; therefore he
shielded him [Hector] with his [Apollo's] golden aegis
continually, that he [Hector] might take no hurt while
Akhilleus was dragging him.*

Homerys sat down, declaring:

"The Gods are great." I can't understand why someone didn't brain the old guy. However, it was a blessing of sorts that the Gods were protecting Hector's corpse. Hector would look good on his funeral pyre. Troilus however, had no time for the Gods. He shook his fists at heaven and cried:

"Oh, you Gods! From your thrones, look down upon Troy! You've done your worst to us; be merciful, and destroy what is left so that there may be an end to our misery." Æneas tried to calm Troilus down. Losing one's temper never did anyone any good.

"Troilus." he said. "You need to get a grip. You'll demoralize our people and, with or without Hector, the war has to go on. And we're not done for yet. You wait and see. Chin up. We need every man!" Troilus turned on him in fury:

"As usual, you don't get it. I'm not talking about death but of the unknowable future. Hector is gone; who is to tell Priam and Hecuba? Who'll now inspire and lead us? Hector was our rock and our star and Hector is gone!" He turned in the general direction of the Dardanian plain and shook his fists. "You vile abominable tents! Why are you here? Why do you stay? No one asked you to come. Just wait, I swear, I swear, no matter how early the sun rises, I'll be waiting for you. Nothing, nothing can now patch up our quarrel. I'll follow you wherever you go and, when I'm dead, I'll haunt you to the end of time." Everyone fell silent and concentrated on their food. It was no doubt sad about Hector but then again everyone must die sometime. The real lesson here, I think, was the danger of putting all your eggs in one basket – depending on one man alone. The man on the white horse. However, in the case of the Trojans, there just had never been anyone else. I left quietly and slipped out of Troy.

4.5 THE UGLY TRUTH

There was a strange silence at *The Greek Olive Tree*. Hector's death was common knowledge by this time but no one talked about it. They all sat around, the Greek High Command, as if waiting. Then the man everyone was waiting for, Akhilleus, came in and sat down at an empty table. Eurybates hurried over with a beaker. Akhilleus drank in silence, the others looking at him. Odysseus broke the silence.

"So, you got Hector at last."

"Indeed," answered Akhilleus. "I killed him myself, well, more or less." Everyone looked up. What did that mean? Akhilleus continued in a dreamy voice: "I met him first alone; but that didn't suit my purposes at all. It would have been too easy – for him, not me. So I left him and called my Myrmidons." The silence became deafening. This wouldn't have a happy ending. Akhilleus continued: "Then we went looking for him again. And we found him, sitting quietly on a rock, taking a break after all that killing." Talk about the pot calling the kettle black. "I said to him: 'Look, Hector, morning is almost over and the sun will soon be at zenith and start sinking into the west. And as sinks, Hector, so does your life.' Replied Hector: 'I am unarmed, Greek, you have me at an unfair advantage'." Akhilleus had left us behind and was deep into his gruesome memories. "I called my Myrmidons and they surrounded Hector and I said: 'This is the man I seek. Strike, fellows, hack and stab'." He breathed in. "And so Hector died." The silence was as dead as Hector. A chill ran down my back. Akhilleus continued: "I looked down at him and thought: 'So, Troy, you are next. Here lies your heart, sinews and bones'. I said to my lads: 'Shout it out to the world, my friends. Akhilleus has the mighty

Hector slain!'" He continued, matter-of-factly. "And so I sheathed my sword. I was done." The silence was broken by Odysseus:

"You had Hector murdered." Akhilleus answered:

"Yes, and then I tied him to my horse's tail and dragged him behind me all around Troy."

Agamemnon was truly shocked:

"Akhilleus, that was not playing the game. This is not how Greeks fight. You have dishonoured us." Akhilleus turned on him fiercely:

"What do you care? Hector is dead, Troy is ours for the taking. Our wars are over." In silence that followed, Odysseus spoke at length.

"Let us all hope, Akhilleus," he said quietly, "that indeed they are."

A footslogger popped in.

"Akhilleus, there's an old man out here wanting to talk to you." He stood aside and old Priam came in, leaning on his stick.

"I have come," he said, "to reclaim my son's body." Akhilleus sneered.

"And why should I give it to you? Let it lie in the sun rotting! Let the dogs have a good meal!" The other Greeks drew in their breaths sharply. Even I, a cat without a conscience, was shocked. This Akhilleus was really too awful to be true. Agamemnon drew himself up and was obviously about to lay down the law but Odysseus stopped him. And, in truth, this was a moment for common sense and diplomacy.

"Lord Priam," said Odysseus gently. "Come and sit down. And can I get you something to drink?" Priam did sit down; he was very shaky. Eurybates brought him a beaker of watered wine, which he sipped slowly. Odysseus turned to Akhilleus:

"My friend and comrade in arms," he said, "we have travelled a long way, both in time and space, to fulfil our oaths of protecting Helen. That we have not yet achieved. Yet you seem to have put it as your ultimately objective the killing of Hector and dishonour of his corpse. This dishonour would reflect on all the Greeks, not only yourself. In the name of humanity, honour and mercy, I ask you to turn Hector's body over to his family, as we would have expected the Trojans to do had it been you, not Hector, who died. There is no glory in holding back a corpse. Show your honour and greatness now, Akhilleus, by returning

Hector's remains to his grieving family. The Gods will applaud you for it." Akhilleus scratched his head and said truculently:

"He killed Patroklos!" Odysseus went on:

"That is very true, Akhilleus. But you must not forget this is war. And in wars people are liable to get killed, even the best of us. So I repeat: to honour the Gods and our adversaries, and not set a precedent we all may later regret, let Priam take Hector back." Akhilleus waved his hands about as if chasing off flies.

"Oh, all right. I suppose I will have to or Agamemnon will raise a stink and I'll never hear the end of it. For Chrissake!" Odysseus turned at once to Diomedes.

"Diomedes, please take the Lord Priam to Akhilleus' tent and see that he returns safely to Troy with his son's body." Diomedes left with the old man. Odysseus sank onto a stool and took a beaker from Eurybates.

"The last straw," he said, "the last effing straw." Of course, Homerys didn't see it like this at all. This is how he has Akhilleus grant a father's wish:

> *He [Akhilleus] frowned and said: "Give not my blood*
> *fresh cause of fury; I know well I must resign thy son,*
> *Zeus by my mother uttered it, and what besides is done,*
> *I know as amply; and thyself, old Priam, I know too*
> *some God [Hermes, although he denies it] has brought*
> *thee: for no man durst use a thought to go on such a*
> *service. I have guards, and I have gates to stay easy*
> *access; do not then presume thy will can sway, like Zeus'*
> *will, and incense again my quenched blood: lest nor*
> *though nor Zeus gets the command of me.*

But I must say this for Homerys: he portrayed Akhilleus for the arrogant bastard he was.

5
AFTERMATH

5.1 FUNERAL MEATS

It took the Trojans nine days to round up enough wood for a decent funeral pyre for Hector, erected on the top of Troy's massive tower. This is how Homerys described the funeral and I don't believe anyone could do it better.

> *On the morning of the tenth day, with many tears,*
> *they took brave Hector forth, laid his dead body upon*
> *the summit of the pyre and set fire thereto. When*
> *dawn appeared on the eleventh day, the people again*
> *assembled round the pyre of mighty Hector. They*
> *quenched the fire with wine and then his brothers and*
> *comrades gathered his white bones, wrapped them*
> *in soft robes of purple and laid them in a golden urn,*
> *which they placed in a grave and covered over with*
> *large stones. Then they built a barrow over it, keeping*
> *guard lest the [Greeks] should attack them before they*
> *had finished. When they had heaped up the barrow, they*
> *went back into the city and held high feast in the house*
> *of Priam their king.*[15]

---

[15]   See Homerys's *The Iliad*, Book XXIV

The Trojan standard with its horse rampant fluttered sadly in the breeze at half mast from the highest point in the tower. At dusk, before the pyre was lit, they sang the national anthem. As if to provide Hector with a stairway to Trojan heaven, should there be one (as a mere cat, I'm not an expert on such things), the flames and sparks from the pyre flew upwards, higher and higher. It was beautiful and uncanny. I am sure there were superb funeral orations but Homerys didn't bother recording them and I was too far off to hear.

Patroklos got a send off too, if not quite in the same style. The Greeks also had difficulties getting enough wood. Personally, I think Agamemnon would have preferred to throw the corpse into the sea to feed the fish but Akhilleus wouldn't have put up with that. So, to appease him, they went through the motions. The funeral pyre was set up on the beach. No one bothered bringing the Greek City States' Stars and Stripes standard. However, everyone was there since a rumour had gone around that there would be open bar at *The Greek Olive Tree* afterwards. Most of the mourners didn't shed any tears although they held their handkerchiefs to their faces, perhaps to keep out the smell of burning flesh. Akhilleus did his best to make up for others' callousness. He wept and wept. He eulogized Patroklos and went on and on until I thought it would continue into the 20th century. Then torches were thrown onto the pyre but the wood would not kindle. This was embarrassing as it implied the Gods were not willing to take Patroklos. Akhilleus became desperate and prayed and called on the Gods. Then unexpectedly, mighty flames roared forth. I looked around and saw Hermes next to me.

"Ah," I said, "it's you." Hermes nodded:

"Enough is enough. Poor Patroklos deserves a proper send-off like anyone else." All night long the flames roared while Akhilleus drew wine from a mixing-bowl of gold and, calling upon the spirit of dead Patroklos, poured it upon the ground until the earth was drenched. Only at dawn did the fire slowly burn itself out. Akhilleus himself put out the last embers with wine and sifted through the ashes to collect Patroklos' bones, which he wrapped in cloth of gold. Homerys, of course, saw it all differently:

> *And now some powers [the Gods] denied consents*
> *[allow] to this solemnity: the fire (for all the oily fuel it*
> *had injected) would not burn; and then the loving cruel*
> *studied for help, and standing off, invoked the two fair*
> *winds (Zephyr and Boreas) to afford the rage of both*
> *their kinds to aid his [Akhilleus] outrage. Precious gifts*
> *his earnest zeal did vow; poured from a golden bowl*
> *much wine, and prayed them both to blow that quickly*
> *his friend' corpse might burn and that heap's [wood]*
> *sturdy breast embrace consumption.*

"Now," I said to Hermes, "he's going to talk about you." Hermes sneered:

"You wish! Why, Homerys wouldn't know the truth if it bit him in the rear." And, indeed, Homerys went on:

> *Iris heard; the winds where at a feast, all in the court*
> *of Zephyrus (that boisterous blowing air) gathered*
> *together. She that wears the thousand coloured hair flew*
> *thither, ... I come to signify that Thetis' son (Akhilleus)*
> *implores your aids (princes north and west) with vows*
> *of much sacrifice, if each will set his breast against his*
> *heap of funeral, and make it quickly burn. Patroklos lies*
> *there, whose decease all the Achaeans [Greeks] mourn.*

"Who on earth is Iris?" I asked. Hermes shrugged:

"She is a minor deity, of no real consequence, goddess of the rainbow. From time to time she also runs errands for Hera."

"Oh," was all I could say.

I was snoozing on the bar later in the day when Agamemnon's raised voice woke me up with a startle.

"Funeral games for Patroklos?" he shouted. "Akhilleus, have you finally lost your mind?" I looked up. Akhilleus was seething with fury.

"Patroklos deserves funeral games. He died a hero's death for the Greek cause and performed acts of valour that will be remembered down the ages." I lay back and closed my eyes. No need to fuss, thinks I, Homerys will give Patroklos spectacular funeral games. But Agamemnon wasn't having any. He did go as far as attempting to reason with Akhilleus instead of just laying down the law as he would have done at any other time.

"Akhilleus," he said, "be reasonable. Here we are, with a war is in its ninth year. We've just been through one hell of a battle, everyone is worn out. Who do you think is fit to compete in funeral games? Also, where would we hold them? Akhilleus, it just isn't practical." Akhilleus looked as if he were about to burst a main artery. He shouted:

"You always hated Patroklos. There was never anything he could do that was any good in your eyes – and that goes for the rest of you, too," he turned furiously around to the rest of the assembled Greeks, who stared fixedly into space. Odysseus walked up. Here comes the peacemaker.

"My dear Akhilleus," he said soothingly, patting him on the shoulder. "We all know what you have suffered and, believe me, there is nothing we, the High Command, would rather do than have funeral games for Patroklos." Akhilleus looked somewhat mollified. "How about this," continued Odysseus. "There is a level space over by that hillock," and he pointed towards the back of the camp. "The audience could sit on the hill. And all contestants would be volunteers. As Agamemnon says, a lot of our boys are veterans. Olympic competitions are for the young and strong." Akhilleus cleared his throat.

"Well," snapped Agamemnon, "what else is it you want?" Akhilleus explained:

"There are those twelve Trojan princes I took prisoners. I want to sacrifice them to Patroklos' shade." Before Agamemnon had a chance of replying, Odysseus turned to Akhilleus in fury:

"Don't even think of it! We are not barbarians!" Akhilleus started shouting:

"I want them to be Patroklos' companions in the Underworld!" Odysseus got right up into Akhilleus' face:

"If you don't want Patroklos to be alone, look!" and he took out his dagger that he handed it to Akhilleus, "stab yourself! Then the two of you can be together forever. Or as long as Hades puts up with your goings on!" I could see Akhilleus wanted to argue but the look on Odysseus' face quelled him! So he had to be content with the games. I have never seen Odysseus so infuriated. "Nestor," he shouted, "send a troop of guards down to Akhilleus' ships and bring up his Trojan prisoners. Put them in the common prison compound." Menelaus murmured, shaking his head sadly:

"Seems never to have heard of the Mesopotamia Convention! What an ignoramus!" Right. Akhilleus was a bull in a china shop. The Greeks would have been better off without him.

On the appointed day, a few soldiers straggled up the hill to see the show. Most of them had bandages here and there, arms in slings and/ or limped. It was not an impressive audience. Akhilleus must have felt it, too, for, all of a sudden he announced that there would be open house at *The Greek Olive Tree* for the spectators later. After that, the side of the hill filled to capacity, washerwomen, army suppliers, camp followers and all. So it turned out to be a jolly affair after all. The main contestants were Akhilleus' Myrmidons who didn't have the option of refusing and some of the higher ups to pacify Akhilleus. Akhilleus did not participate since he said it would be unfair as he was bound to win all the prizes himself. The contestants quarreled and fought among themselves about all sorts of technicalities so a good time was had by all. And so, at last, the story of Patroklos came to an end.

6

ON THE BEACH

It was a peaceful afternoon. Neither too hot nor too cold. The sun was halfway to the horizon, its rays streaming towards me over a calm sea, waves lapping gently on the white sands. In the bay, off the island of Tenedos, the Greek fleet rode at anchor, sails furled, oars stowed, the ships moving with the gentle rock of the waves,.

Two biremes were anchored closer to shore. Rowboats plied back and forth, ferrying people out, mostly wounded returning to Greece. I wondered if they would be bringing fresh troops back. Some of the Greek boys who had been children ten years ago would now be old enough to become cannon fodder – well, you know what I mean. Then I saw Calchas and Cressida heading over the sand and towards the sea. Well, I knew Calchas planned to leave. Diomedes was with them. This boded well for Cressida's future as I quite liked Diomedes. And being married to a warrior was a good deal for a woman since he was hardly ever home. I thought of Troilus and decided, PACE Romeo and Juliet, it was difficult to have a relationship when the parties concerned are on different sides of a nasty war. Suddenly, Diomedes rose on his toes and leaned backwards into a very awkward position. I looked up in surprise. Had he received an arrow from Troy's walls? But no, that would have been an impossible shot. Then I looked sideways and there was Eros, bow in hand, clearly just having fired. Diomedes straightened up. Cressida and Calchas didn't seemed to have noticed anything. Eros looked at me, somewhat embarrassed.

"I did it to please you," he muttered. I nodded in agreement:

"Thanks, Eros, the girl needs a break. But what about an arrow for her?" Eros shook his head.

"She'll have to make up her own mind," and then he left.

Just as the sun was setting, the biremes were ready to leave, sails unfurled, oars unshipped, gliding out of the bay, past the Isle of Tenedos and into the Ægean sea. I watched them sail away. Should I have gone with them?

I looked out over the Ægean. All was peace and quiet. I really should move on. But curiosity, as is well known, is a cat's besetting sin. As I watched the fleet sail, I took stock. To summarise:

- Cressida and Troilus love-that-would-last-forever was a wash-out;
- Two attempts to end the war by single combat went nowhere;
- The Trojans attempted to burn the Greek ships, no luck;
- The Greeks tried to scale Troy's walls, no;
- The Trojans lost Hector, their top commander; and
- The Greeks lost Patroklos, Akhilleus friend.

I looked at these results from all sides. No matter how you cut it, the Greeks had come out on top. I returned to my tree for a snooze and to await the next developments.

7
EPILOGUE

Zeus and Hera were having tea on the terrace outside their temple. Everything was very quiet and peaceful. Herakles was asleep behind a column, his snoring the only audible sound. Zeus gave me a benign look and sipped his tea. He seemed to be over his latest hangover. Hera was busy with crochet work and did not look up. She said:

"So glad you could come to tea, Gaius. What can I get you: Earl Grey or India?" My thought: none of the above. But one must be polite so I chose Earl Grey. India really does not agree with me. My tea arrived and Hera continued: "Do have a tuna sandwich." I had the tuna but left the sandwich. One must not be greedy. To change the subject, I asked:

"Where are all the other Gods and Goddesses?" Hermes, who was also there, answered:

"They've gone to a second-tier two-week Gods conference in Memphis, Egypt." Hera sighed:

"It's so wonderful and peaceful without them. Those youngsters do make such a racket and it never seems to stop. What was the title of the conference, Hermes?"

"Climbing the Corporate Ladder in an Immortal Society." Hera sighed:

"Of course. How could I forget. Artemis is delivering the keynote speech – *Immortality and Invincibility – Exclusive or Inclusive?*" Zeus snorted:

"Rubbish. They'll come back with their heads full of plans and stratagems and we'll all have a merry time of it. To say nothing of the hangovers."

"What sort of other Gods will be there?" I asked. "Perhaps Bastet, the cat-God of the Egyptians?" Always cheer for the home team.

"No doubt," answered Hermes. "Also Baal and Ashtoreth, and from as far away as India – Shiva and so on. But the meeting will probably be dominated by those peculiar Egyptian Gods in the forms of animals. Sobek whom I believe is a crocodile and Sekhmet, the lioness. Most odd." Before I could express my indignation at this slight at the animal kingdom, Hermes brought the conversation back to the essentials:

"It seems, Great Zeus, that the poet Homerys is convinced that the Olympians were at the last battle and it was their interference that decided the outcome." Zeus shook his head vigorously.

"No, indeed. That Homerys, don't believe anything he writes. Humans started it all and they can finish it. If it isn't poetic enough for Homerys, there's nothing I can do about it." He added: "and I must say I have never been too sure what it is all about – some girl, isn't it?"

"Said to be your daughter, my dear Zeus," said Hera in a sweet voice but with a nasty undertone. "Remember Leda, my love? And the swan? And there's the bull, to say nothing of the shower of gold. So imaginative of you. All those artistic ways of getting into a girl's knickers."

"Wild oats, my dear," replied Zeus hastily, "young men need to sow them, you know." There was something menacing about the way Hera's hands moved over her crochet work.

"Indeed, and no one was a young man longer than you were." Ouch, below the belt. I tried to tidy up.

"Boys will be boys," I said with a smirk. Hera glared at me.

"And toms will be toms unless they're neutered." Remind me to keep on the good side of this lady. I decided that the war was a safer subject.

"So the two of you are not on anyone's side?" Hera glared.

"My dear Gaius," she said, "this is not a football match, although sometimes I have my doubts. But I do confess a slight partiality for the Trojans. Hector was such a handsome lad. And Paris, of course. You, my dear," turning to her husband , "have a partiality for the Greeks although I cannot see why since they have no interesting women with them." Zeus looked at her sideways. If boys will be boys, I wouldn't be surprised if girls will be girls and Hera had got up to some interesting tricks in her youth. Zeus, of course, did not comment but shook his great head.

"My love," he patted her knee and I was afraid she'd drive the crochet needle into his hand. "You really mustn't exaggerate. You know that both the Greeks and Trojans are my children and one doesn't take sides in children's quarrels." Hera gave him a sideways look of her own over her spectacles.

"But a little betting here and there in all innocent fun," she said, "who's keeping the book this week? And what was the outcome?" Hermes cleared his throat and we all knew who had the book.

"As a matter of fact," he said, "we're in a bit of a dilemma. The bet was whether Akhilleus would kill Hector or Hector Akhilleus. Now, Hector thought he had killed Akhilleus but it turned out to be Patroklos. But those who laid their bets on Hector might have a case to demand some of the winnings." I turned to Zeus:

"As a supreme God, I take it you know how this war is going to end. I mean, who wins, the Greeks or Trojans?" Zeus stroked his beard.

"Let's put it this way," he said after a bit. "If everything works out the way it should, I do know, but..." I raised my eyebrows:

"But?"

"My dear Gaius, there is always the matter of chance. The unexpected. The unforeseen that not even the Gods can see." Accountants call it incidentals. "But if you, as you say, come from the future, you must know the answer to that question yourself."

"That would be true, Great Zeus; however, the future has no record of what really happened. In fact, the scientific community is still arguing whether the Trojan War took place at all or if there ever was a Troy. You see, all we have to go on is this long epic by Homerys written about three thousand years ago and, as you said yourself, of doubtful authenticity. Impossible to validate, don't you know."

"Yes," said Zeus, "I see humanity has a problem. Besides, he's blind so how could he ever be a credible witness?"

"I am told he gets his information straight from the gods," I remarked. Both Zeus and Hera sighed. Hera said:

"I do so hate all this name dropping! Really, it's so ... so false, if you know what I mean." I did. But name dropping is not going to go out of fashion anytime soon. I got back on track:

"So we have to take Homerys's word for it that the Greeks come out on top." I thought for a bit. "On the other hand, there is a saying: the truth belongs to the victor. Ergo, the Greeks did win."

"Good point, Gaius," exclaimed Zeus. I looked at Zeus. I wanted to ask a question but was not quite sure how to phrase it. I started carefully:

"You know, Zeus, in my time you have become a myth. Very famous, no doubt, but the temples once dedicated to you are now only used to fleece the tourists and keep the archaeologists busy and out of the bars. So, what happened to you? How can you suddenly no longer be a God?" There was a twinkle in Zeus' eye as he answered.

"You agree with me," he said, "that Gods are immortal?" That was a difficult one.

"Well," I answered, "I believe you if you say so. I have no direct evidence myself."

"And in your day and age, there are still religions around?" I was on firmer ground here:

"Lots, Great Zeus. Anyone can start up a religion; it's like a franchise of sorts. Religion and faith remain essentially unchanged from the here and now. Only the outer trappings are different."

"So, Gaius, what you are telling me is that all the world believe in a God." I thought for a bit.

"Well, Great Zeus, I suppose I can agree on that but most humans wouldn't. Each one thinks his or her One God to be unique and goes under different names – Allah, Buddha, Zen, Yahweh." Zeus combed his beard with his fingers.

"Therefore," he said, "a God remains. And would you say God has created humanity in His image?" I demurred. This was like having a conversation with Socrates.

"Well, if I were to have any opinion at all, I would think humanity created God in their image so humanity would feel, so to speak, at home with him." Zeus patted me.

"Good cat. Go to the front of the class. So, if we agree that humanity created God in his own image, is that not why I am here, in Greek dress? But, should I wear another type of clothing from another time, would I still be a God?"

"I suppose so."

"And, instead of being called Zeus I were to be called, let us say, Yahweh or Zoroaster, I would still be the same God?" This was making me tired.

"Yes," I agreed, trying to get this thing over.

"Therefore," continued Zeus, "God may come under different names and dressed in different clothes but he is still God, immortal. Call him what you will, portray him as you like."

I digested this and couldn't find fault with it. There would always be a God and I was seeing him as the faithful believers of the time believed him to be. So, what's in a name? A rose by any other name will smell as sweet and so on. Names come and go. But the One God is forever.

The Greek Gods

Aphrodite – Latin: Venus.

Goddess of love, beauty and fertility. She is also known as the mother of Æneas, the Trojan who founded Rome.

Apollo – Latin: unknown.

Twin brother to Artemis, God of plague and healing, music, oracle and archery. Represented as a handsome, athletic young man.

Ares – Latin: Mars.

Son of Zeus and Hera, God of War.

Artemis – Latin: Diana.

Twin sister of Apollo. She is known as the Virgin Goddess of the Hunt, whose arrows bring sudden death.

Athena Latin: Minerva.

A war Goddess, her main temple was on the Acropolis in Athens. She is represented usually as a Goddess of severe beauty, dressed in armor, with helmet.

Eros: Latin: Cupid.

God of love, personifying physical desire, cruel and unpredictable. He is depicted as a handsome young man, armed with bows and arrows. Eros had a cult in many ancient cities.

Hera – Latin: Juno.

Wife of Zeus and his Queen. Worshipped all over Greece as goddess of marriage and married women. Also represented as a jealous and vengeful wife

Demeter – Latin:

Ceres. Goddess of Agriculture, sister of Zeus and mother of Persephone, who was abducted by Hades, king of the Underworld.

Dionysus – Latin: Bacchus.]God of wine and ecstasy, often represented as an happy-go-lucky youth, reclining with a bunch of grapes.

Ganymede – Latin: Catamitus.

Cup bearer of the Gods, linked to the zodiac sign of Aquarius.
Hermes – Latin: Mercury. Messenger/herald of the Gods, known
also as furtive and for being a trickster.

Hephaestus – No Roman equivalent.

God of fire and crafts, particularly those that employed fire. He
created the first woman, Pandora.

Herakles – Latin: Hercules.

Most famous of the Greek heroes, his exploits widely known
and his cult observed throughout the Greek world. He is most
famous for the twelve labors imposed upon his by the oracle of
Delphi, after he had killed his wife and children following a fit of
madness sent by Hera (see below). After his death, he was carried
to Olympus and reconciled with the Gods.

Thetis – No Latin equivalent.

Mother of Akhilleus (Latin: Achilles). Daughter of the sea-
god Nereus (no Latin equivalent), and one of the Nereids, the
sea-maidens.

Zeus – Latin: Jupiter.

Supreme Deity, king of the Gods. He is also Cloud gatherer,
thunderer on high, hurler of thunderbolts.